PIXEL+INK

Pixel+Ink is an imprint of TGM Development Corp.
www.pixelandinkbooks.com
Printed and bound in June 2022 at Toppan Leefung, DongGuan, China.
Cover design by Richard Fairgray, Tyler Nevins, and Jay Colvin
Interior design by Richard Fairgray

Cataloging-in-Publication information is available from the Library of Congress.

Hardcover ISBN: 978-1-64595-041-7
PB ISBN: 978-1-64595-111-7
E-book ISBN: 978-1-64595-112-4

First Edition

1 3 5 7 9 10 8 6 4 2

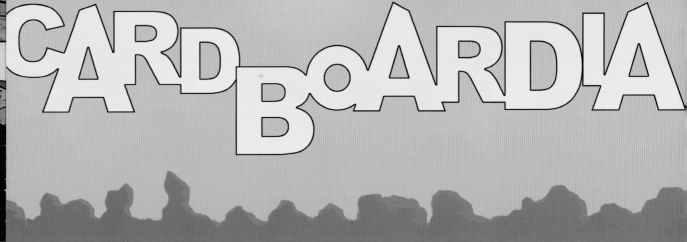

CARDBOARDIA

THIS SIDE UP

Written by **RICHARD FAIRGRAY**
and **LUCY CAMPAGNOLO**

Illustrated by **RICHARD FAIRGRAY**

PIXEL + INK

New York

Lucy

Richarc
peo

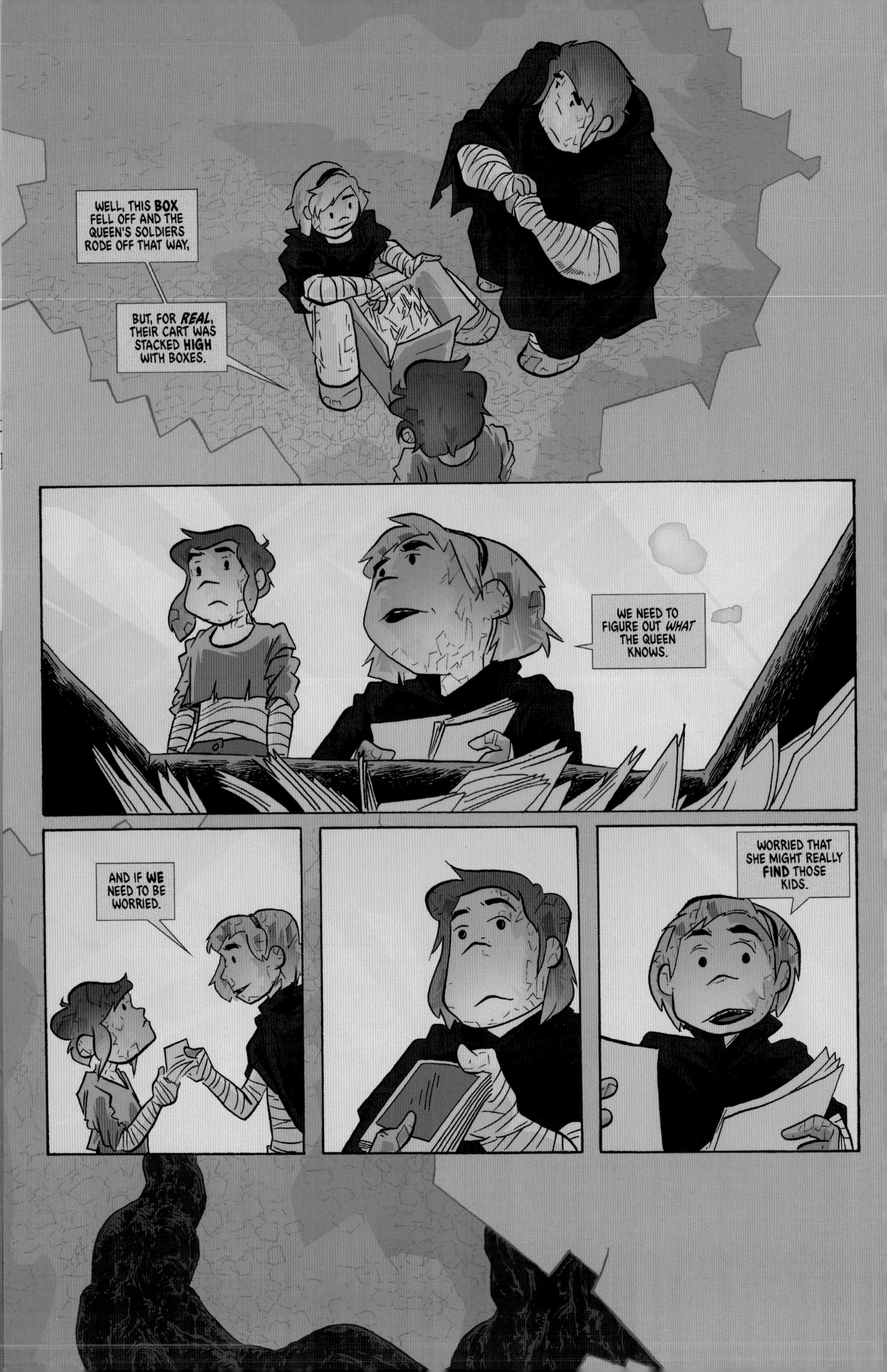

WELL, THIS BOX FELL OFF AND THE QUEEN'S SOLDIERS RODE OFF THAT WAY.
BUT, FOR REAL, THEIR CART WAS STACKED HIGH WITH BOXES.
WE NEED TO FIGURE OUT WHAT THE QUEEN KNOWS.
AND IF WE NEED TO BE WORRIED.
WORRIED THAT SHE MIGHT REALLY FIND THOSE KIDS.

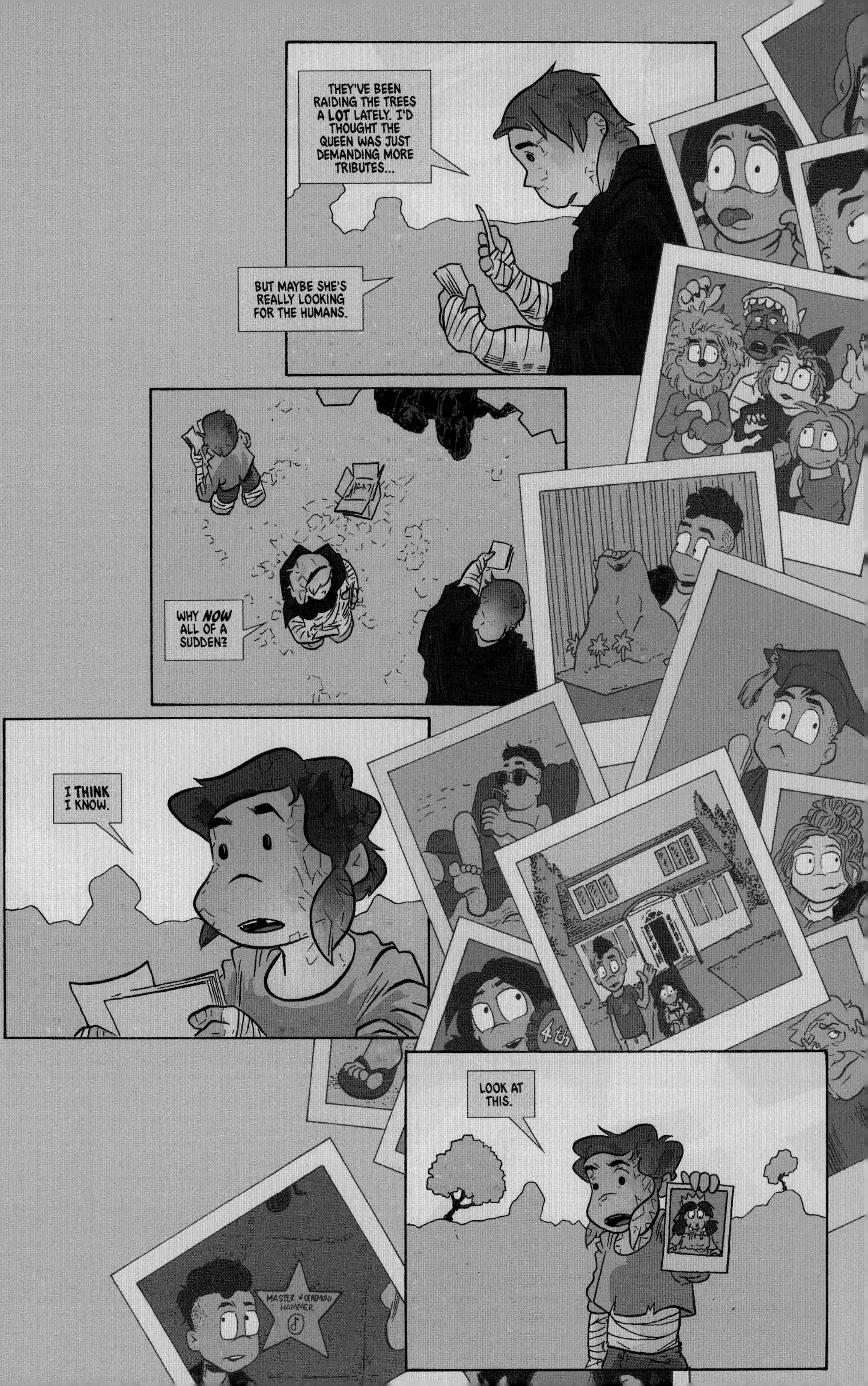
THEY'VE BEEN RAIDING THE TREES A LOT LATELY. I'D THOUGHT THE QUEEN WAS JUST DEMANDING MORE TRIBUTES...
BUT MAYBE SHE'S REALLY LOOKING FOR THE HUMANS.
WHY NOW ALL OF A SUDDEN?
I THINK I KNOW.
4th
LOOK AT THIS.
MASTER of CEREMONY HAMMER

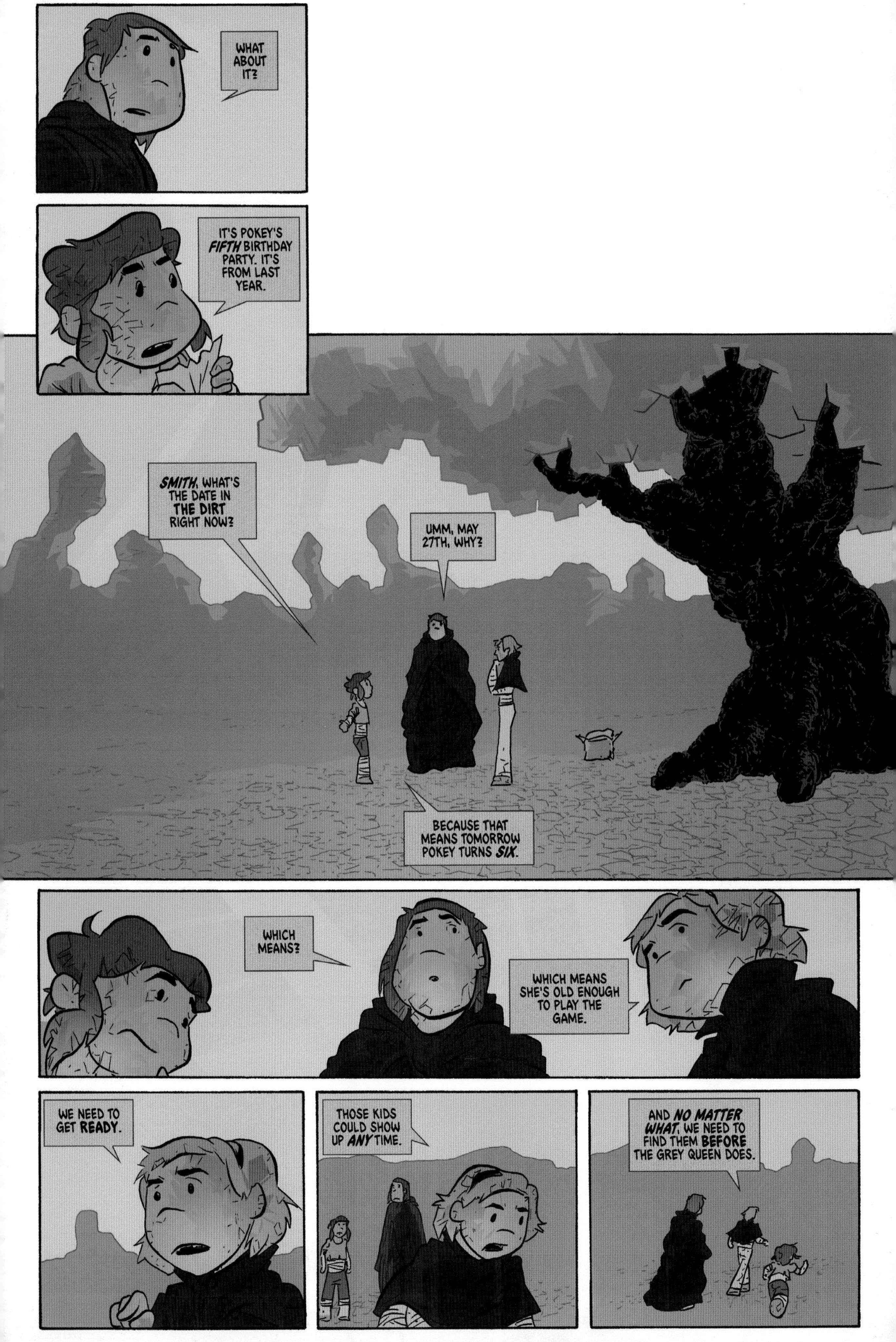
WHAT ABOUT IT?
IT'S POKEY'S ***FIFTH*** BIRTHDAY PARTY. IT'S FROM LAST YEAR.
SMITH, WHAT'S THE DATE IN **THE DIRT** RIGHT NOW?
UMM, MAY 27TH, WHY?
BECAUSE THAT MEANS TOMORROW POKEY TURNS ***SIX***.
WHICH MEANS?
WHICH MEANS SHE'S OLD ENOUGH TO PLAY THE GAME.
WE NEED TO GET **READY**.
THOSE KIDS COULD SHOW UP ***ANY*** TIME.
AND ***NO MATTER WHAT***, WE NEED TO FIND THEM **BEFORE** THE GREY QUEEN DOES.

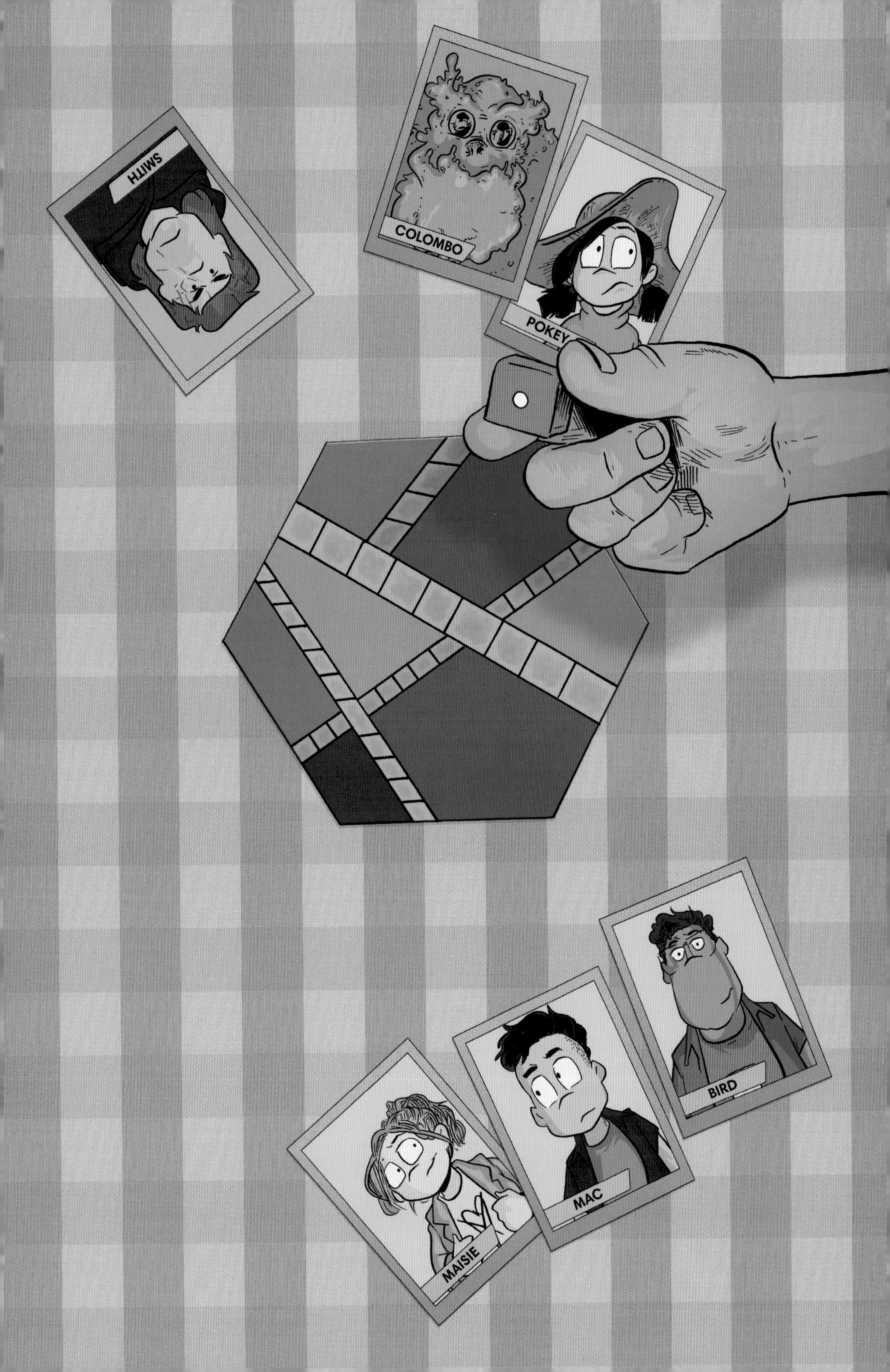
SMITH
COLOMBO
POKEY
BIRD
MAC
MAISIE

COLOMBO
POKEY

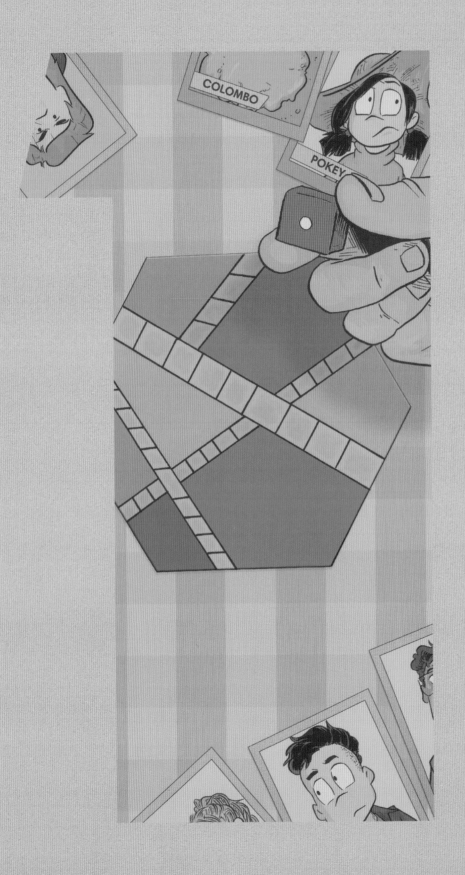

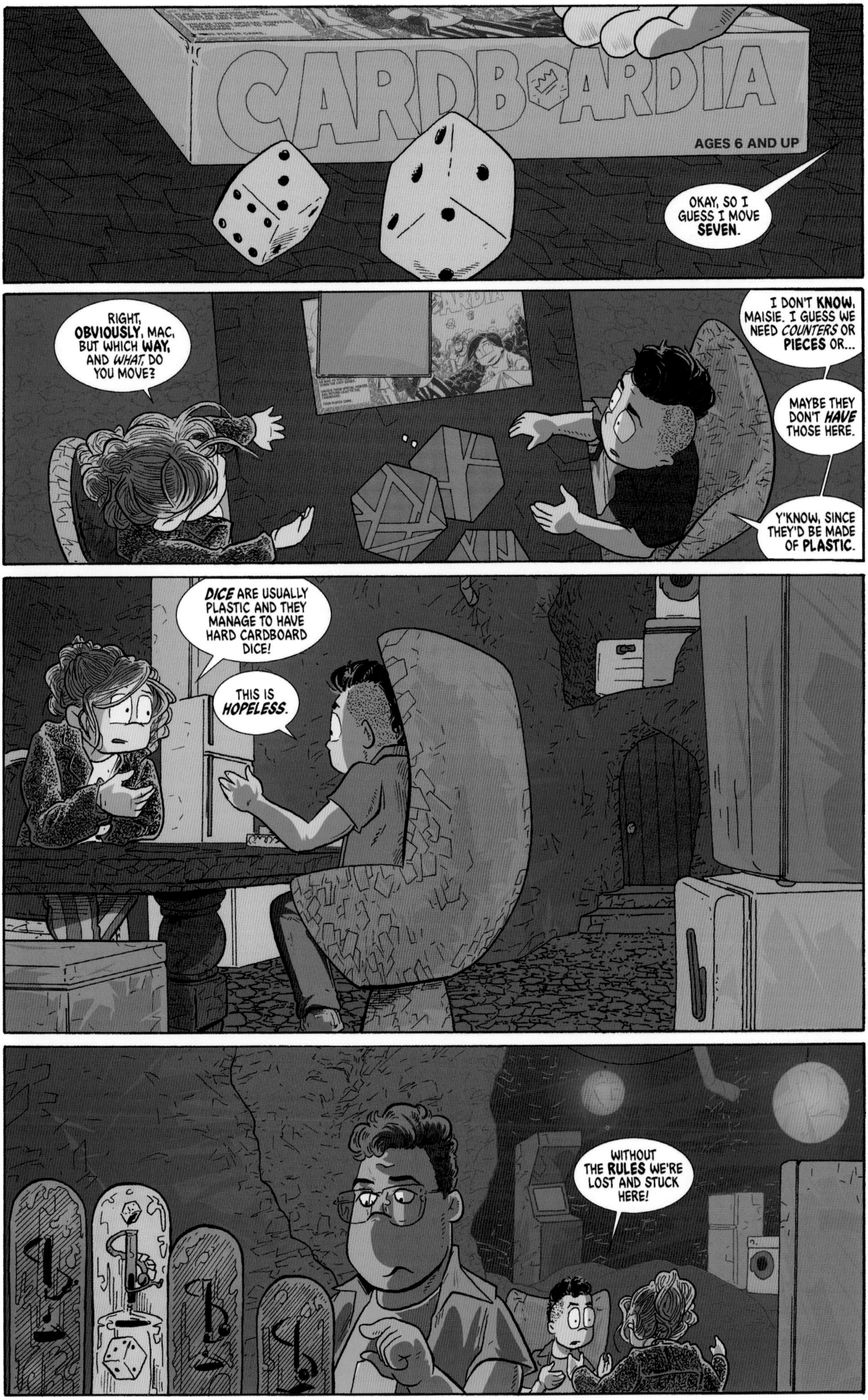
CARDBOARDIA
AGES 6 AND UP
OKAY, SO I GUESS I MOVE SEVEN.
RIGHT, OBVIOUSLY, MAC, BUT WHICH WAY, AND WHAT, DO YOU MOVE?
I DON'T KNOW, MAISIE. I GUESS WE NEED COUNTERS OR PIECES OR...
MAYBE THEY DON'T HAVE THOSE HERE.
Y'KNOW, SINCE THEY'D BE MADE OF PLASTIC.
DICE ARE USUALLY PLASTIC AND THEY MANAGE TO HAVE HARD CARDBOARD DICE!
THIS IS HOPELESS.
WITHOUT THE RULES WE'RE LOST AND STUCK HERE!

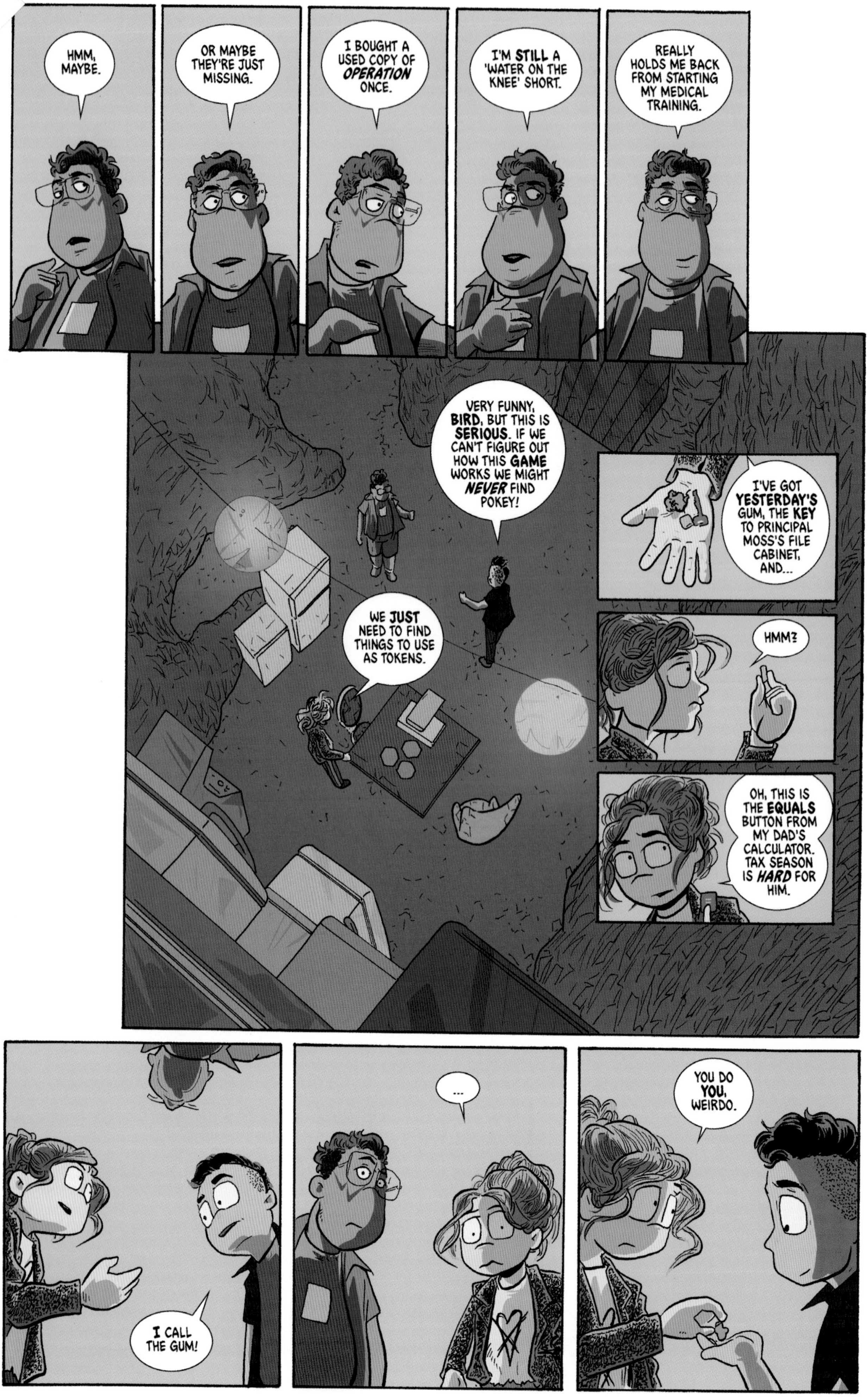
HMM, MAYBE.
OR MAYBE THEY'RE JUST MISSING.
I BOUGHT A USED COPY OF OPERATION ONCE.
I'M STILL A 'WATER ON THE KNEE' SHORT.
REALLY HOLDS ME BACK FROM STARTING MY MEDICAL TRAINING.
VERY FUNNY, BIRD, BUT THIS IS SERIOUS. IF WE CAN'T FIGURE OUT HOW THIS GAME WORKS WE MIGHT NEVER FIND POKEY!
WE JUST NEED TO FIND THINGS TO USE AS TOKENS.
I'VE GOT YESTERDAY'S GUM, THE KEY TO PRINCIPAL MOSS'S FILE CABINET, AND...
HMM?
OH, THIS IS THE EQUALS BUTTON FROM MY DAD'S CALCULATOR. TAX SEASON IS HARD FOR HIM.
I CALL THE GUM!
...
YOU DO YOU, WEIRDO.

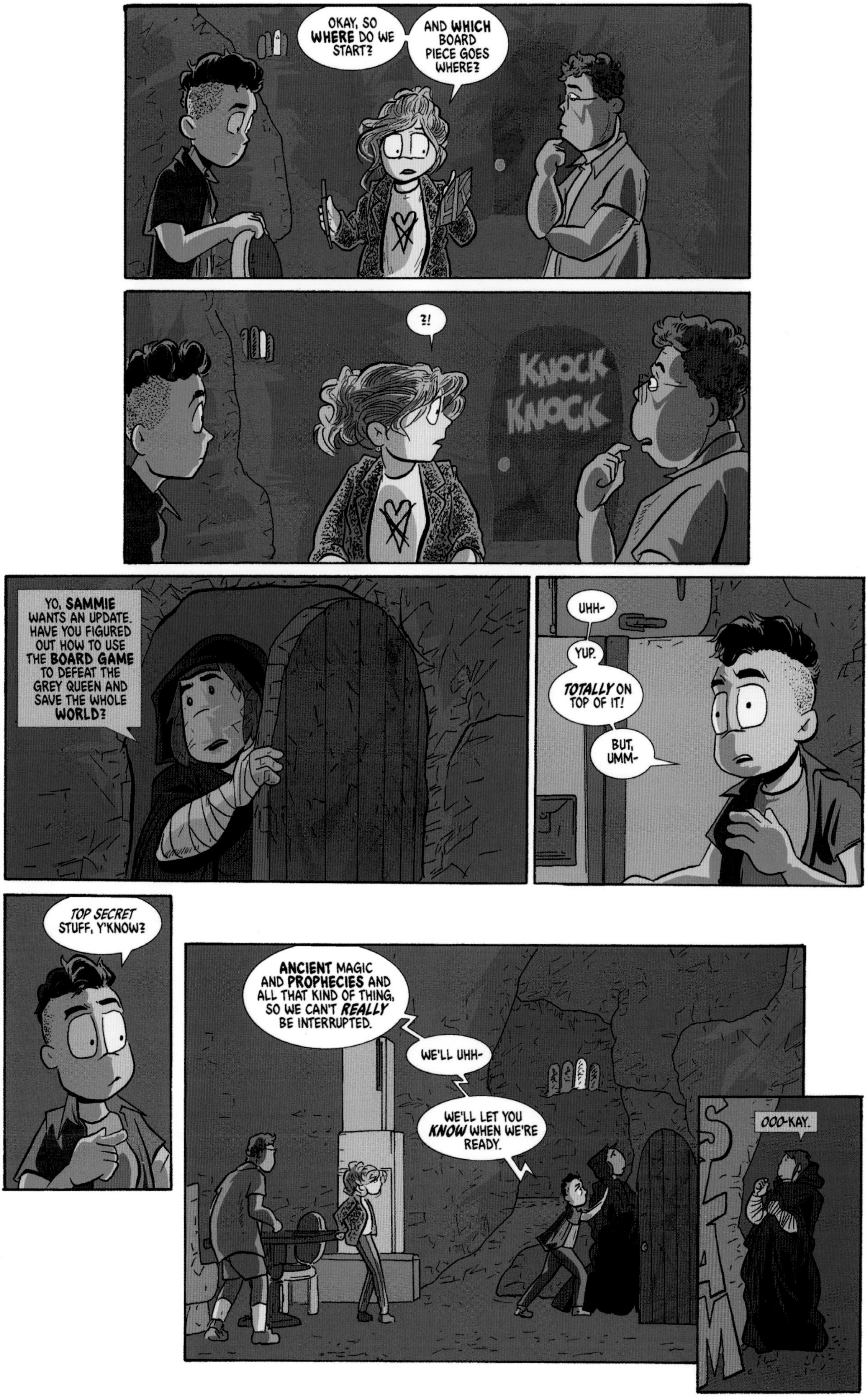
OKAY, SO WHERE DO WE START?
AND WHICH BOARD PIECE GOES WHERE?
?!
KNOCK KNOCK
YO, SAMMIE WANTS AN UPDATE. HAVE YOU FIGURED OUT HOW TO USE THE BOARD GAME TO DEFEAT THE GREY QUEEN AND SAVE THE WHOLE WORLD?
UHH-
YUP.
TOTALLY ON TOP OF IT!
BUT, UMM-
TOP SECRET STUFF, Y'KNOW?
ANCIENT MAGIC AND PROPHECIES AND ALL THAT KIND OF THING, SO WE CAN'T REALLY BE INTERRUPTED.
WE'LL UHH-
WE'LL LET YOU KNOW WHEN WE'RE READY.
OOO-KAY.

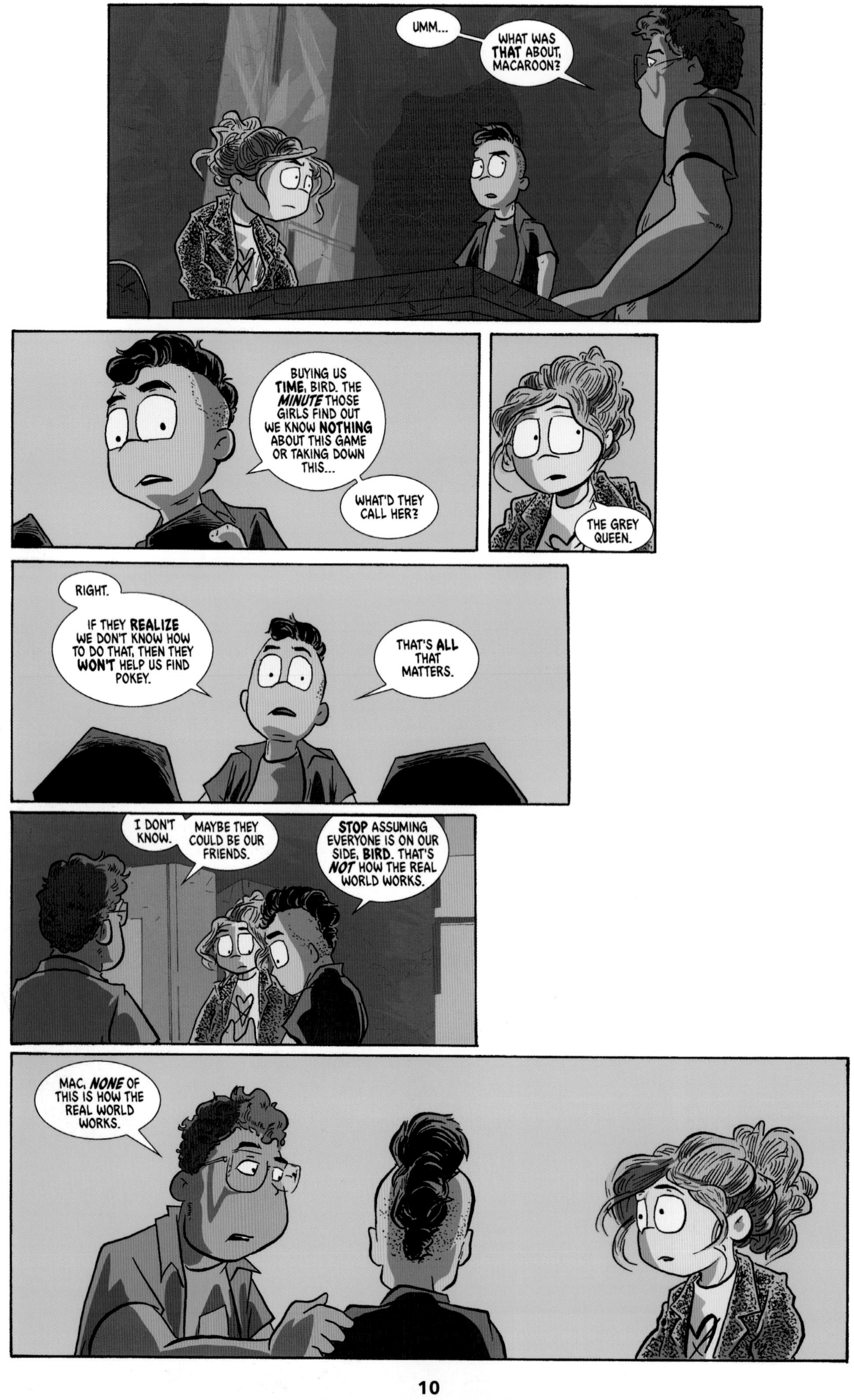
UMM...
WHAT WAS THAT ABOUT, MACAROON?
BUYING US TIME, BIRD. THE MINUTE THOSE GIRLS FIND OUT WE KNOW NOTHING ABOUT THIS GAME OR TAKING DOWN THIS...
WHAT'D THEY CALL HER?
THE GREY QUEEN.
RIGHT.
IF THEY REALIZE WE DON'T KNOW HOW TO DO THAT, THEN THEY WON'T HELP US FIND POKEY.
THAT'S ALL THAT MATTERS.
I DON'T KNOW.
MAYBE THEY COULD BE OUR FRIENDS.
STOP ASSUMING EVERYONE IS ON OUR SIDE, BIRD. THAT'S NOT HOW THE REAL WORLD WORKS.
MAC, NONE OF THIS IS HOW THE REAL WORLD WORKS.

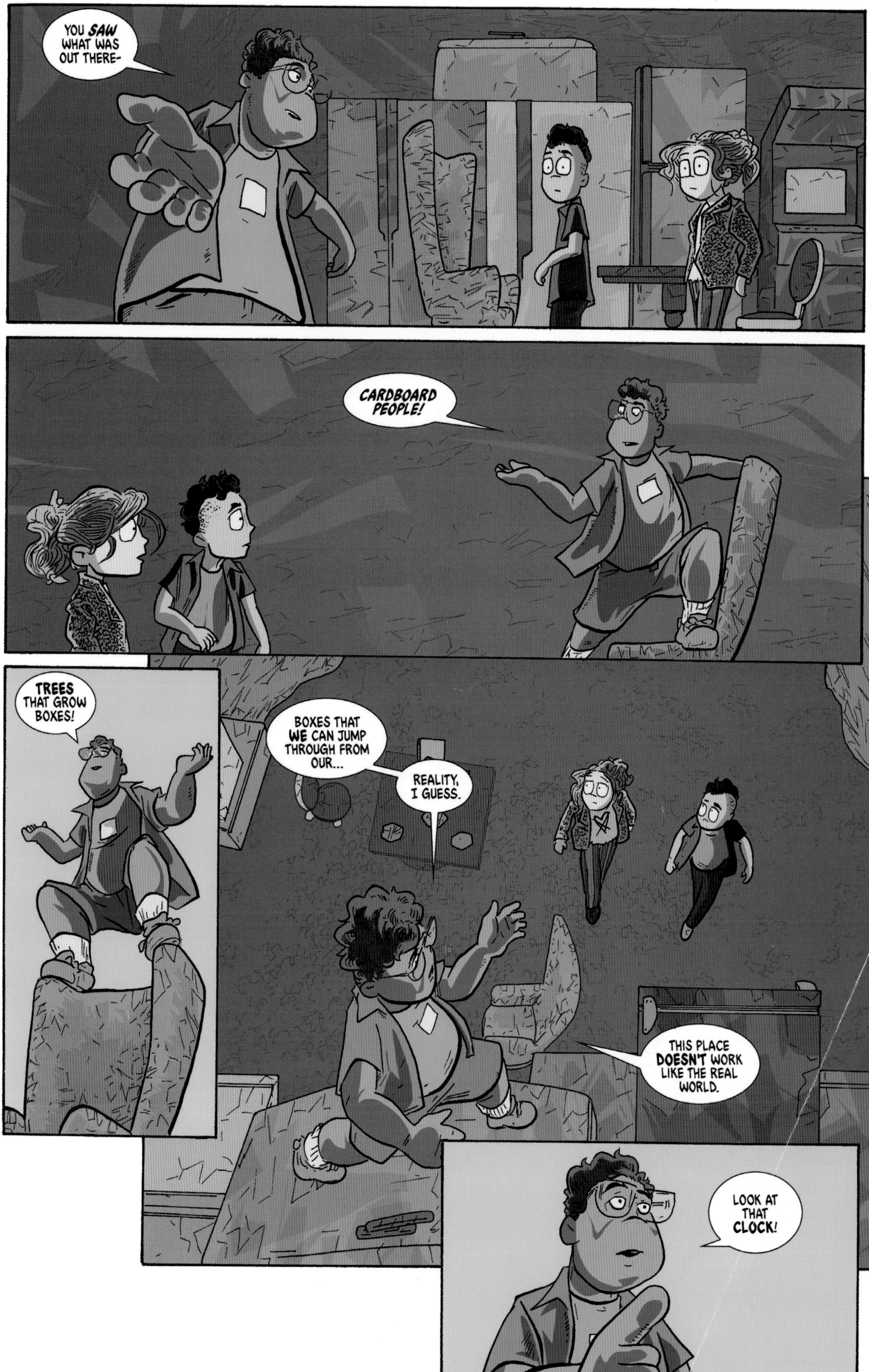
YOU SAW WHAT WAS OUT THERE-
CARDBOARD PEOPLE!
TREES THAT GROW BOXES!
BOXES THAT WE CAN JUMP THROUGH FROM OUR...
REALITY, I GUESS.
THIS PLACE DOESN'T WORK LIKE THE REAL WORLD.
LOOK AT THAT CLOCK!

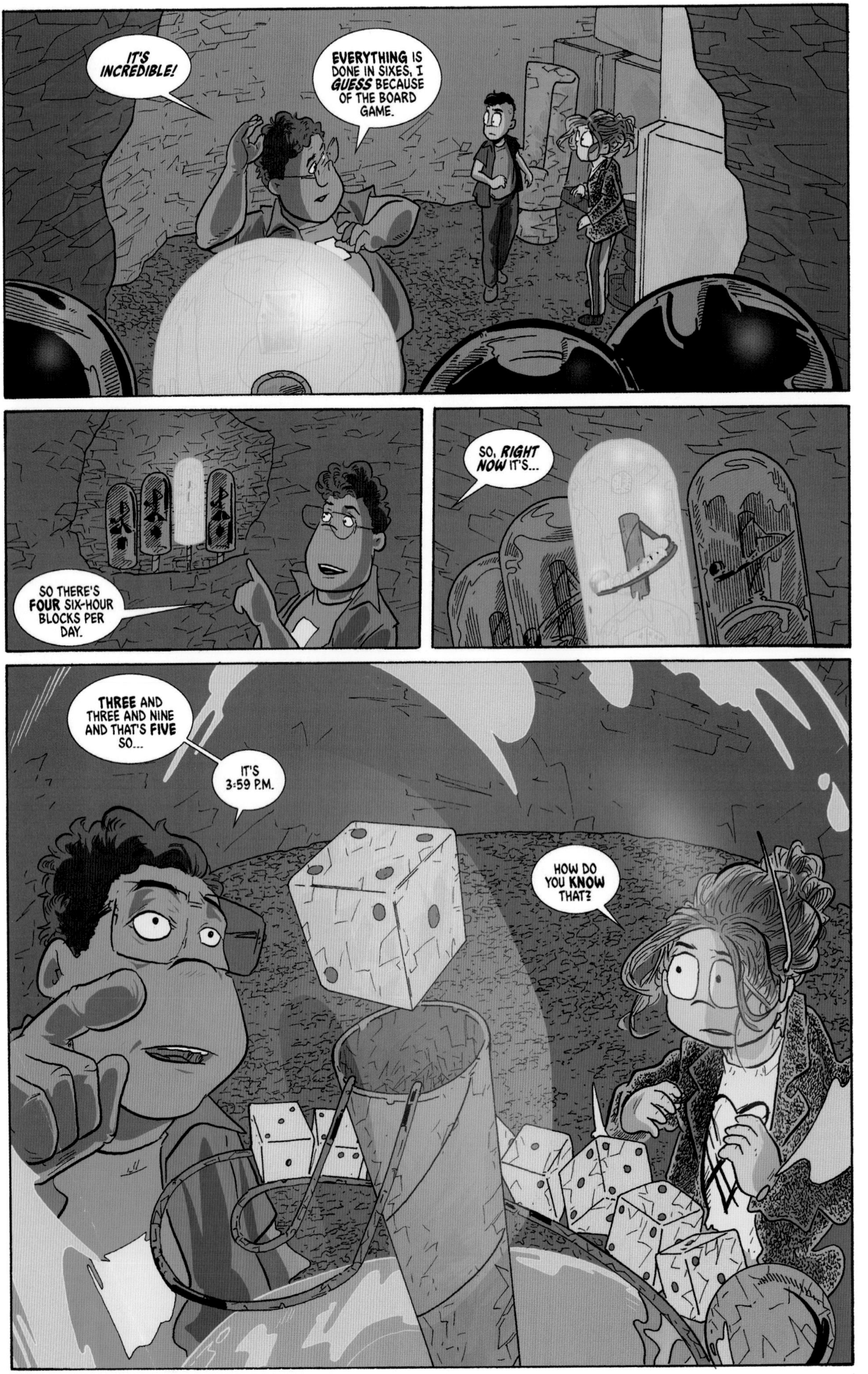
IT'S INCREDIBLE!
EVERYTHING IS DONE IN SIXES, I GUESS BECAUSE OF THE BOARD GAME.
SO THERE'S FOUR SIX-HOUR BLOCKS PER DAY.
SO, RIGHT NOW IT'S...
THREE AND THREE AND NINE AND THAT'S FIVE SO...
IT'S 3:59 P.M.
HOW DO YOU KNOW THAT?

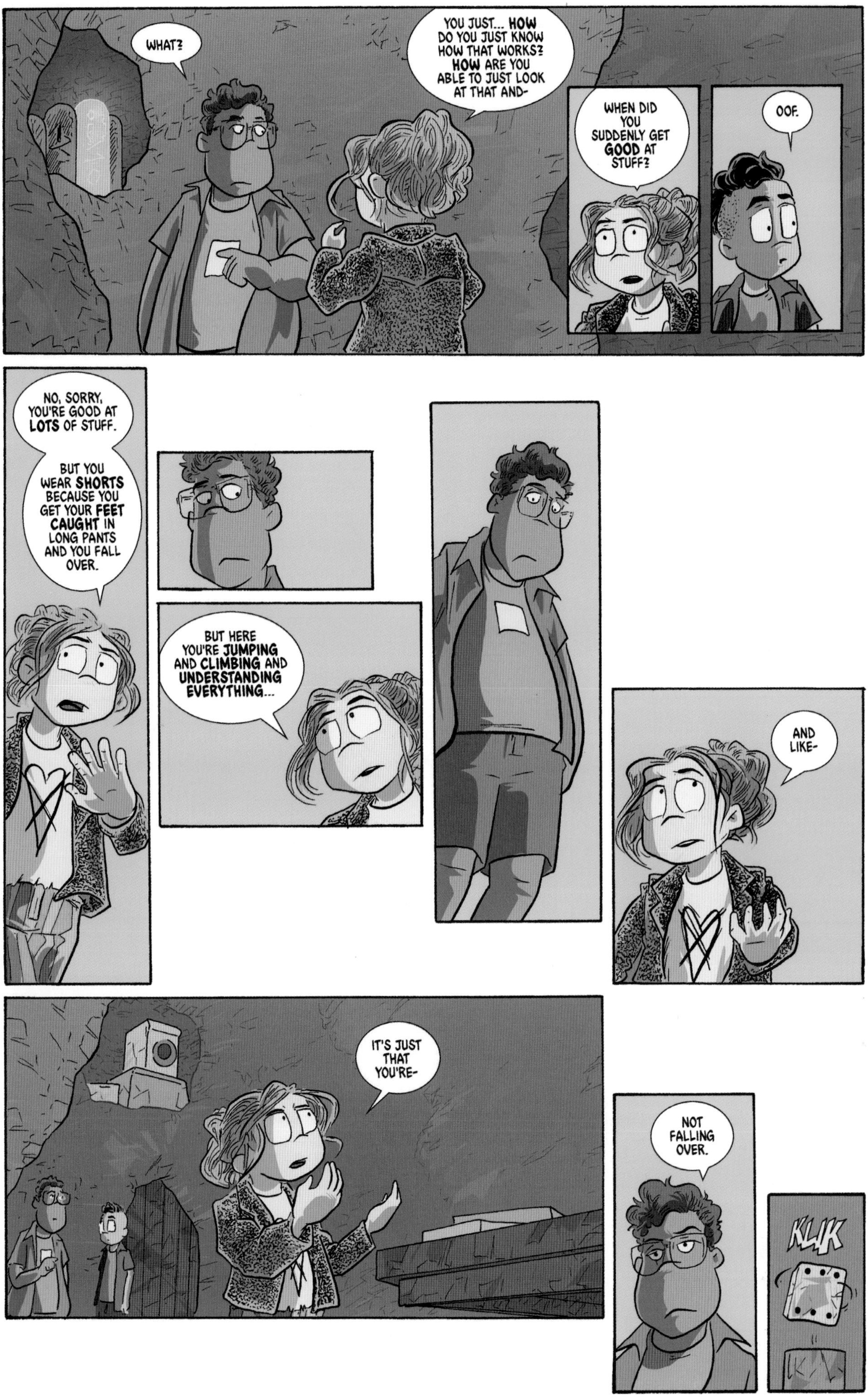
WHAT?
YOU JUST... HOW DO YOU JUST KNOW HOW THAT WORKS? HOW ARE YOU ABLE TO JUST LOOK AT THAT AND-
WHEN DID YOU SUDDENLY GET GOOD AT STUFF?
OOF.
NO, SORRY, YOU'RE GOOD AT LOTS OF STUFF.
BUT YOU WEAR SHORTS BECAUSE YOU GET YOUR FEET CAUGHT IN LONG PANTS AND YOU FALL OVER.
BUT HERE YOU'RE JUMPING AND CLIMBING AND UNDERSTANDING EVERYTHING...
AND LIKE-
IT'S JUST THAT YOU'RE-
NOT FALLING OVER.
KLIK

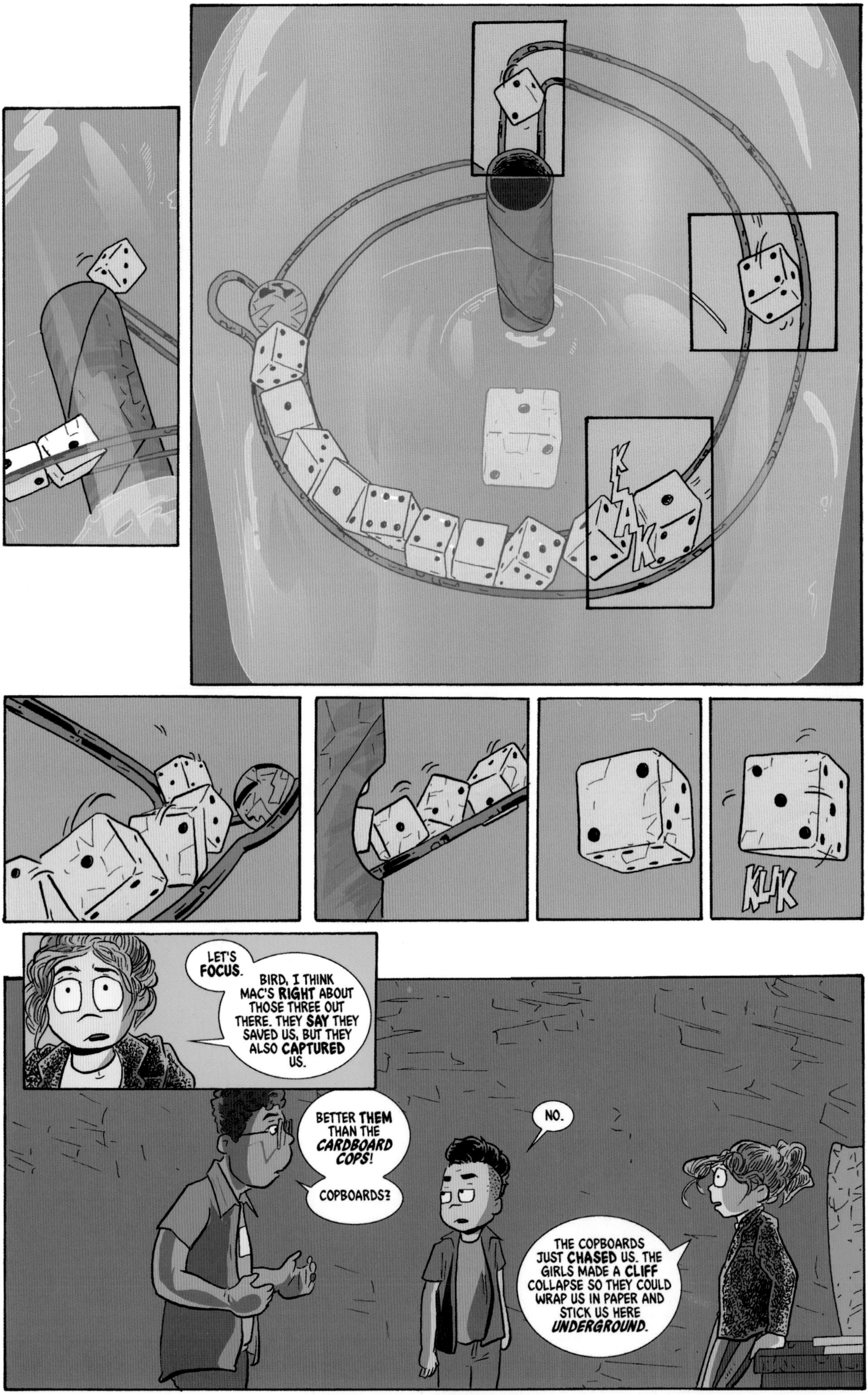
KLAK
KLIK
LET'S FOCUS.
BIRD, I THINK MAC'S RIGHT ABOUT THOSE THREE OUT THERE. THEY SAY THEY SAVED US, BUT THEY ALSO CAPTURED US.
BETTER THEM THAN THE CARDBOARD COPS!
NO.
COPBOARDS?
THE COPBOARDS JUST CHASED US. THE GIRLS MADE A CLIFF COLLAPSE SO THEY COULD WRAP US IN PAPER AND STICK US HERE UNDERGROUND.

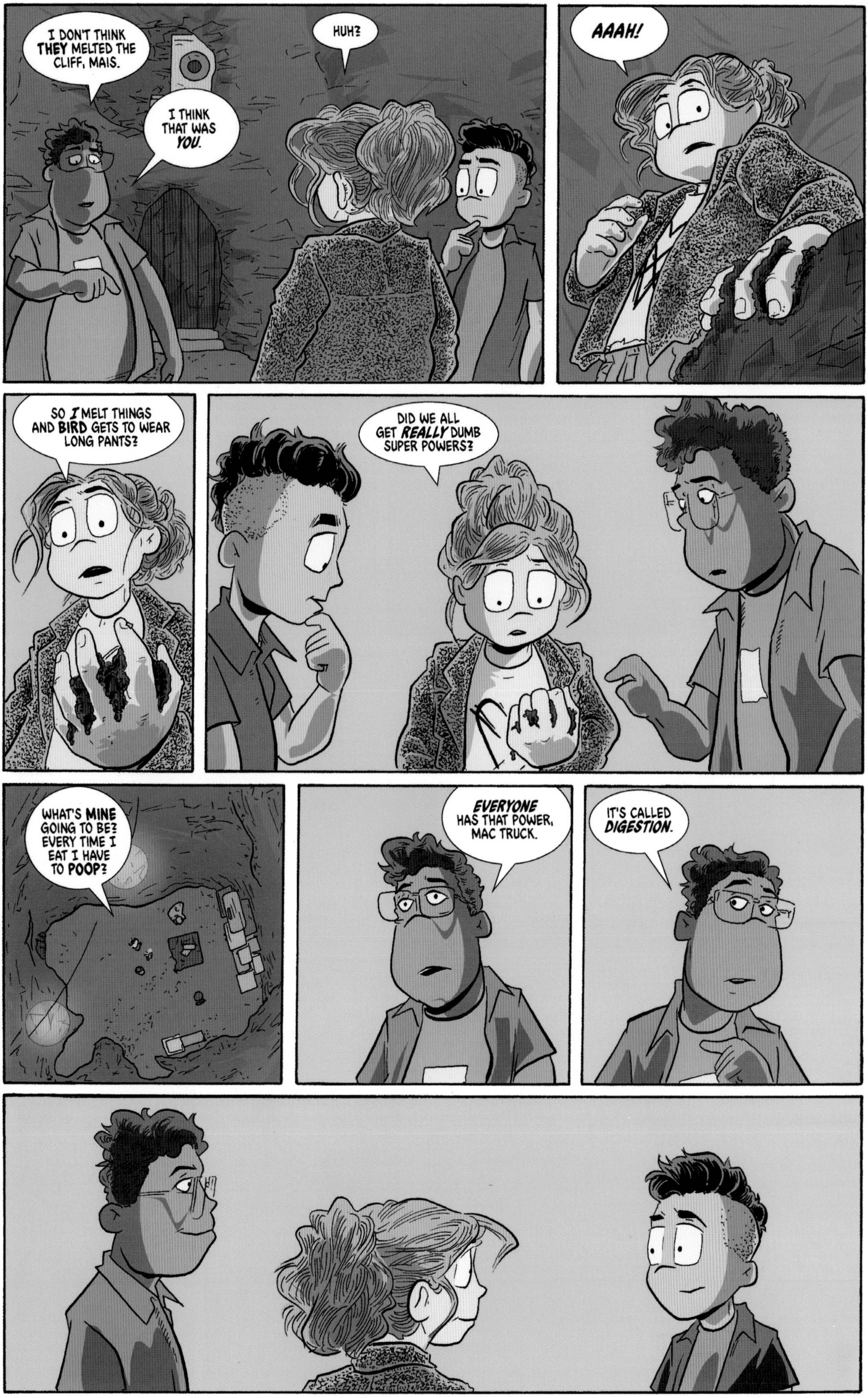
I DON'T THINK THEY MELTED THE CLIFF, MAIS.
I THINK THAT WAS YOU.
HUH?
AAAH!
SO I MELT THINGS AND BIRD GETS TO WEAR LONG PANTS?
DID WE ALL GET REALLY DUMB SUPER POWERS?
WHAT'S MINE GOING TO BE? EVERY TIME I EAT I HAVE TO POOP?
EVERYONE HAS THAT POWER, MAC TRUCK.
IT'S CALLED DIGESTION.

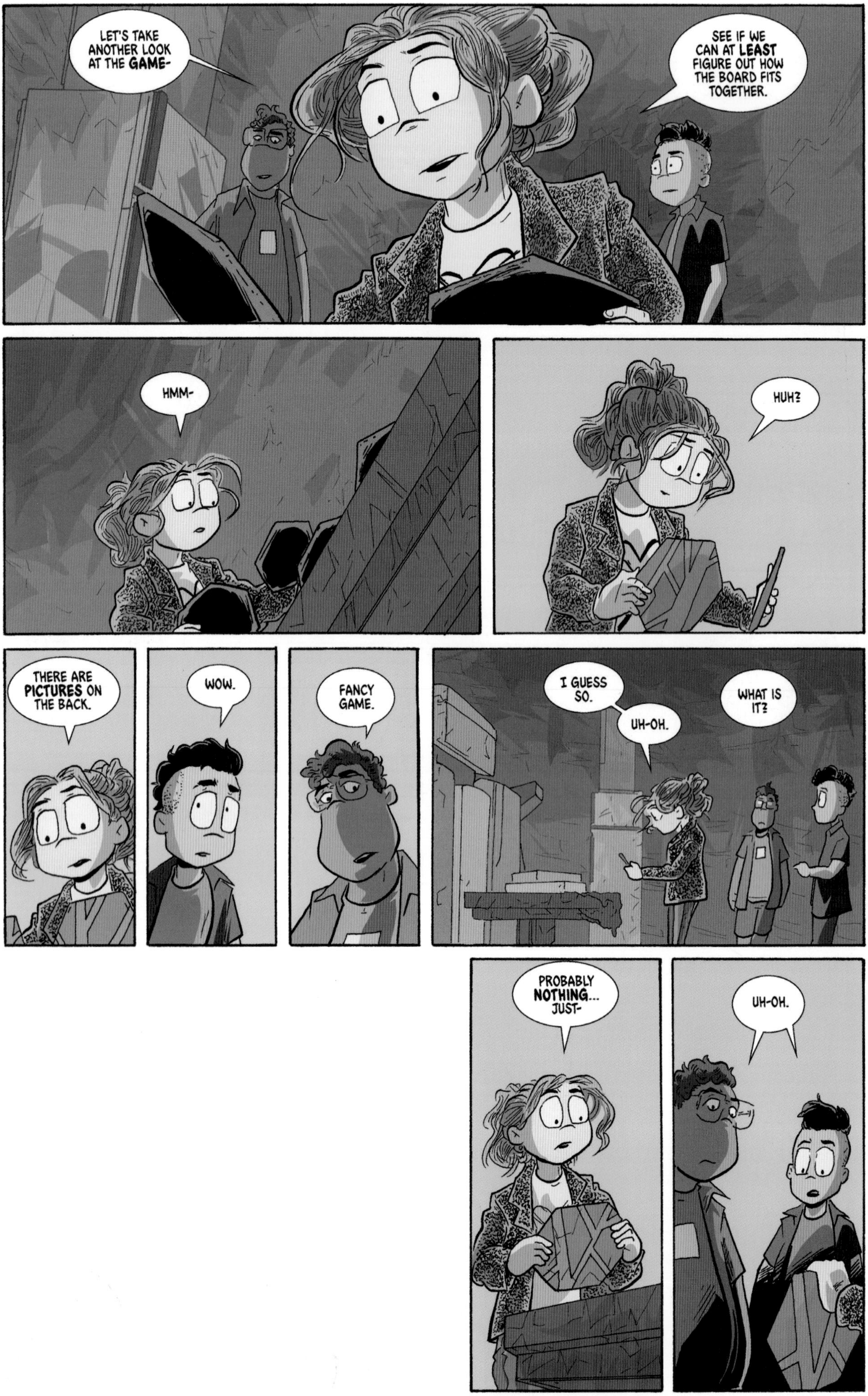
LET'S TAKE ANOTHER LOOK AT THE GAME-
SEE IF WE CAN AT LEAST FIGURE OUT HOW THE BOARD FITS TOGETHER.
HMM-
HUH?
THERE ARE PICTURES ON THE BACK.
WOW.
FANCY GAME.
I GUESS SO.
UH-OH.
WHAT IS IT?
PROBABLY NOTHING... JUST-
UH-OH.

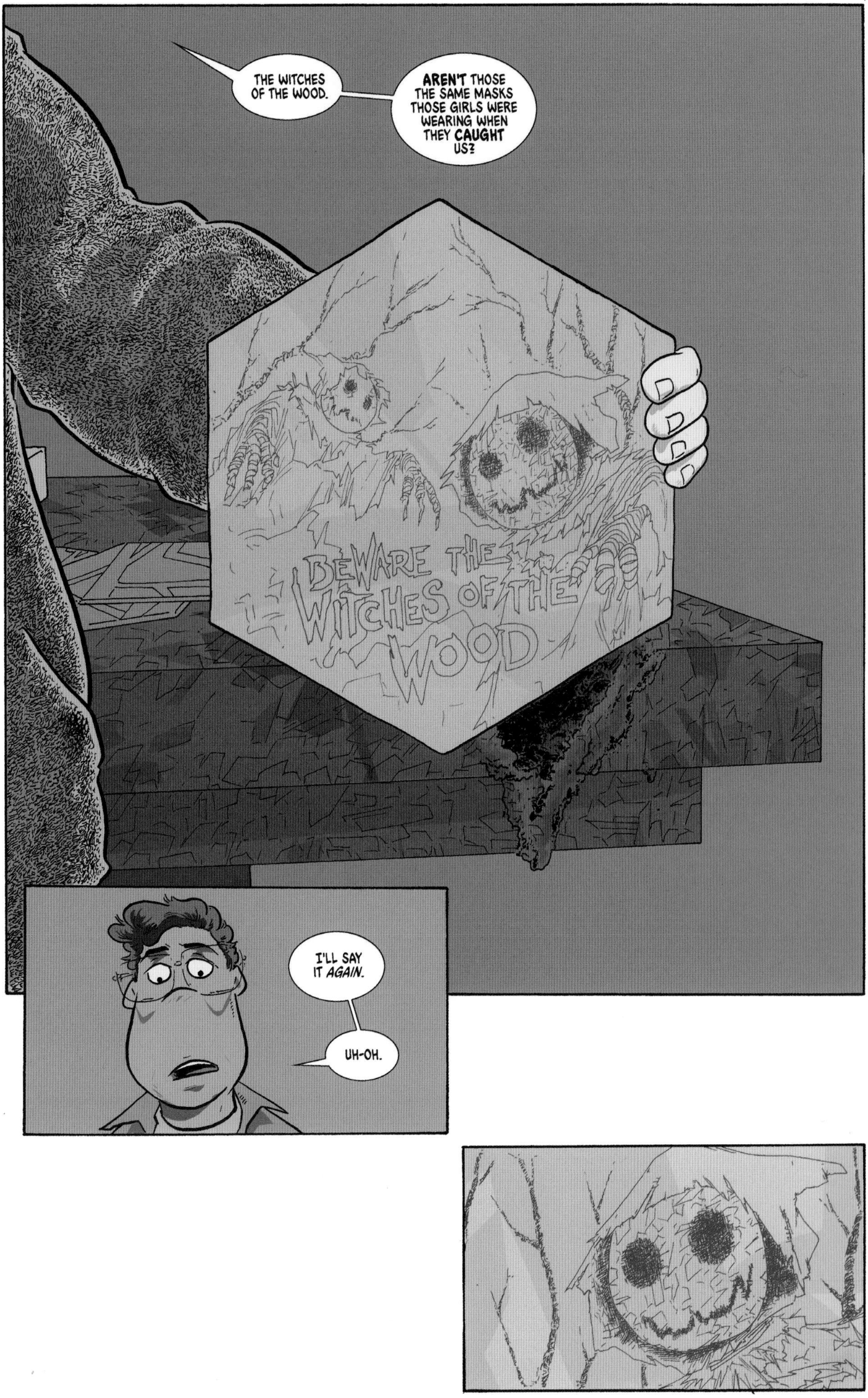
THE WITCHES OF THE WOOD.
AREN'T THOSE THE SAME MASKS THOSE GIRLS WERE WEARING WHEN THEY CAUGHT US?
BEWARE THE WITCHES OF THE WOOD
I'LL SAY IT AGAIN.
UH-OH.

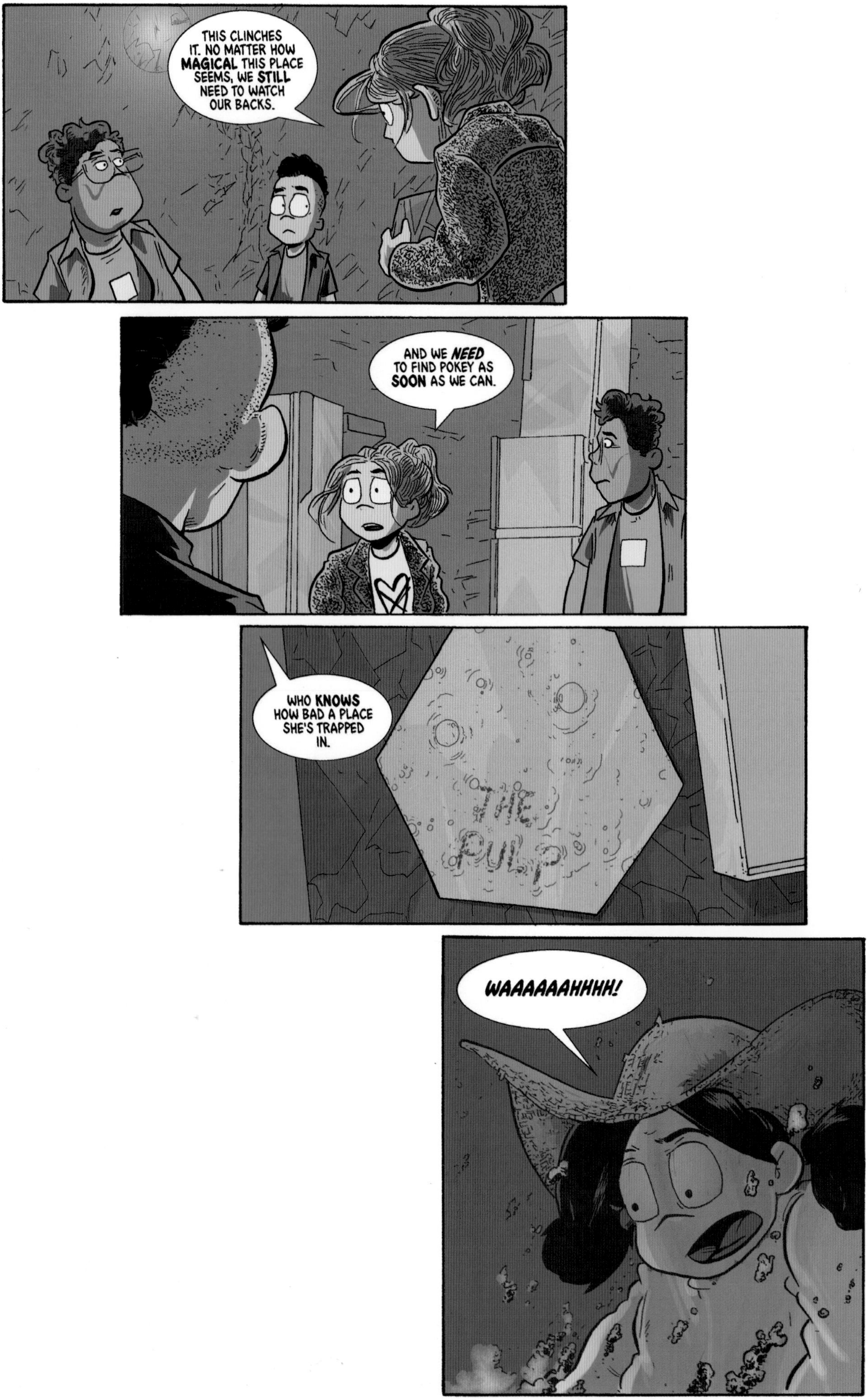
THIS CLINCHES IT. NO MATTER HOW MAGICAL THIS PLACE SEEMS, WE STILL NEED TO WATCH OUR BACKS.
AND WE NEED TO FIND POKEY AS SOON AS WE CAN.
WHO KNOWS HOW BAD A PLACE SHE'S TRAPPED IN.
THE PULP
WAAAAAAHHHH!

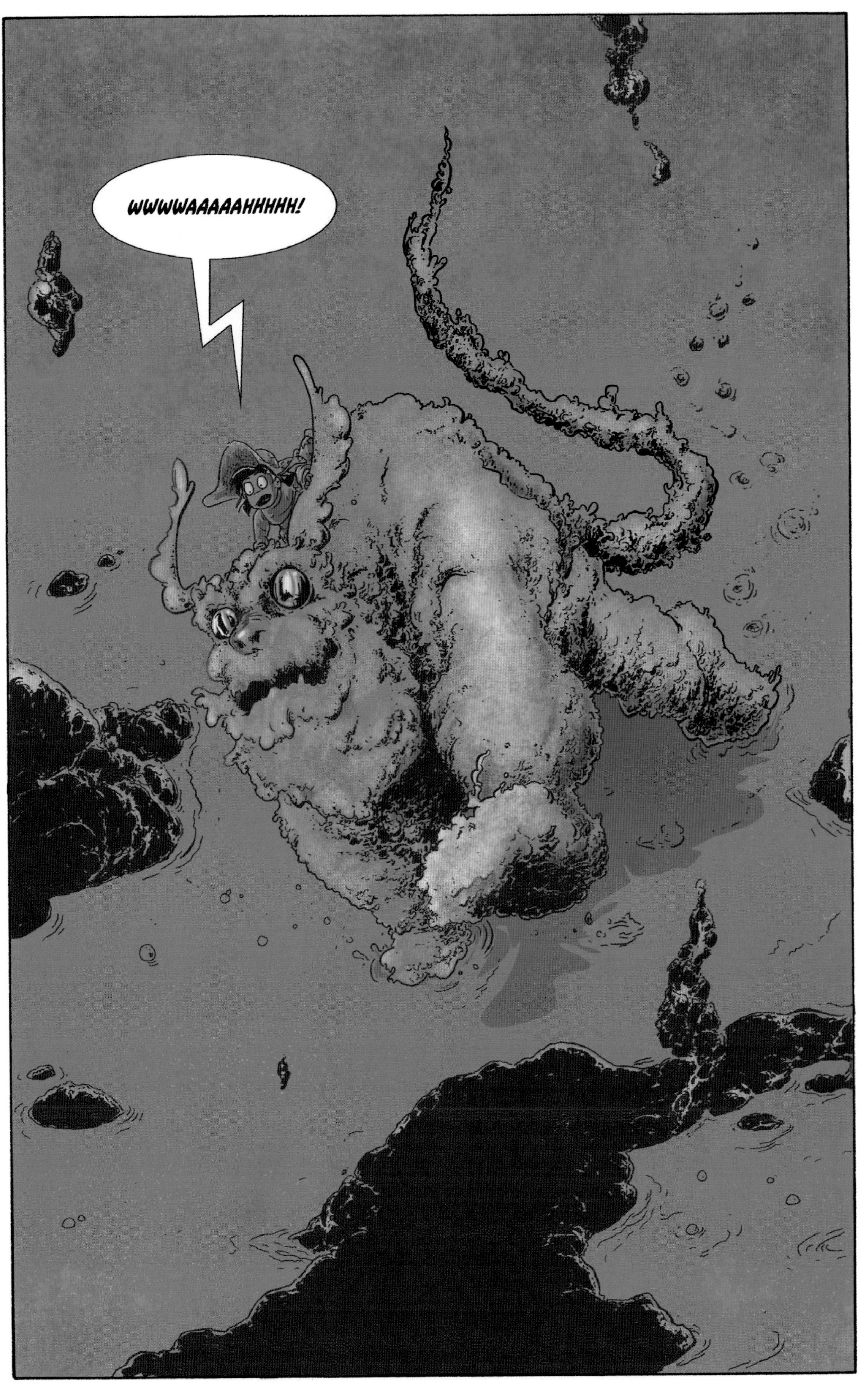
WWWWAAAAAHHHHH!

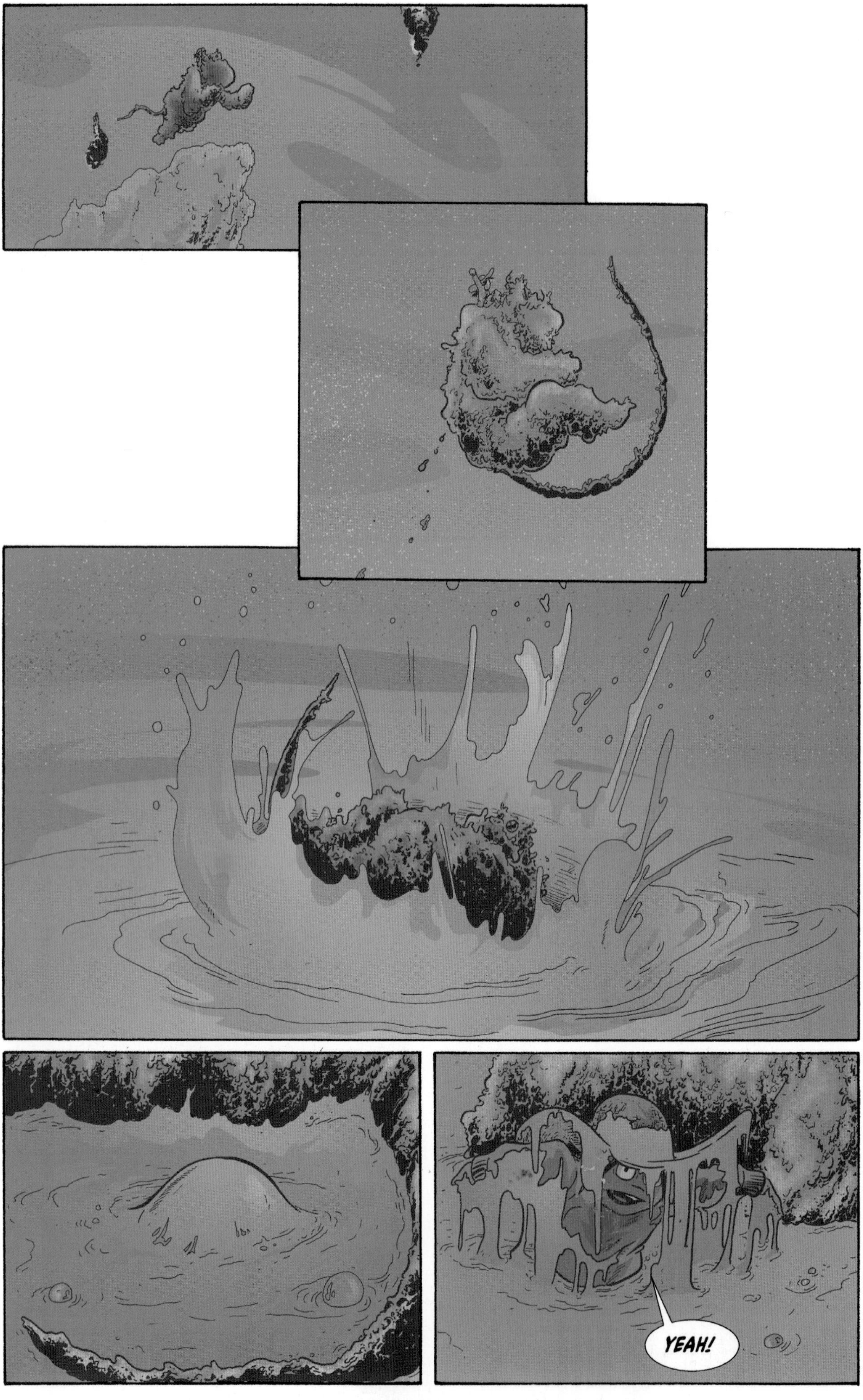
YEAH!

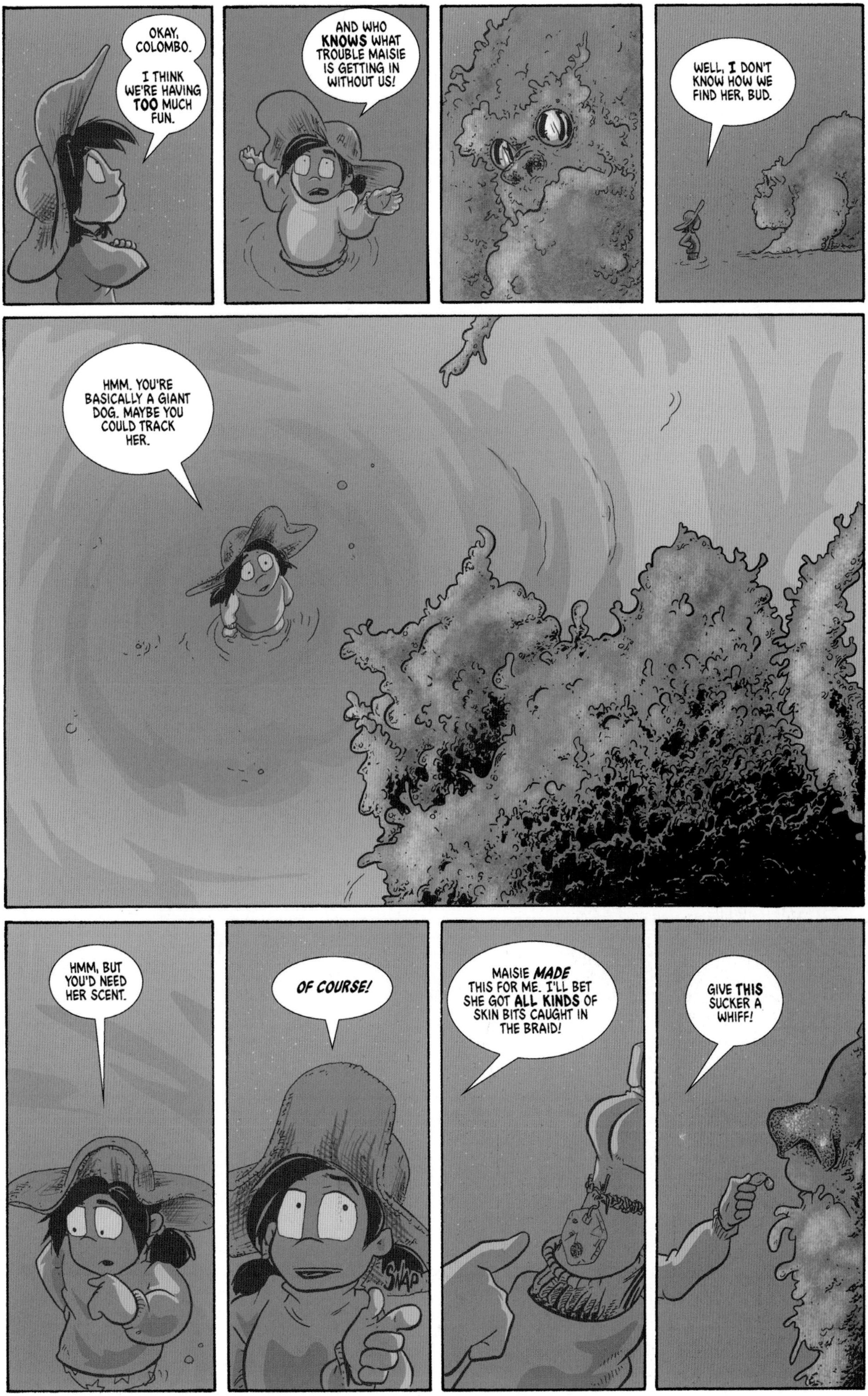
OKAY, COLOMBO.
I THINK WE'RE HAVING TOO MUCH FUN.
AND WHO KNOWS WHAT TROUBLE MAISIE IS GETTING IN WITHOUT US!
WELL, I DON'T KNOW HOW WE FIND HER, BUD.
HMM. YOU'RE BASICALLY A GIANT DOG. MAYBE YOU COULD TRACK HER.
HMM, BUT YOU'D NEED HER SCENT.
OF COURSE!
SNAP
MAISIE MADE THIS FOR ME. I'LL BET SHE GOT ALL KINDS OF SKIN BITS CAUGHT IN THE BRAID!
GIVE THIS SUCKER A WHIFF!

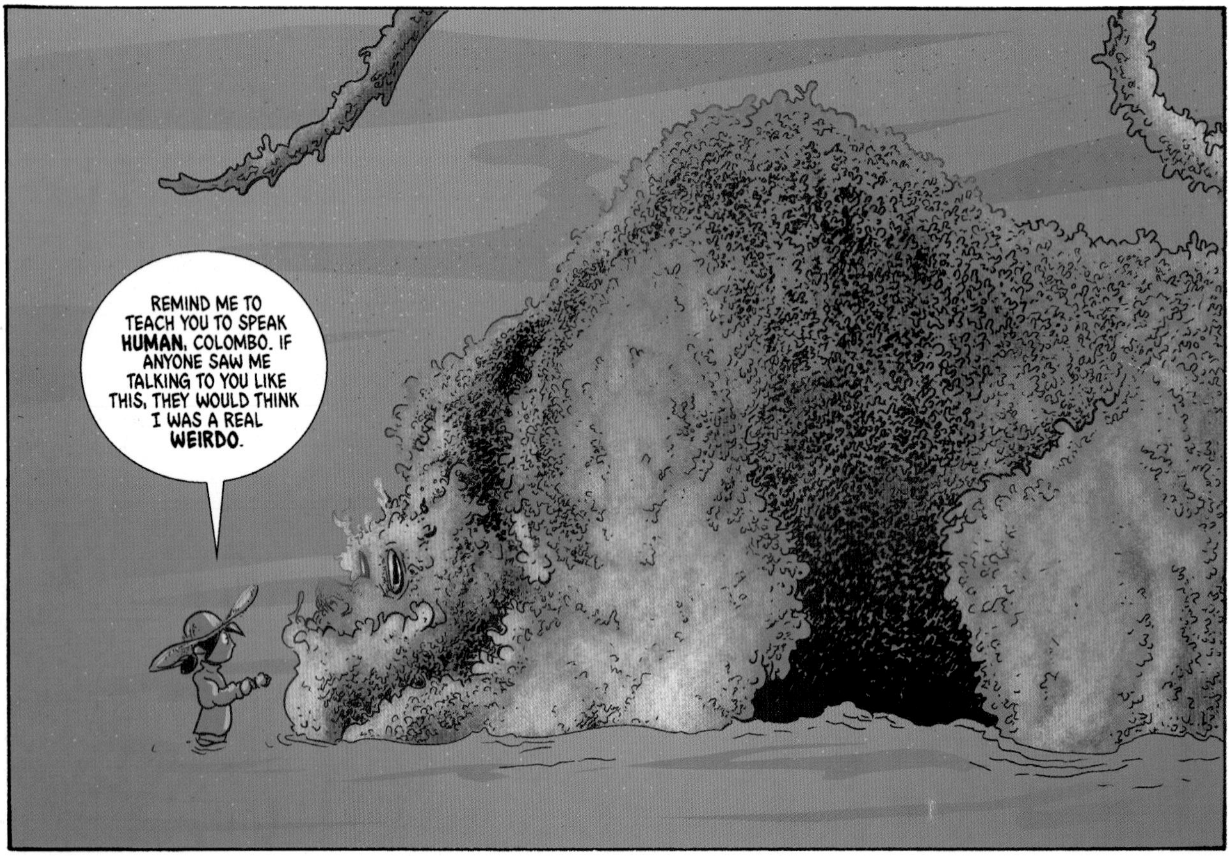
REMIND ME TO TEACH YOU TO SPEAK **HUMAN**, COLOMBO. IF ANYONE SAW ME TALKING TO YOU LIKE THIS, THEY WOULD THINK I WAS A REAL **WEIRDO**.

TO BE CONTINUED.

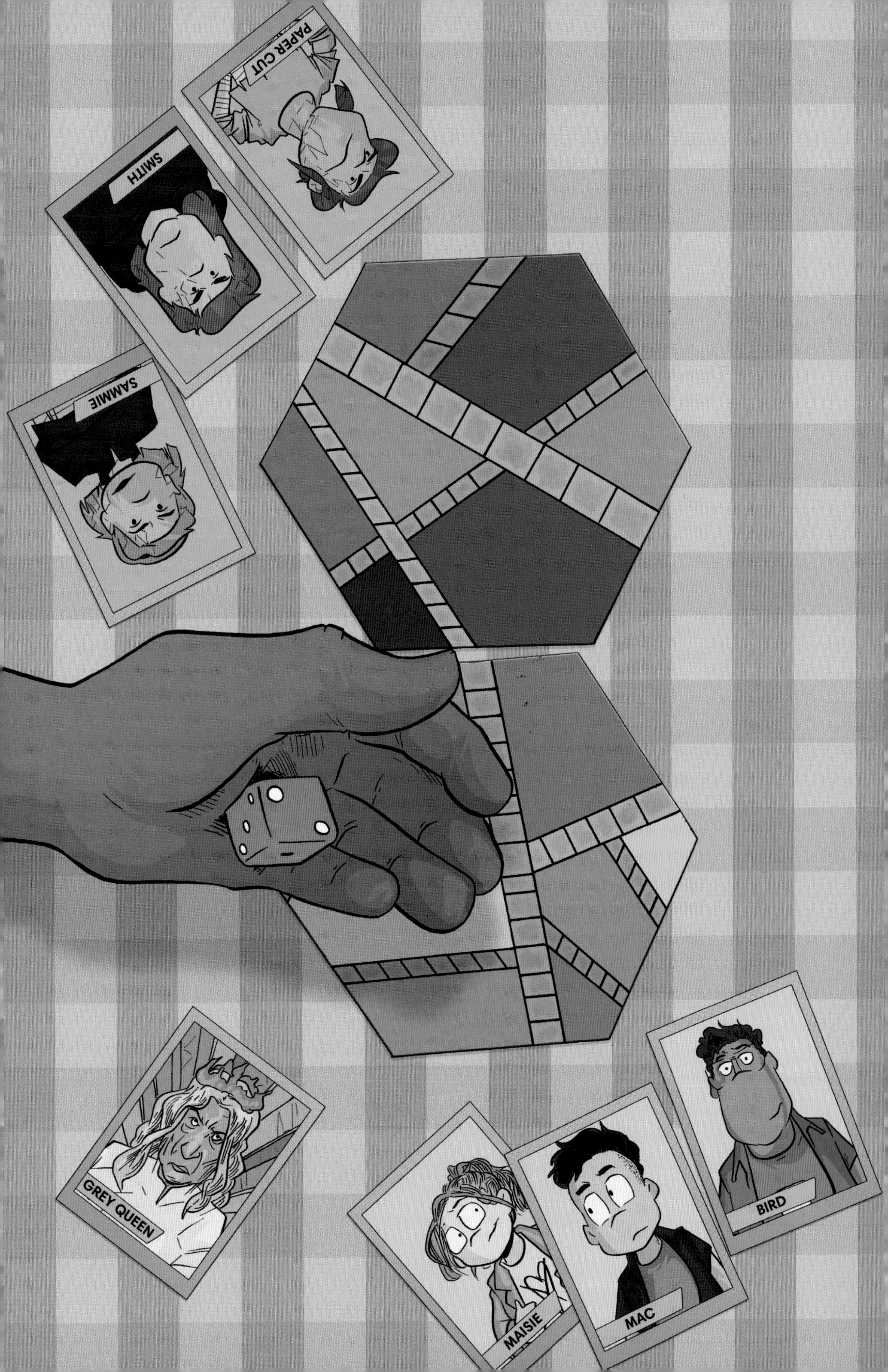
PAPER CUT
SMITH
SAMMIE
GREY QUEEN
MAISIE
MAC
BIRD

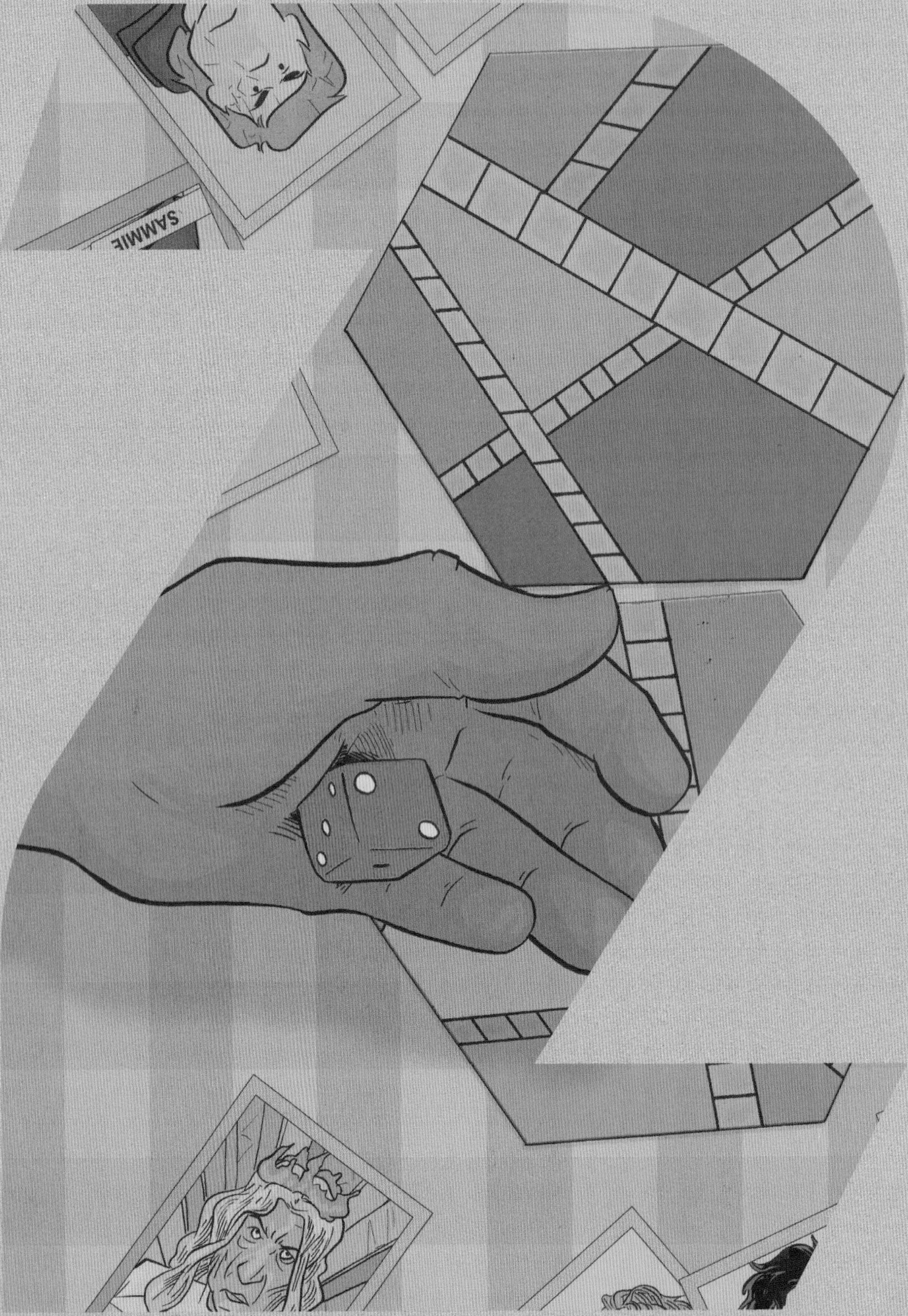
SAMMIE

ANCIENT MAGIC AND PROPHECIES AND ALL THAT KIND OF THING, SO WE CAN'T *REALLY* BE INTERRUPTED.

WE'LL UHH—

WE'LL LET YOU *KNOW* WHEN WE'RE READY.

OOO-KAY.

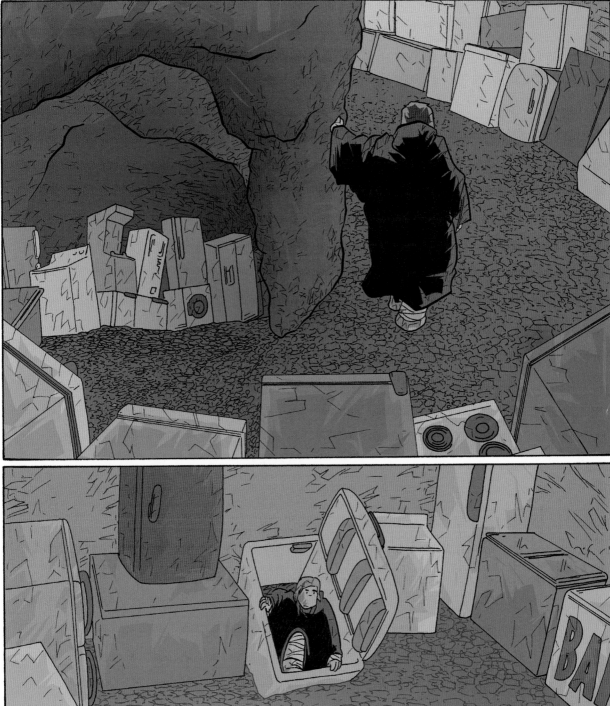

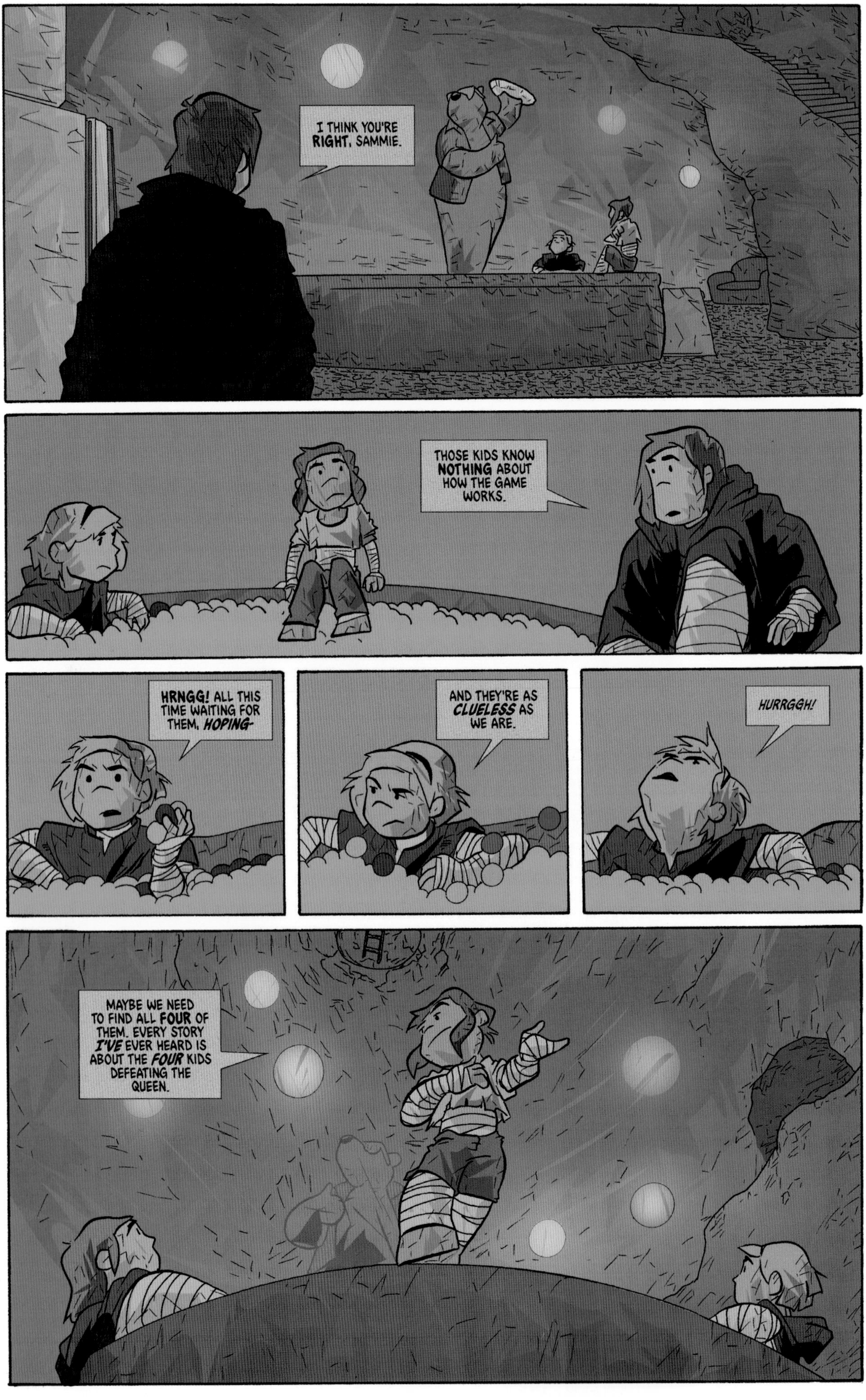

I THINK YOU'RE RIGHT, SAMMIE.
THOSE KIDS KNOW NOTHING ABOUT HOW THE GAME WORKS.
HRNGG! ALL THIS TIME WAITING FOR THEM, HOPING-
AND THEY'RE AS CLUELESS AS WE ARE.
HURRGGH!
MAYBE WE NEED TO FIND ALL FOUR OF THEM. EVERY STORY I'VE EVER HEARD IS ABOUT THE FOUR KIDS DEFEATING THE QUEEN.

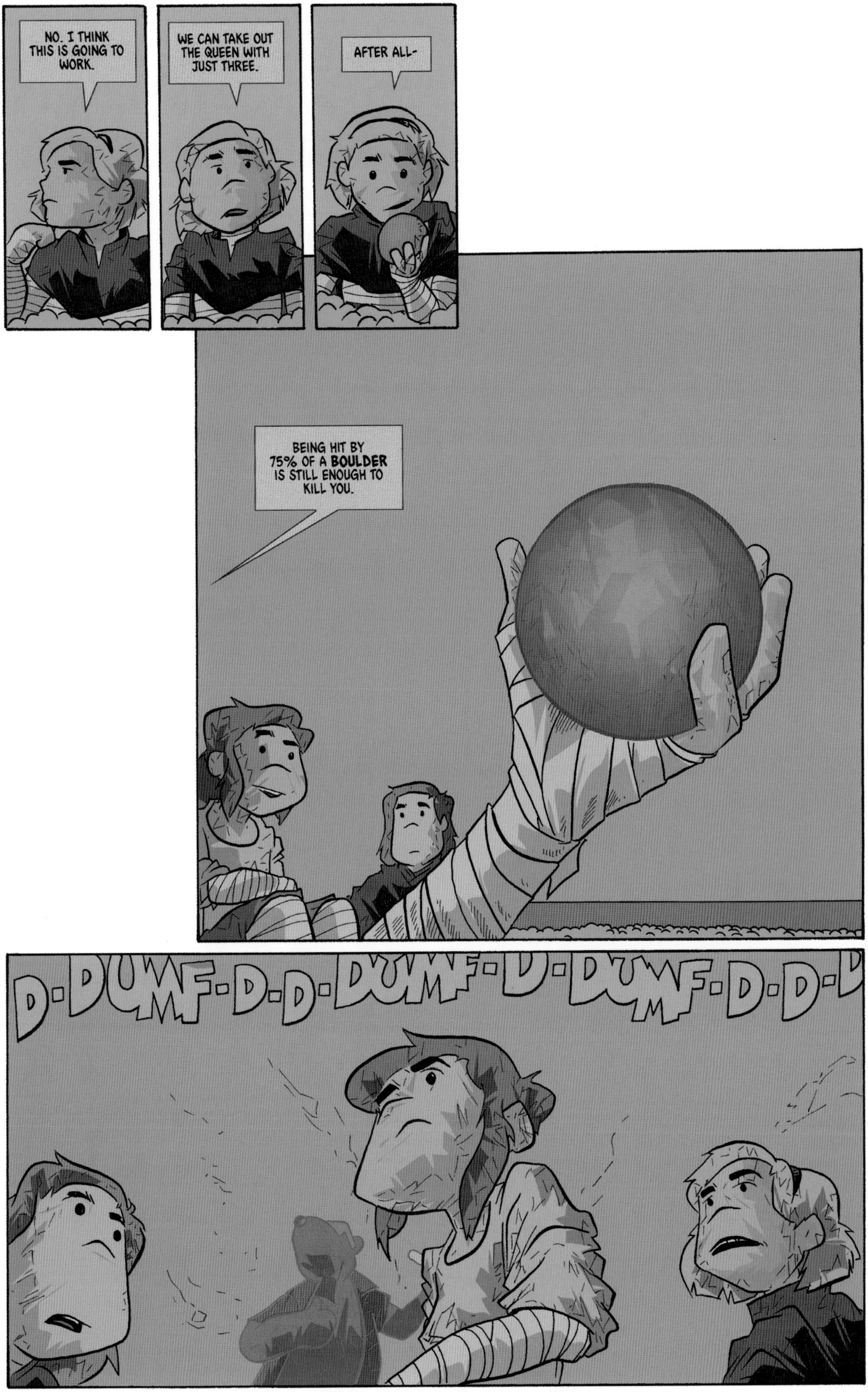
NO. I THINK THIS IS GOING TO WORK.
WE CAN TAKE OUT THE QUEEN WITH JUST THREE.
AFTER ALL-
BEING HIT BY 75% OF A BOULDER IS STILL ENOUGH TO KILL YOU.
D-DUMF-D-D-DUMF-D-DUMF-D-D-D

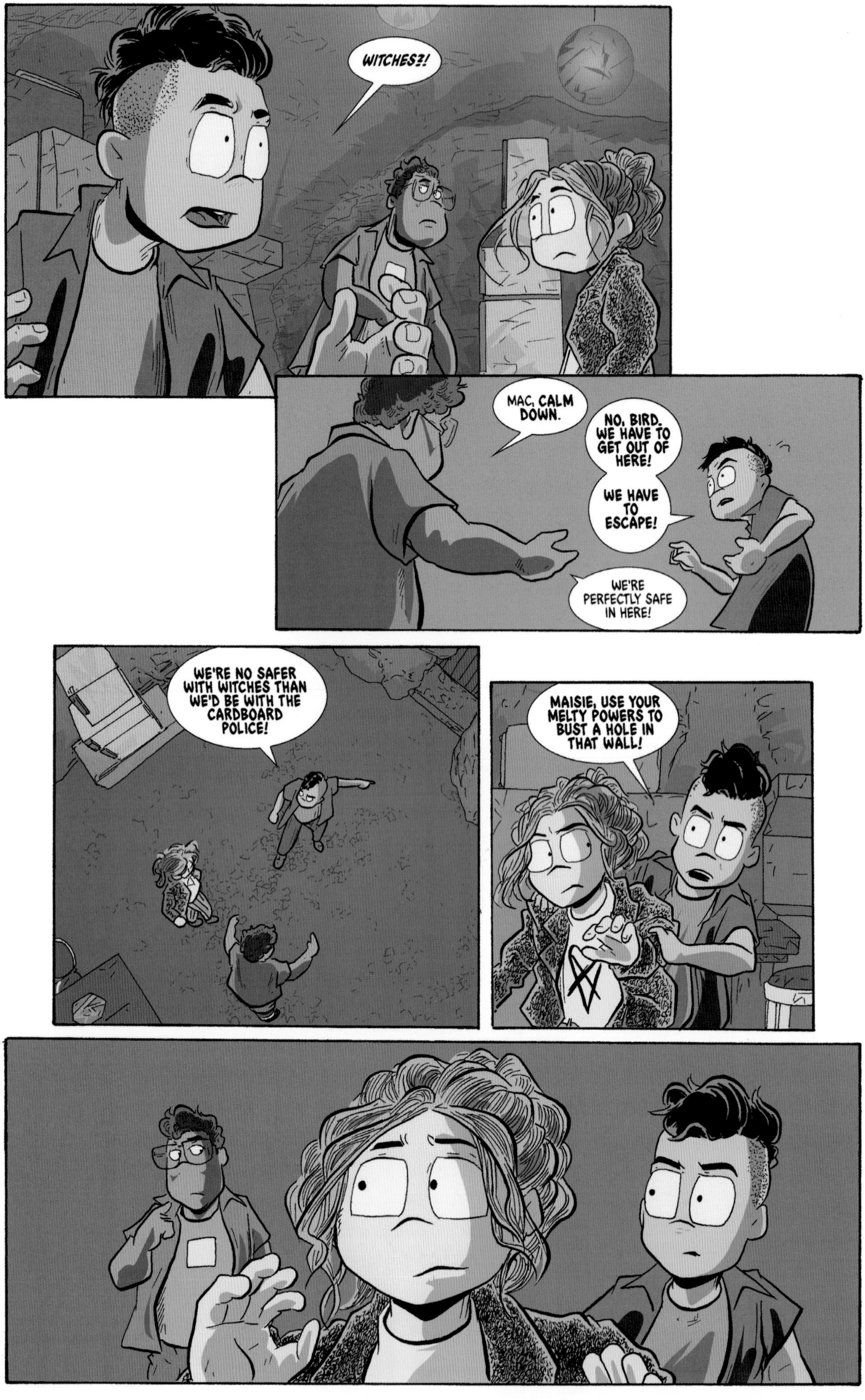
WITCHES?!
MAC, CALM DOWN.
NO, BIRD. WE HAVE TO GET OUT OF HERE!
WE HAVE TO ESCAPE!
WE'RE PERFECTLY SAFE IN HERE!
WE'RE NO SAFER WITH WITCHES THAN WE'D BE WITH THE CARDBOARD POLICE!
MAISIE, USE YOUR MELTY POWERS TO BUST A HOLE IN THAT WALL!

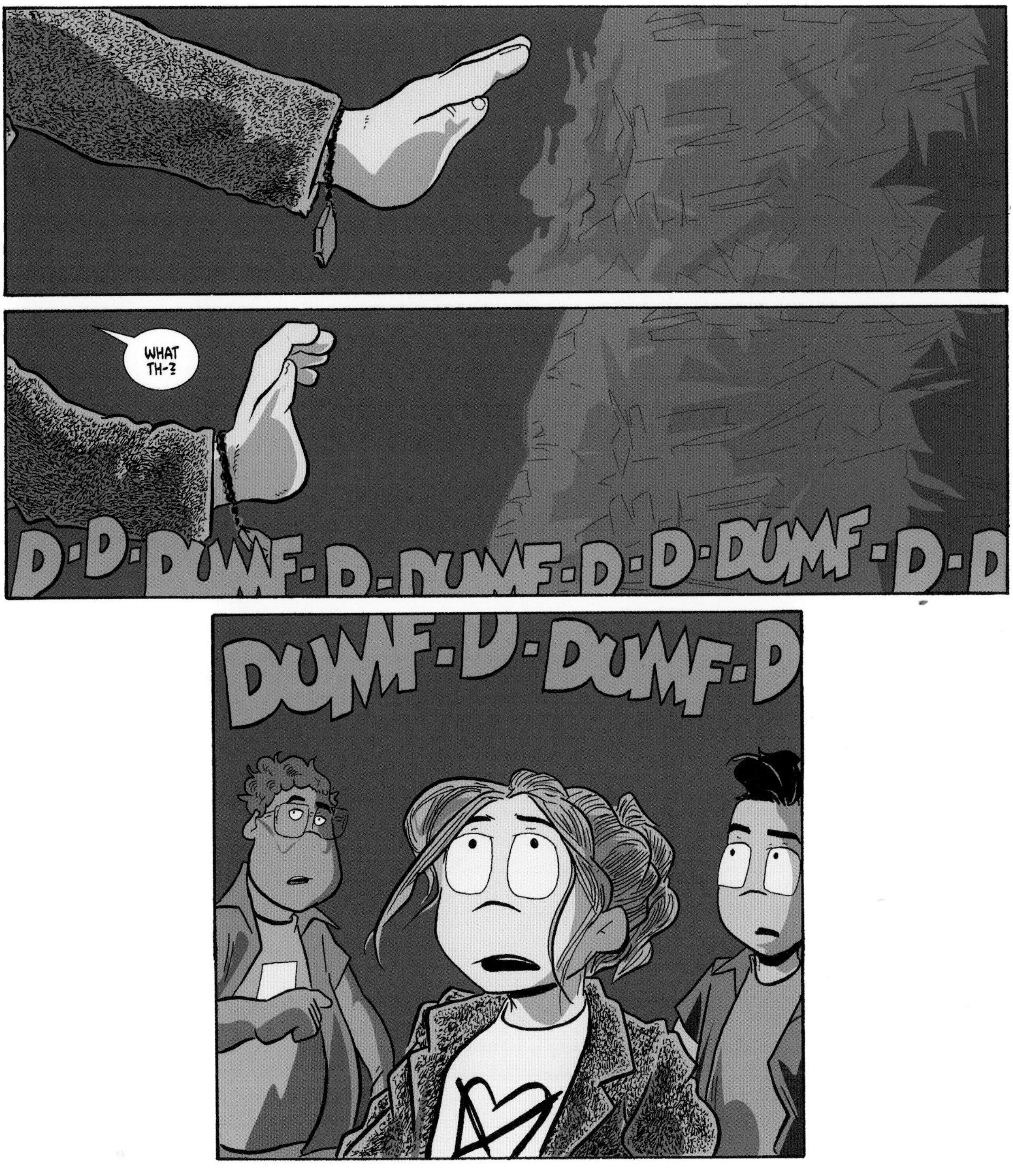
WHAT TH-?
D-D-DUMF-D-DUMF-D-D-DUMF-D-D
DUMF-D-DUMF-D

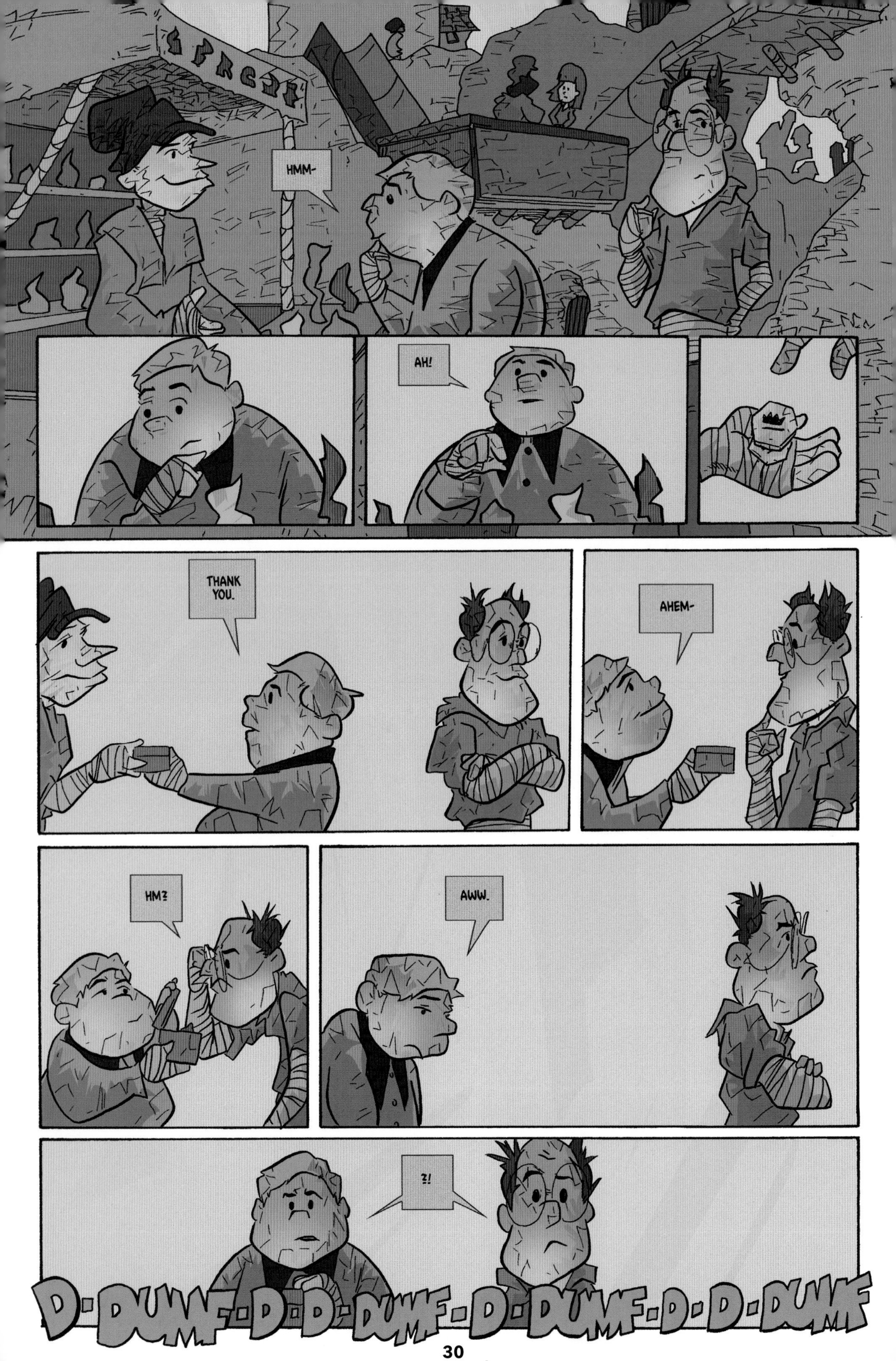
SPRCE
HMM-
AH!
THANK YOU.
AHEM-
HM?
AWW.
?!
D-DUMF-D-D-DUMF-D-DUMF-D-D-DUMF

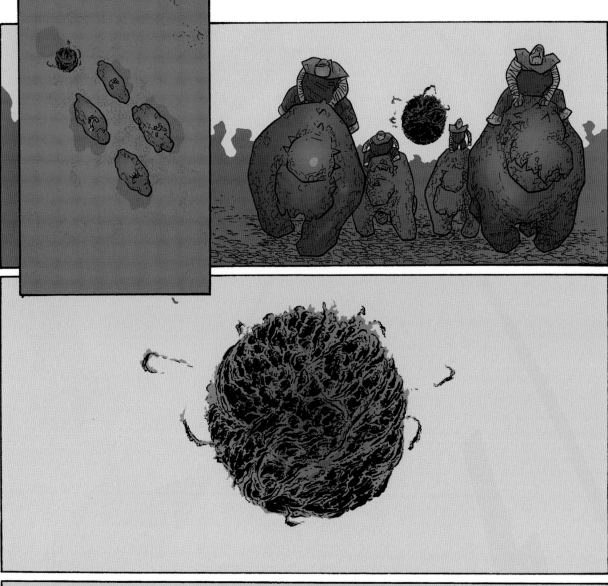

HMPH!

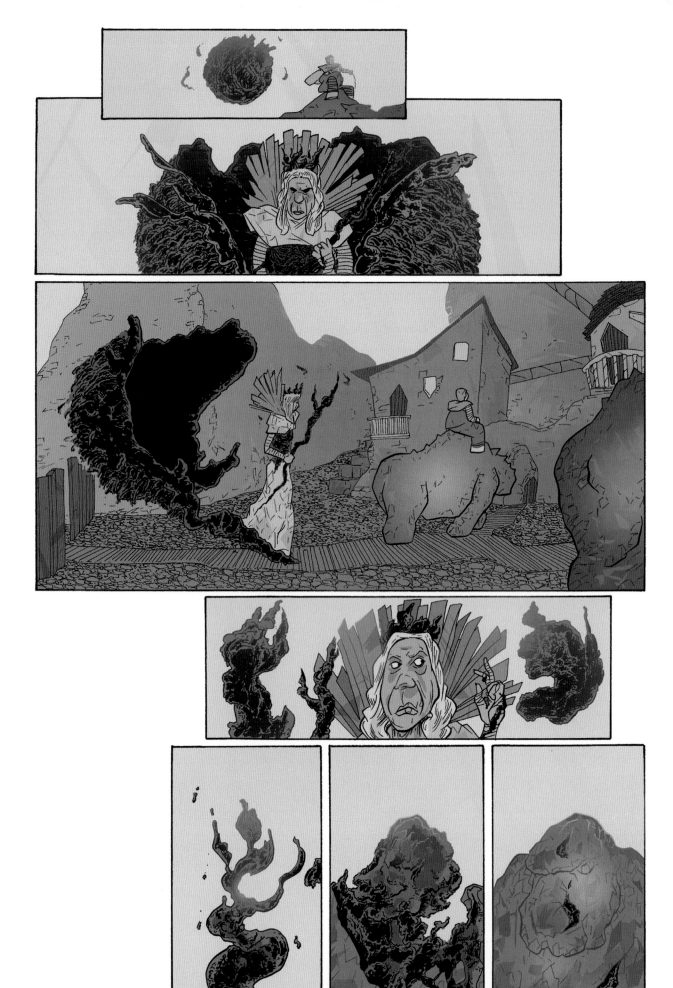

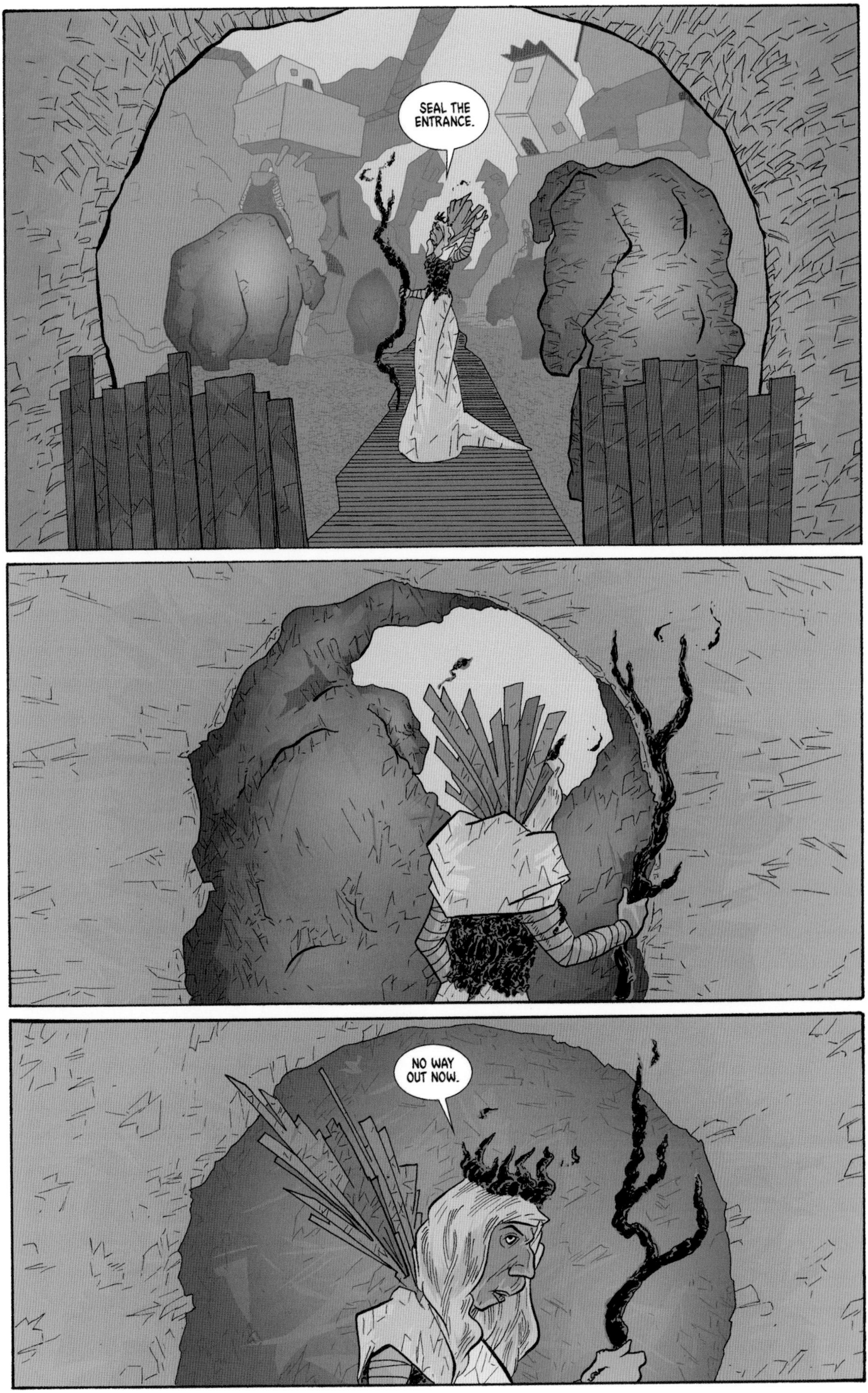
SEAL THE ENTRANCE.
NO WAY OUT NOW.

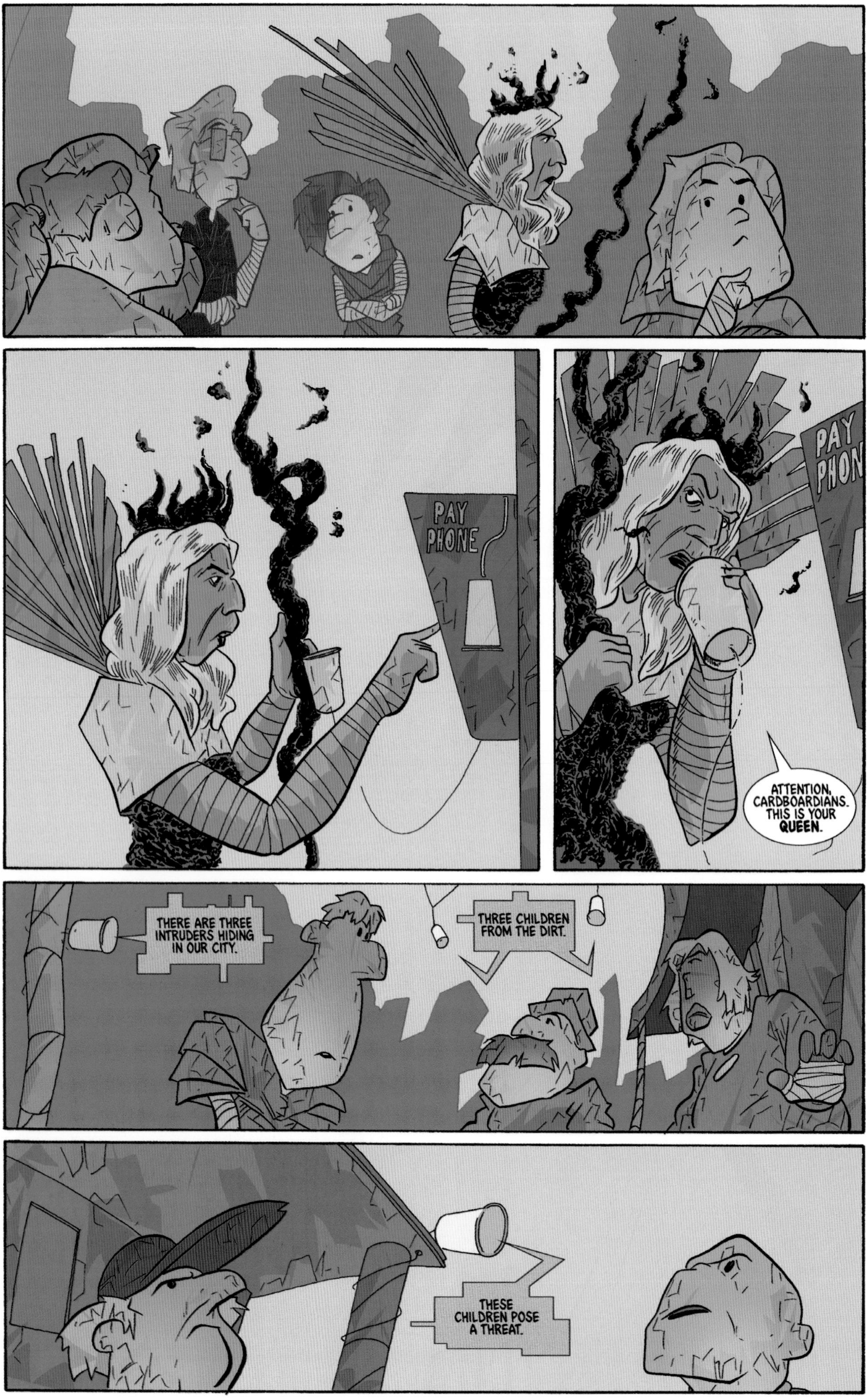
PAY PHONE
PAY PHONE
ATTENTION, CARDBOARDIANS. THIS IS YOUR QUEEN.
THERE ARE THREE INTRUDERS HIDING IN OUR CITY.
THREE CHILDREN FROM THE DIRT.
THESE CHILDREN POSE A THREAT.

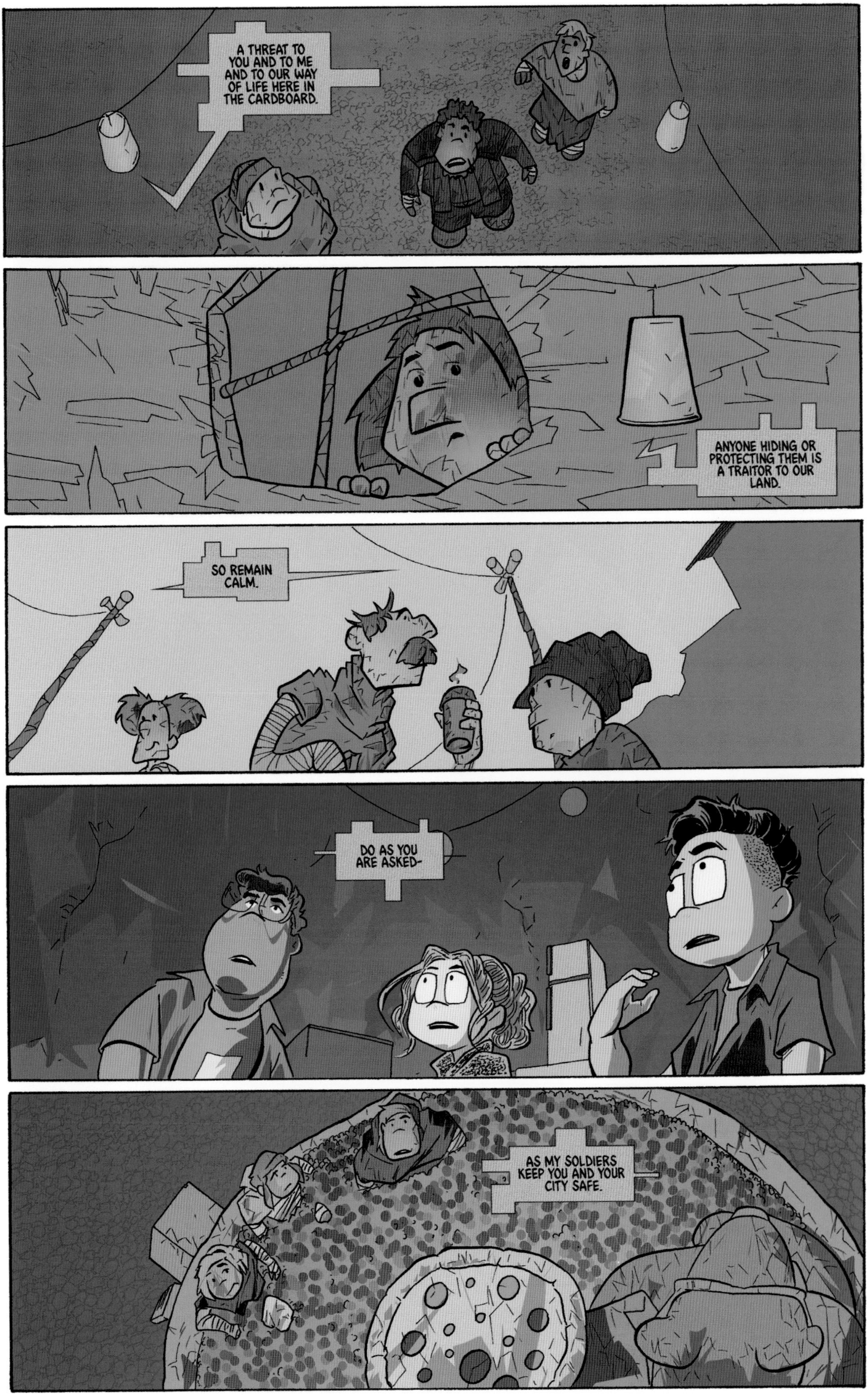
A THREAT TO YOU AND TO ME AND TO OUR WAY OF LIFE HERE IN THE CARDBOARD.
ANYONE HIDING OR PROTECTING THEM IS A TRAITOR TO OUR LAND.
SO REMAIN CALM.
DO AS YOU ARE ASKED-
AS MY SOLDIERS KEEP YOU AND YOUR CITY SAFE.

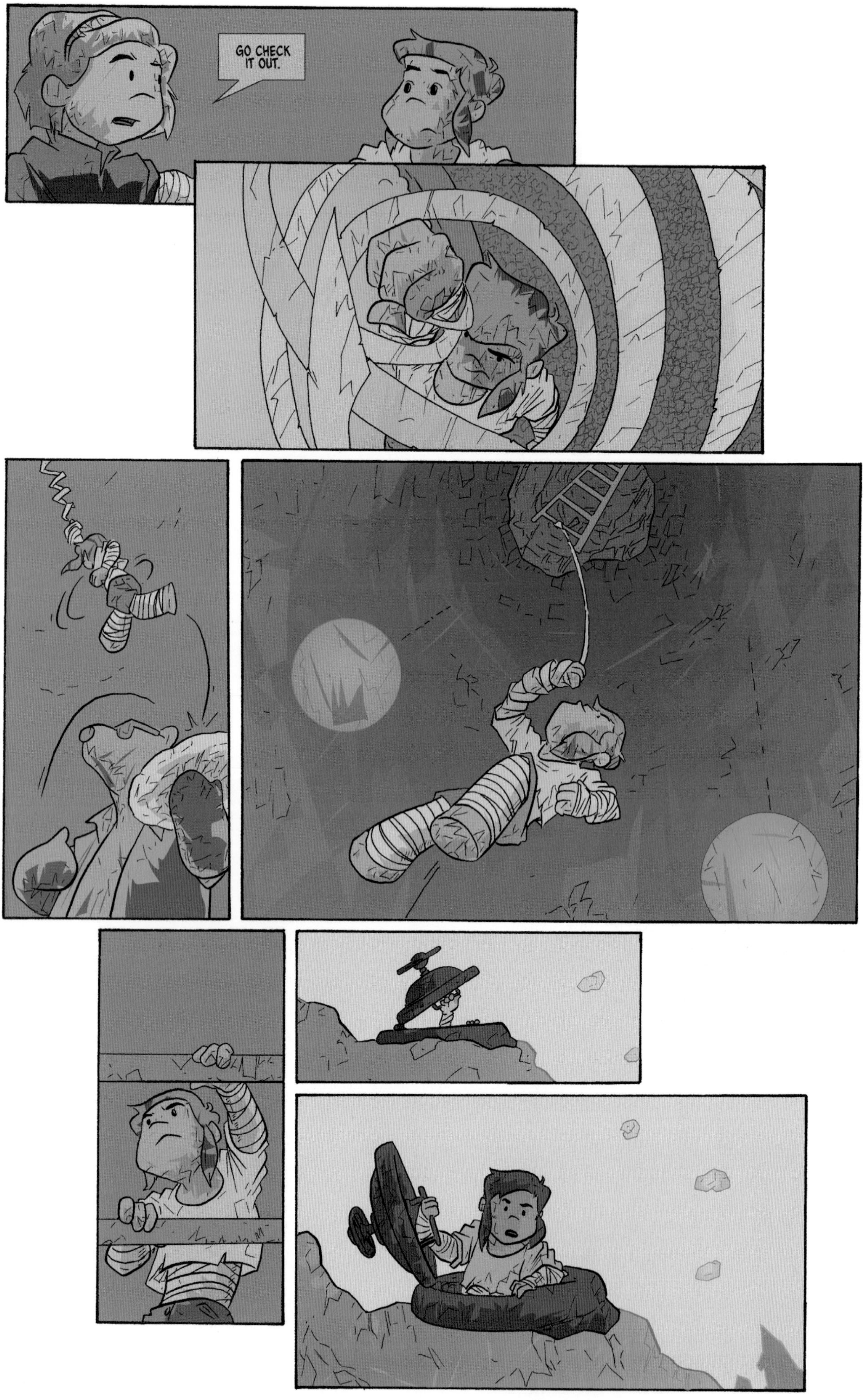
GO CHECK IT OUT.

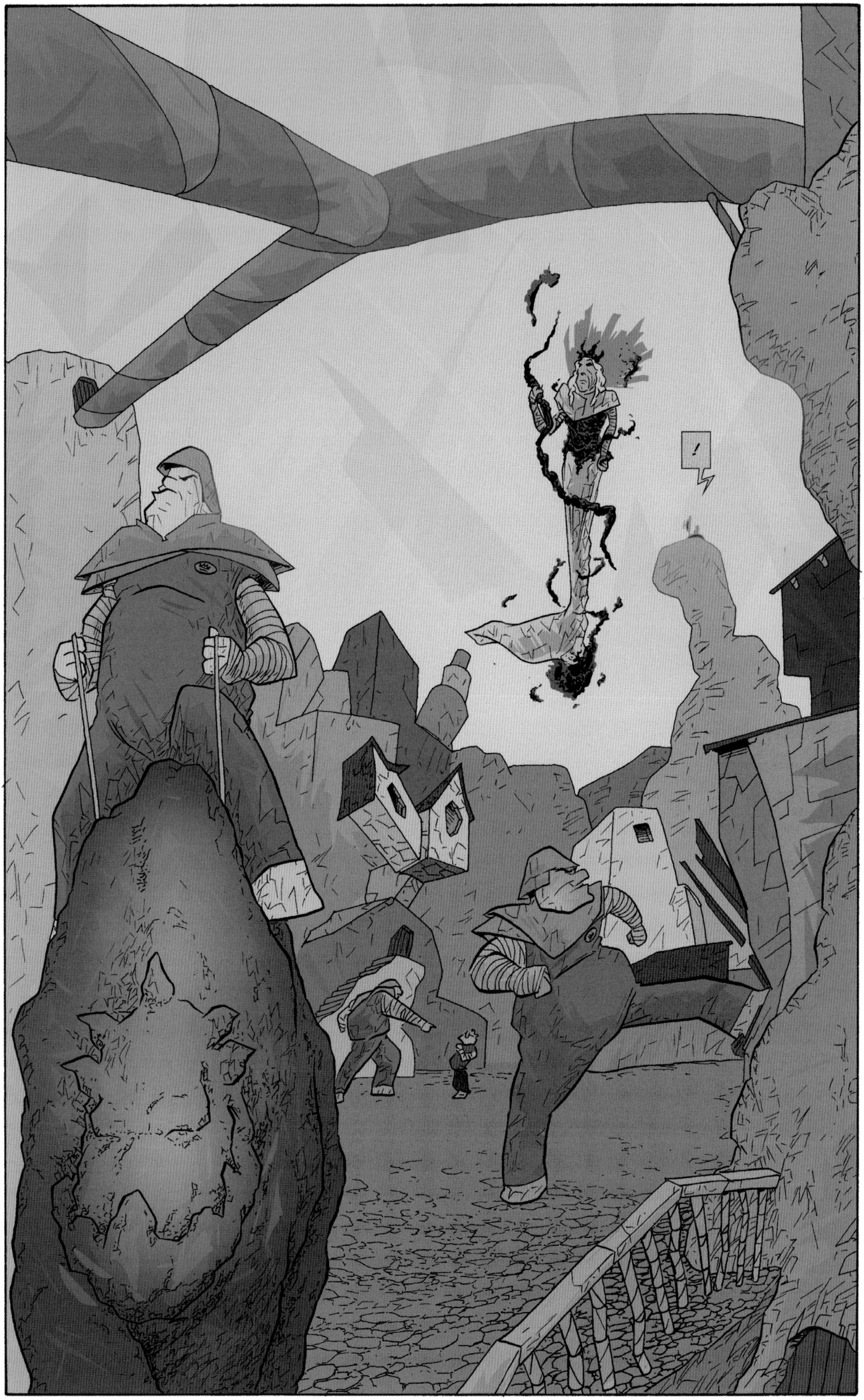
!

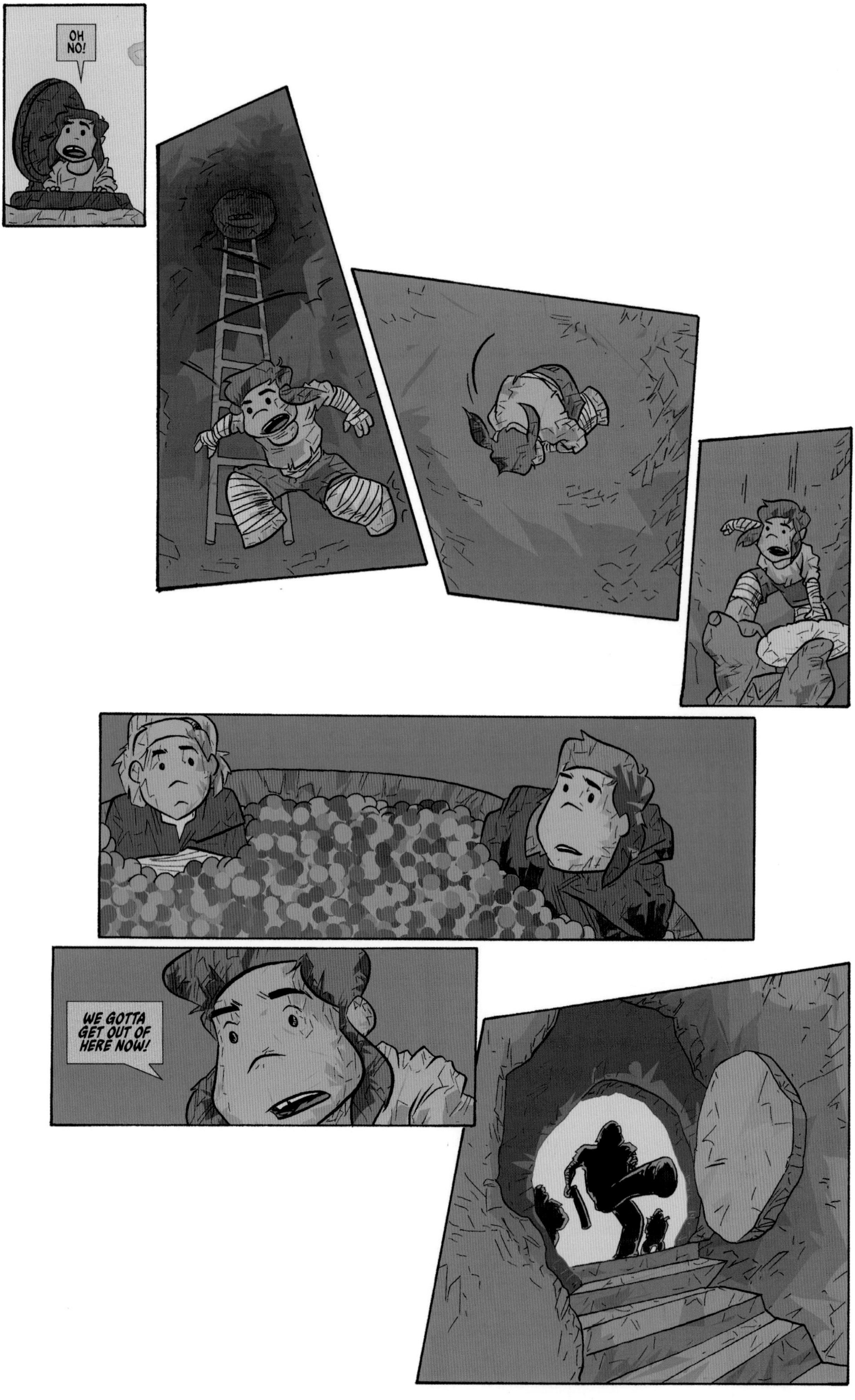
OH NO!
WE GOTTA GET OUT OF HERE NOW!

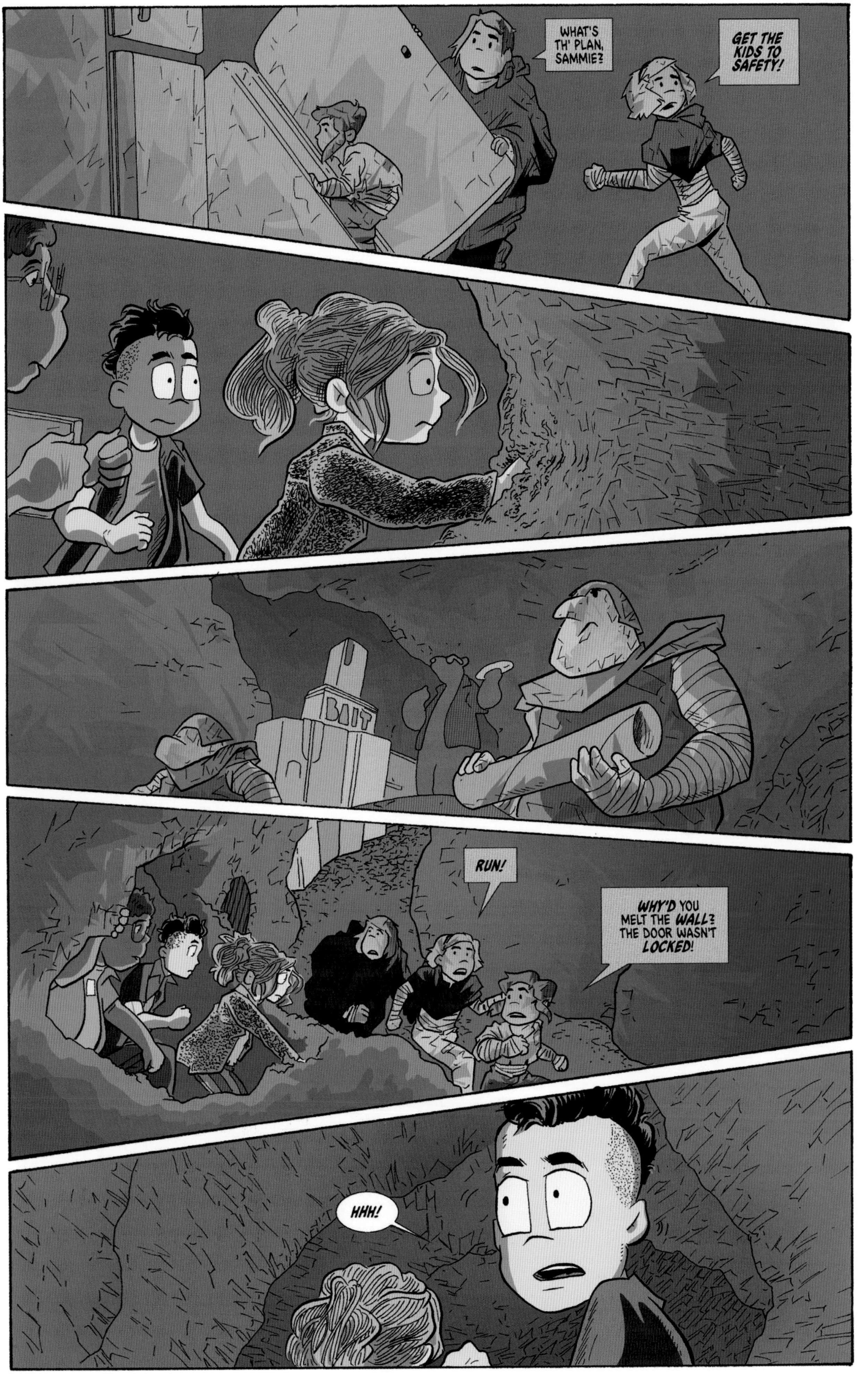
WHAT'S TH' PLAN, SAMMIE?
GET THE KIDS TO SAFETY!
BAIT
RUN!
WHY'D YOU MELT THE WALL? THE DOOR WASN'T LOCKED!
HHH!

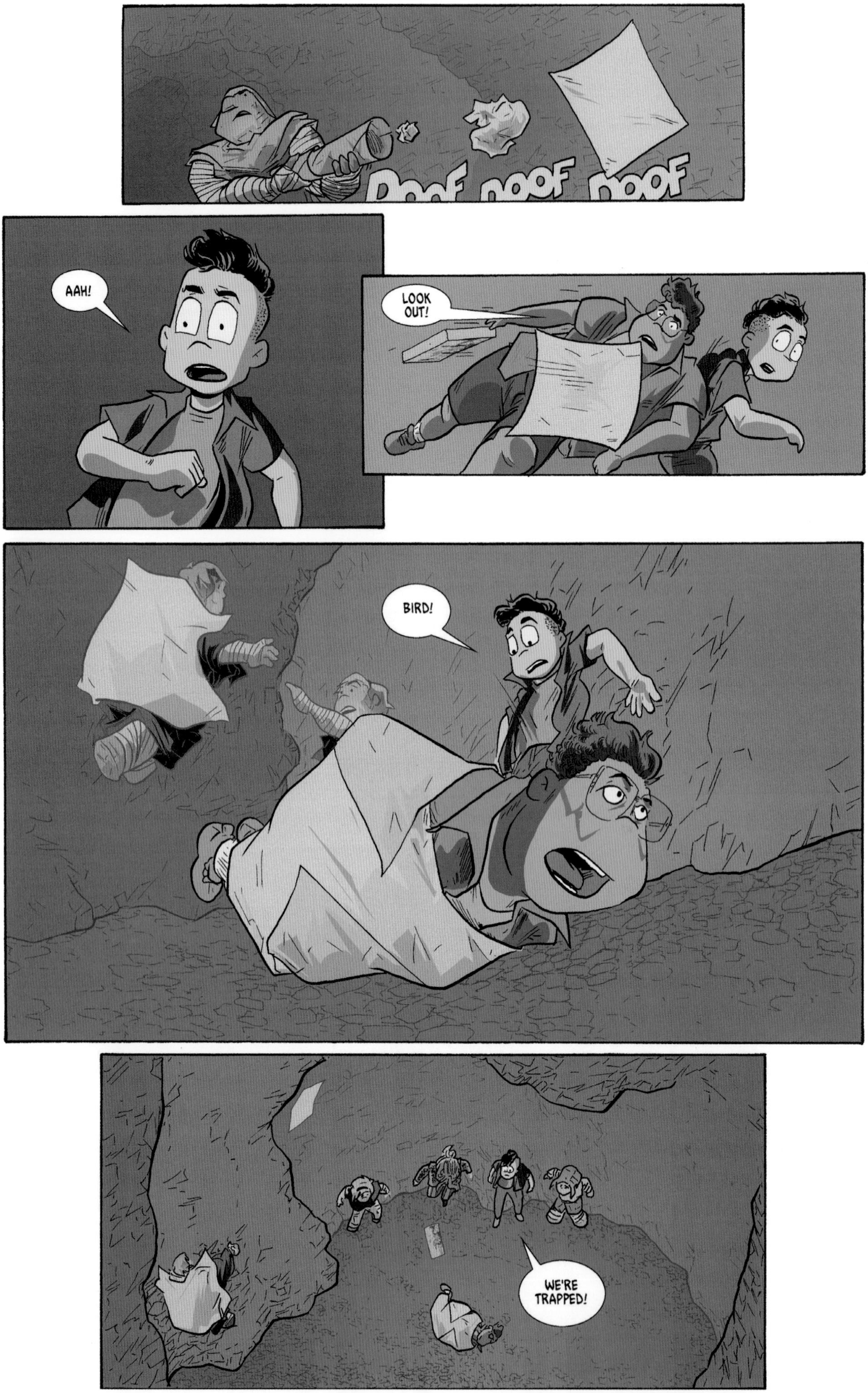
POOF POOF POOF
AAH!
LOOK OUT!
BIRD!
WE'RE TRAPPED!

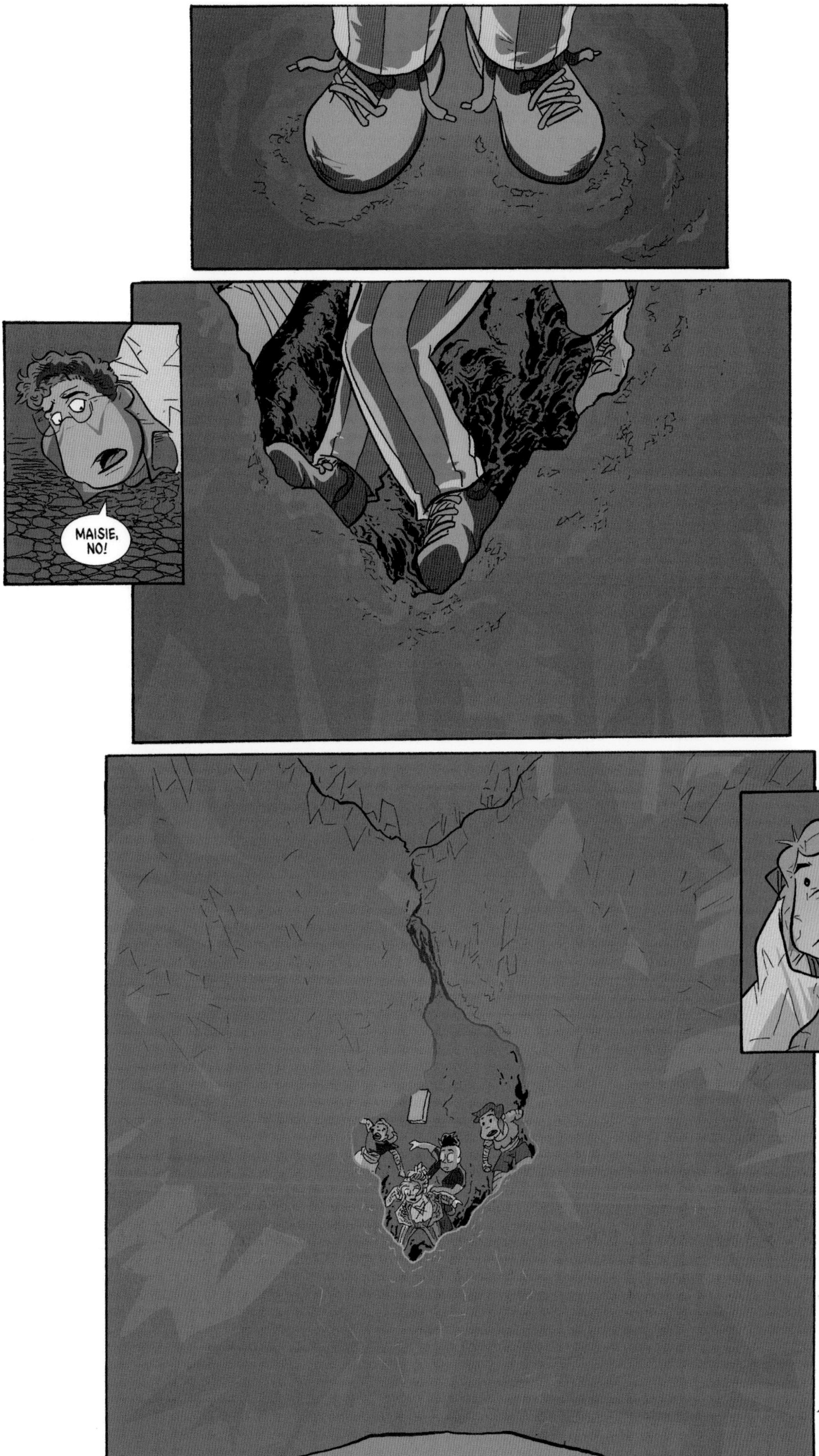
MAISIE, NO!

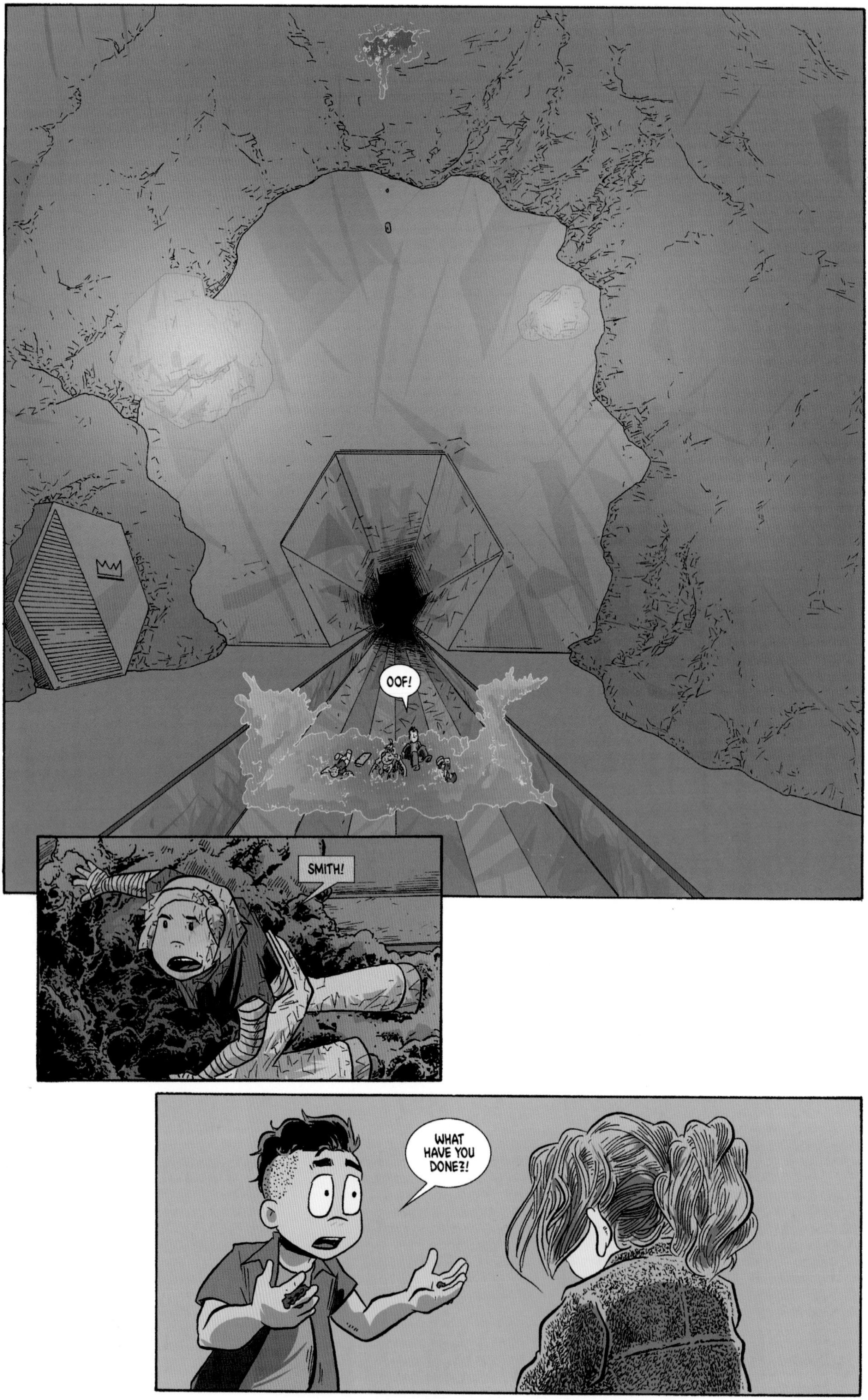
OOF!
SMITH!
WHAT HAVE YOU DONE?!

TO BE CONTINUED.

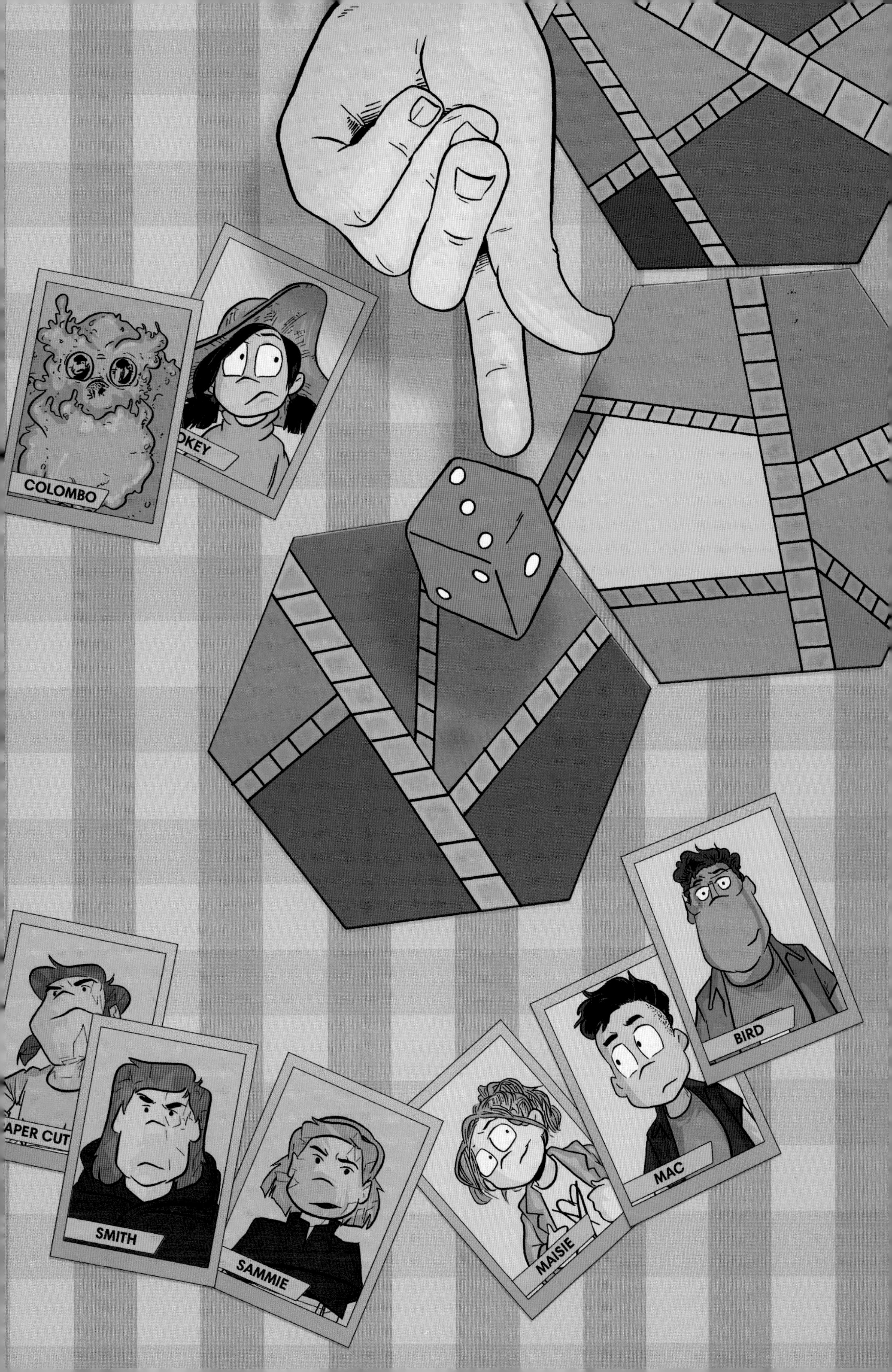
COLOMBO
OKEY
APER CUT
SMITH
SAMMIE
MAISIE
MAC
BIRD

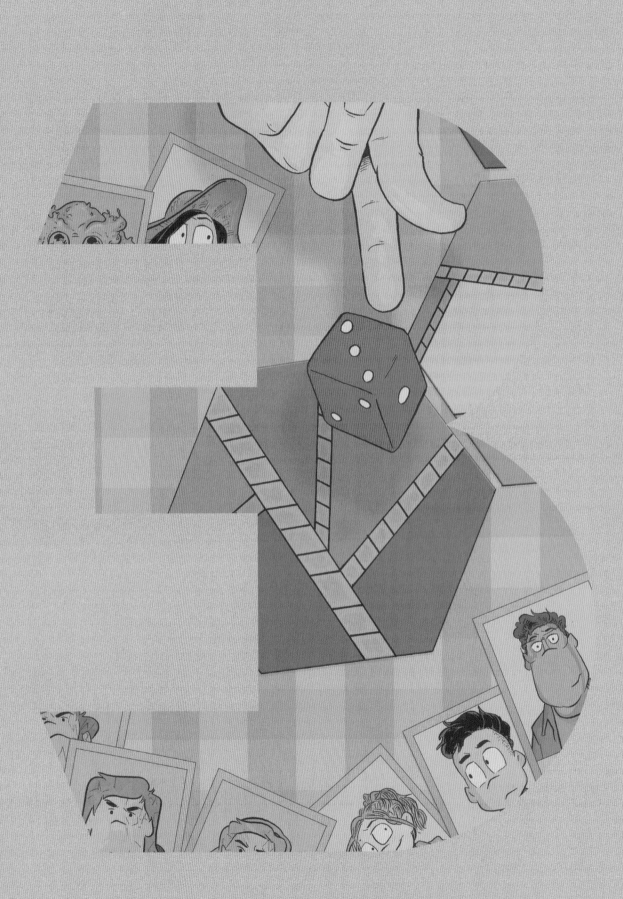

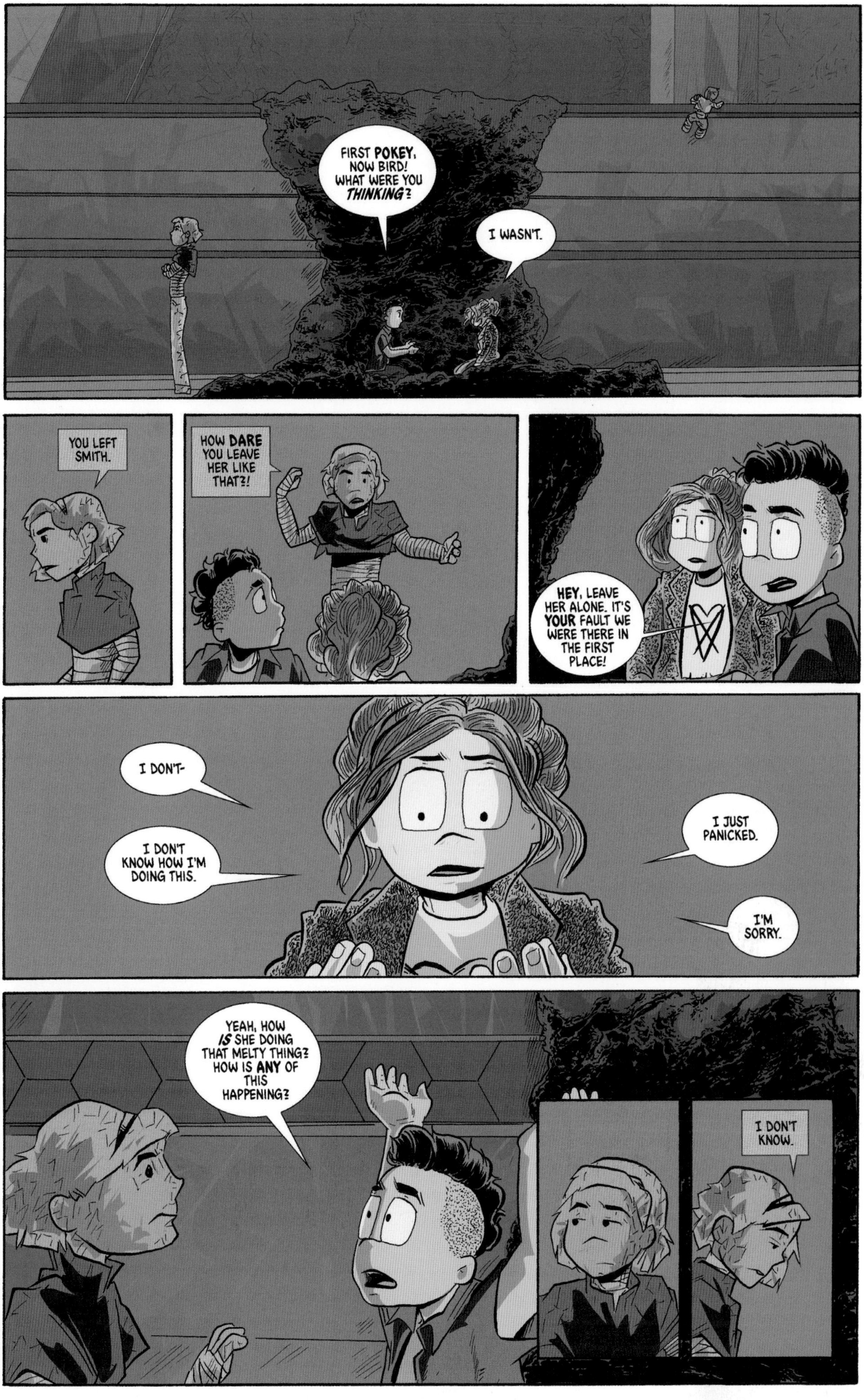
FIRST POKEY, NOW BIRD! WHAT WERE YOU THINKING?
I WASN'T.
YOU LEFT SMITH.
HOW DARE YOU LEAVE HER LIKE THAT?!
HEY, LEAVE HER ALONE. IT'S YOUR FAULT WE WERE THERE IN THE FIRST PLACE!
I DON'T-
I DON'T KNOW HOW I'M DOING THIS.
I JUST PANICKED.
I'M SORRY.
YEAH, HOW IS SHE DOING THAT MELTY THING? HOW IS ANY OF THIS HAPPENING?
I DON'T KNOW.

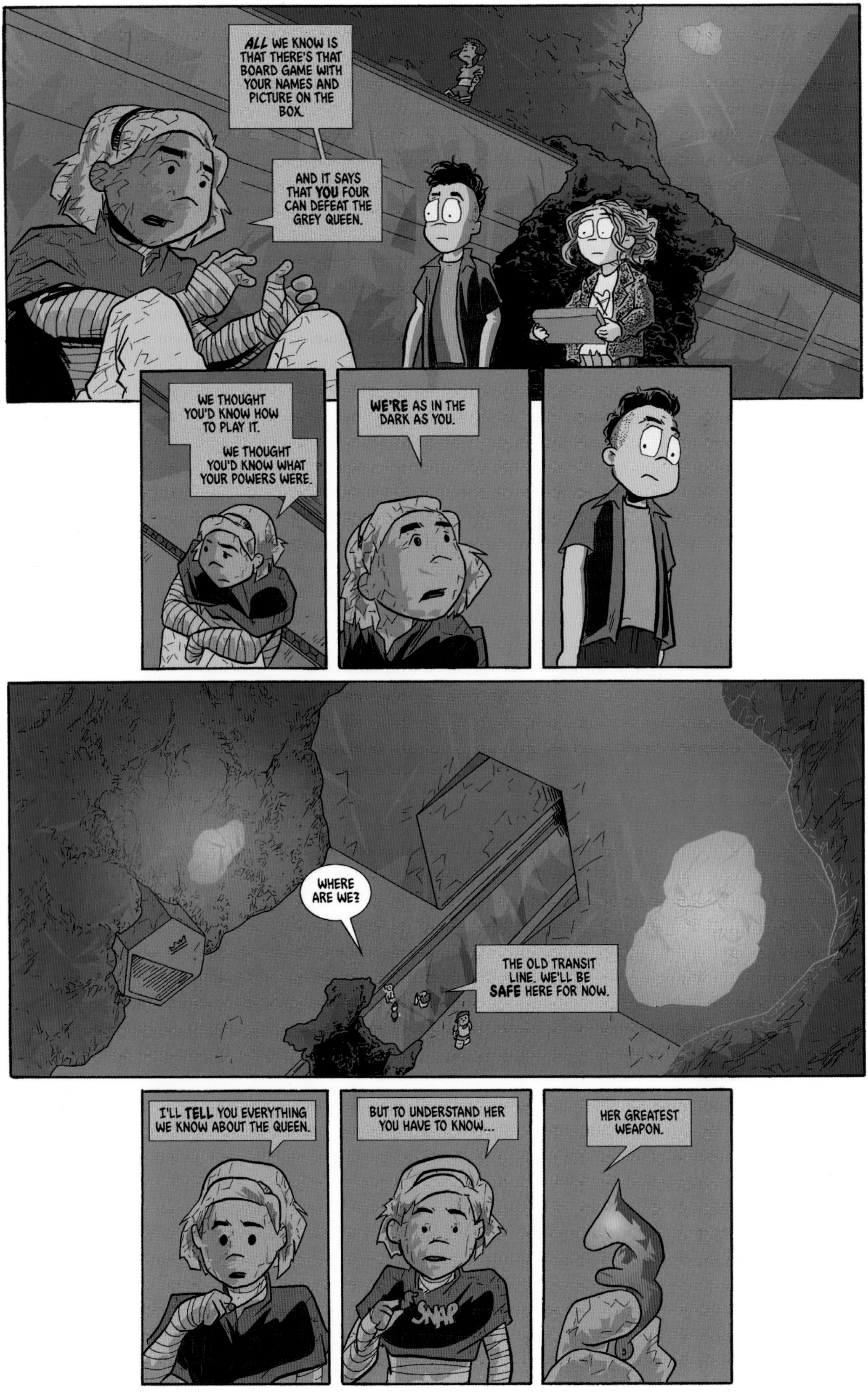
ALL WE KNOW IS THAT THERE'S THAT BOARD GAME WITH YOUR NAMES AND PICTURE ON THE BOX.
AND IT SAYS THAT YOU FOUR CAN DEFEAT THE GREY QUEEN.
WE THOUGHT YOU'D KNOW HOW TO PLAY IT.
WE THOUGHT YOU'D KNOW WHAT YOUR POWERS WERE.
WE'RE AS IN THE DARK AS YOU.
WHERE ARE WE?
THE OLD TRANSIT LINE. WE'LL BE SAFE HERE FOR NOW.
I'LL TELL YOU EVERYTHING WE KNOW ABOUT THE QUEEN.
BUT TO UNDERSTAND HER YOU HAVE TO KNOW...
HER GREATEST WEAPON.
SNAP

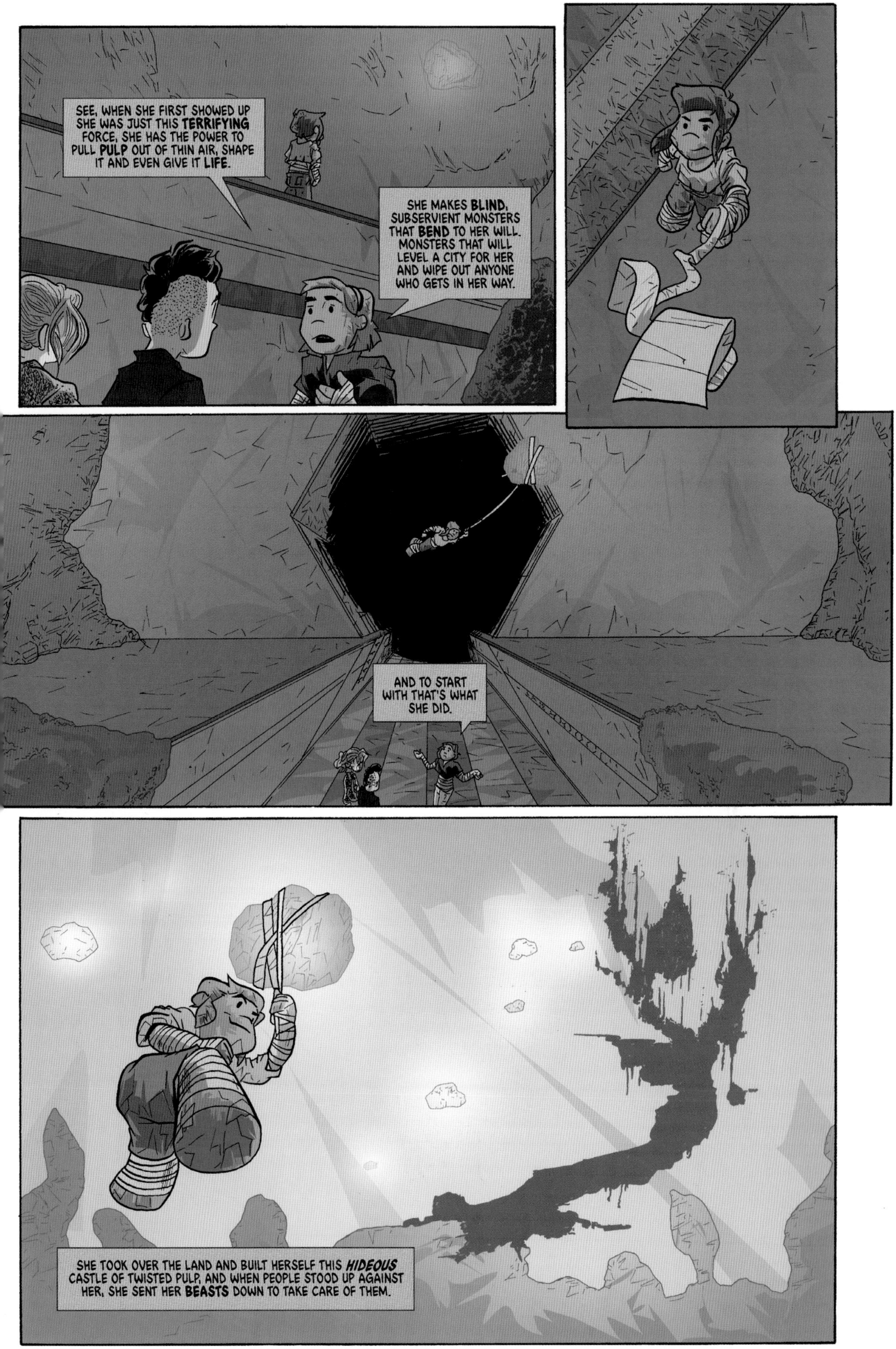
SEE, WHEN SHE FIRST SHOWED UP SHE WAS JUST THIS **TERRIFYING** FORCE, SHE HAS THE POWER TO PULL **PULP** OUT OF THIN AIR, SHAPE IT AND EVEN GIVE IT **LIFE**.
SHE MAKES **BLIND**, SUBSERVIENT MONSTERS THAT **BEND** TO HER WILL. MONSTERS THAT WILL LEVEL A CITY FOR HER AND WIPE OUT ANYONE WHO GETS IN HER WAY.
AND TO START WITH THAT'S WHAT SHE DID.
SHE TOOK OVER THE LAND AND BUILT HERSELF THIS ***HIDEOUS*** CASTLE OF TWISTED PULP, AND WHEN PEOPLE STOOD UP AGAINST HER, SHE SENT HER **BEASTS** DOWN TO TAKE CARE OF THEM.

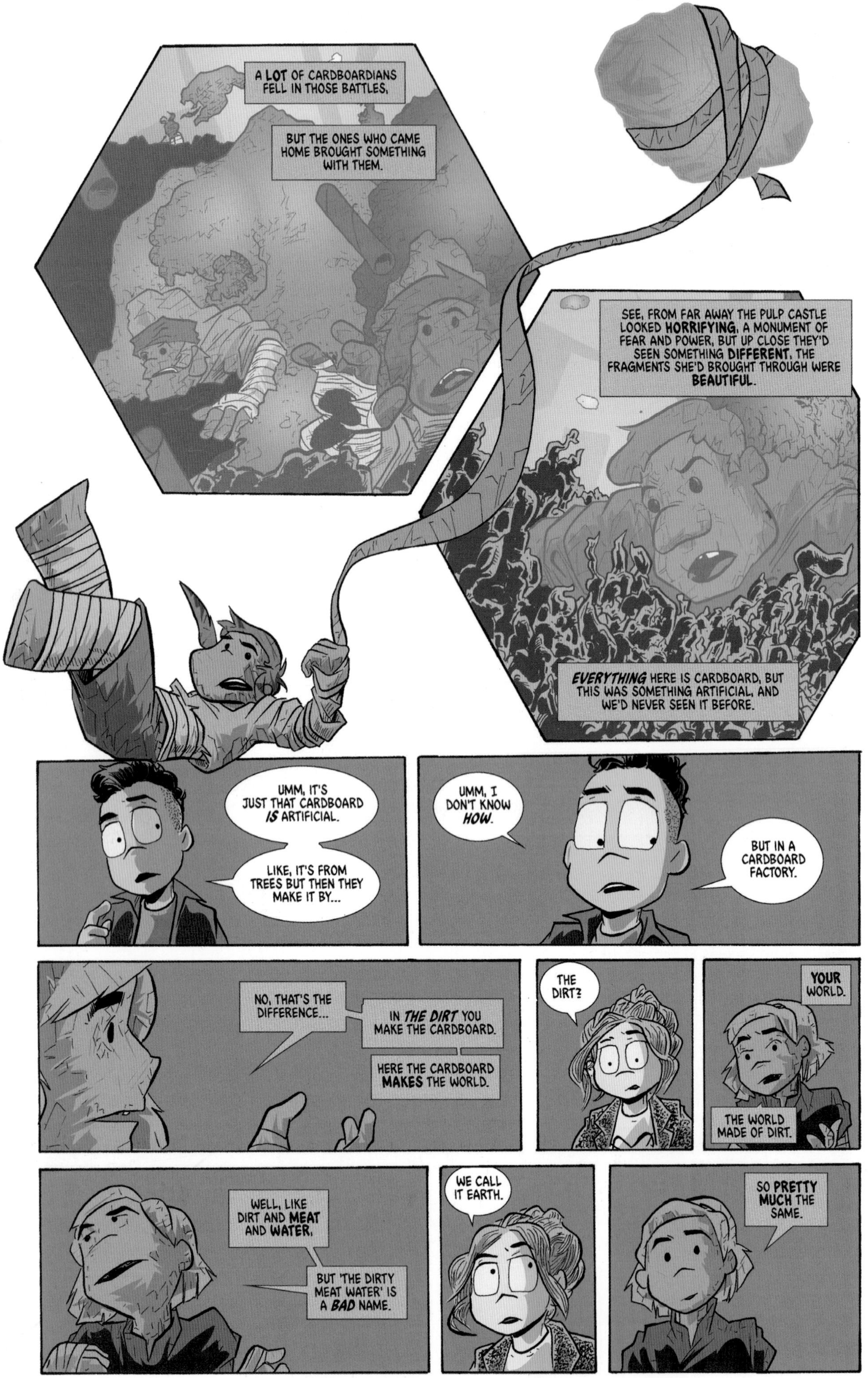
A LOT OF CARDBOARDIANS FELL IN THOSE BATTLES.
BUT THE ONES WHO CAME HOME BROUGHT SOMETHING WITH THEM.
SEE, FROM FAR AWAY THE PULP CASTLE LOOKED HORRIFYING, A MONUMENT OF FEAR AND POWER, BUT UP CLOSE THEY'D SEEN SOMETHING DIFFERENT. THE FRAGMENTS SHE'D BROUGHT THROUGH WERE BEAUTIFUL.
EVERYTHING HERE IS CARDBOARD, BUT THIS WAS SOMETHING ARTIFICIAL, AND WE'D NEVER SEEN IT BEFORE.
UMM, IT'S JUST THAT CARDBOARD IS ARTIFICIAL.
LIKE, IT'S FROM TREES BUT THEN THEY MAKE IT BY...
UMM, I DON'T KNOW HOW.
BUT IN A CARDBOARD FACTORY.
NO, THAT'S THE DIFFERENCE...
IN THE DIRT YOU MAKE THE CARDBOARD.
HERE THE CARDBOARD MAKES THE WORLD.
THE DIRT?
YOUR WORLD.
THE WORLD MADE OF DIRT.
WELL, LIKE DIRT AND MEAT AND WATER.
BUT 'THE DIRTY MEAT WATER' IS A BAD NAME.
WE CALL IT EARTH.
SO PRETTY MUCH THE SAME.

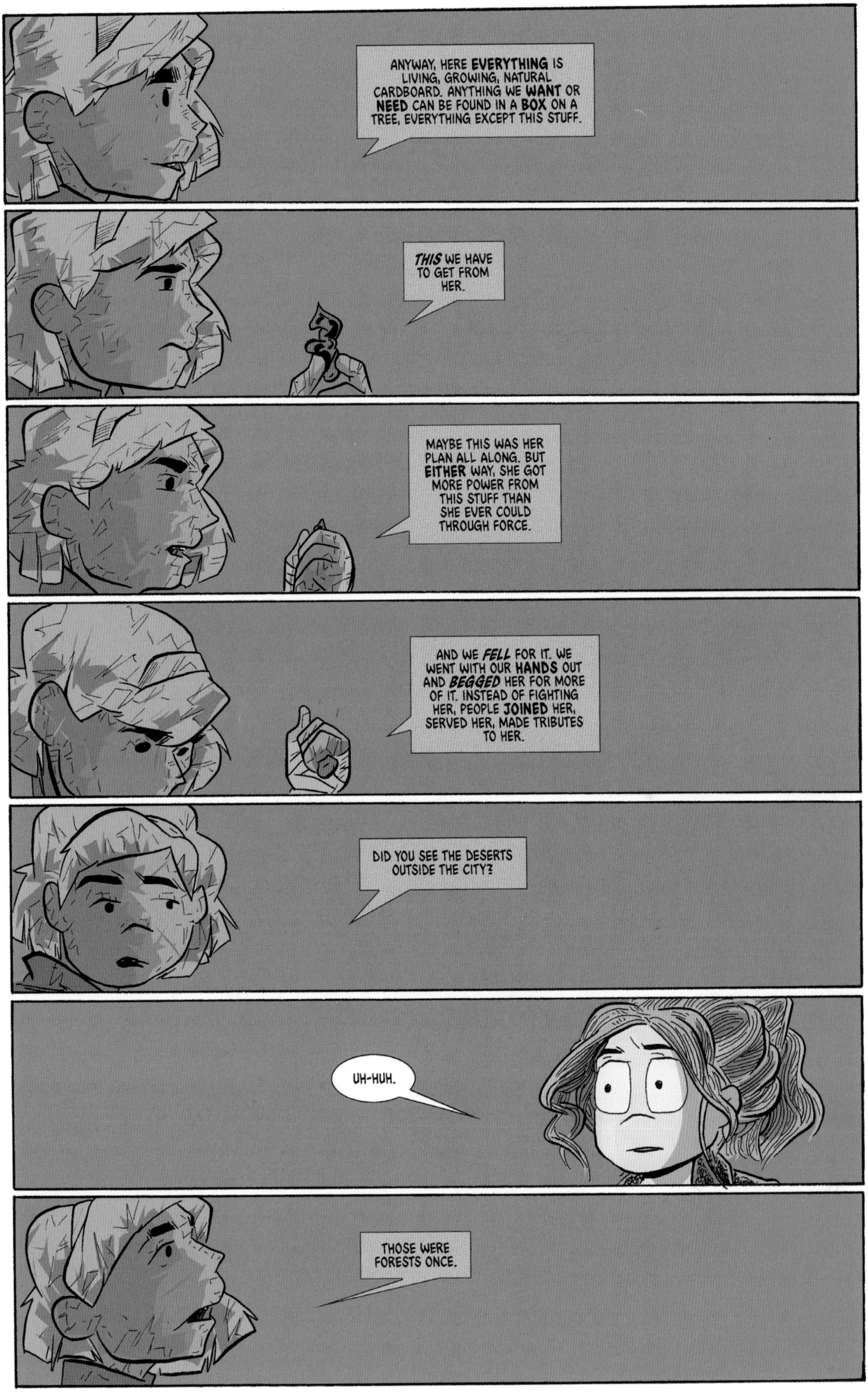
ANYWAY, HERE EVERYTHING IS LIVING, GROWING, NATURAL CARDBOARD. ANYTHING WE WANT OR NEED CAN BE FOUND IN A BOX ON A TREE, EVERYTHING EXCEPT THIS STUFF.
THIS WE HAVE TO GET FROM HER.
MAYBE THIS WAS HER PLAN ALL ALONG. BUT EITHER WAY, SHE GOT MORE POWER FROM THIS STUFF THAN SHE EVER COULD THROUGH FORCE.
AND WE FELL FOR IT. WE WENT WITH OUR HANDS OUT AND BEGGED HER FOR MORE OF IT. INSTEAD OF FIGHTING HER, PEOPLE JOINED HER, SERVED HER, MADE TRIBUTES TO HER.
DID YOU SEE THE DESERTS OUTSIDE THE CITY?
UH-HUH.
THOSE WERE FORESTS ONCE.

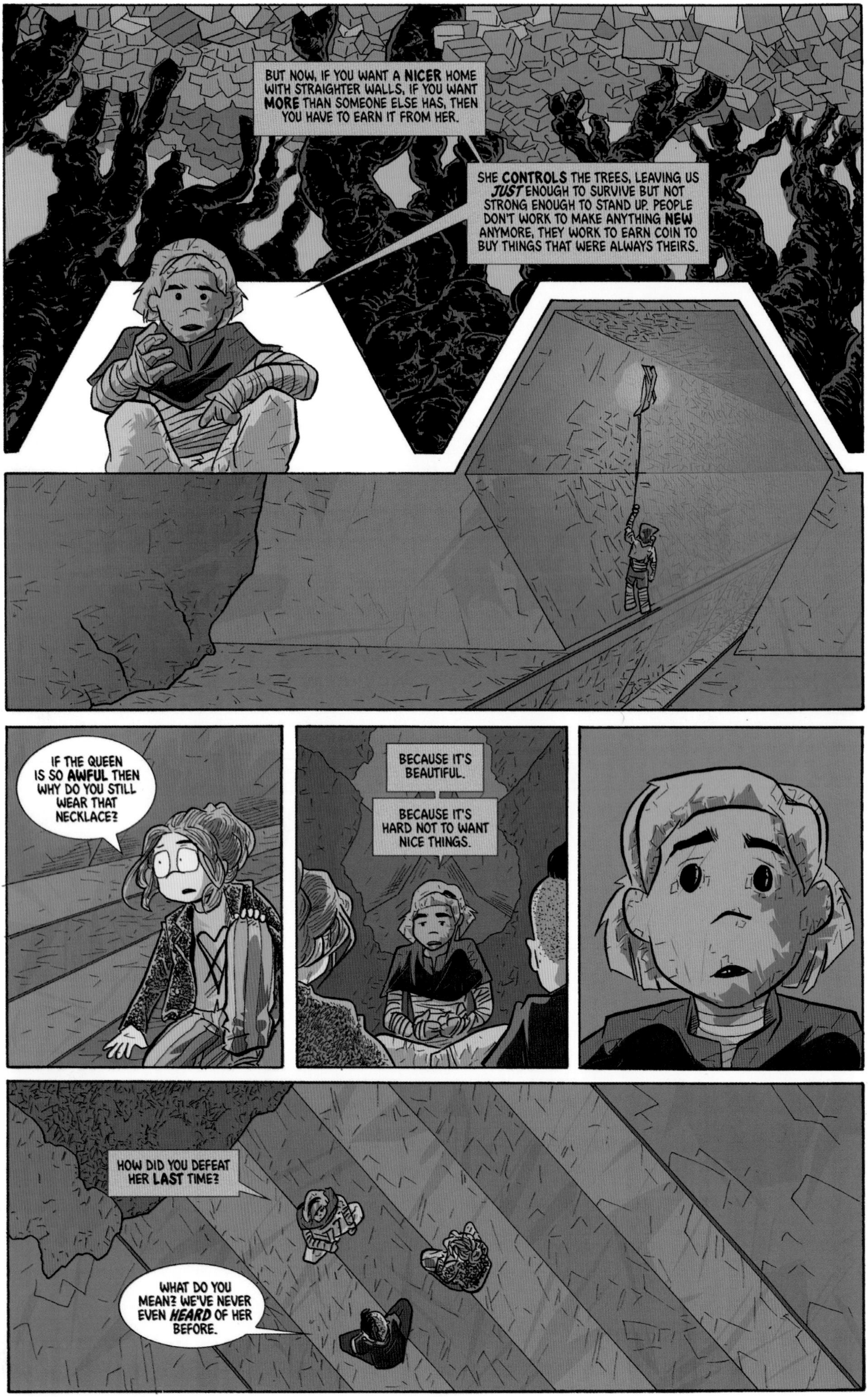

BUT NOW, IF YOU WANT A NICER HOME WITH STRAIGHTER WALLS, IF YOU WANT MORE THAN SOMEONE ELSE HAS, THEN YOU HAVE TO EARN IT FROM HER.
SHE CONTROLS THE TREES, LEAVING US JUST ENOUGH TO SURVIVE BUT NOT STRONG ENOUGH TO STAND UP. PEOPLE DON'T WORK TO MAKE ANYTHING NEW ANYMORE, THEY WORK TO EARN COIN TO BUY THINGS THAT WERE ALWAYS THEIRS.
IF THE QUEEN IS SO AWFUL THEN WHY DO YOU STILL WEAR THAT NECKLACE?
BECAUSE IT'S BEAUTIFUL.
BECAUSE IT'S HARD NOT TO WANT NICE THINGS.
HOW DID YOU DEFEAT HER LAST TIME?
WHAT DO YOU MEAN? WE'VE NEVER EVEN HEARD OF HER BEFORE.

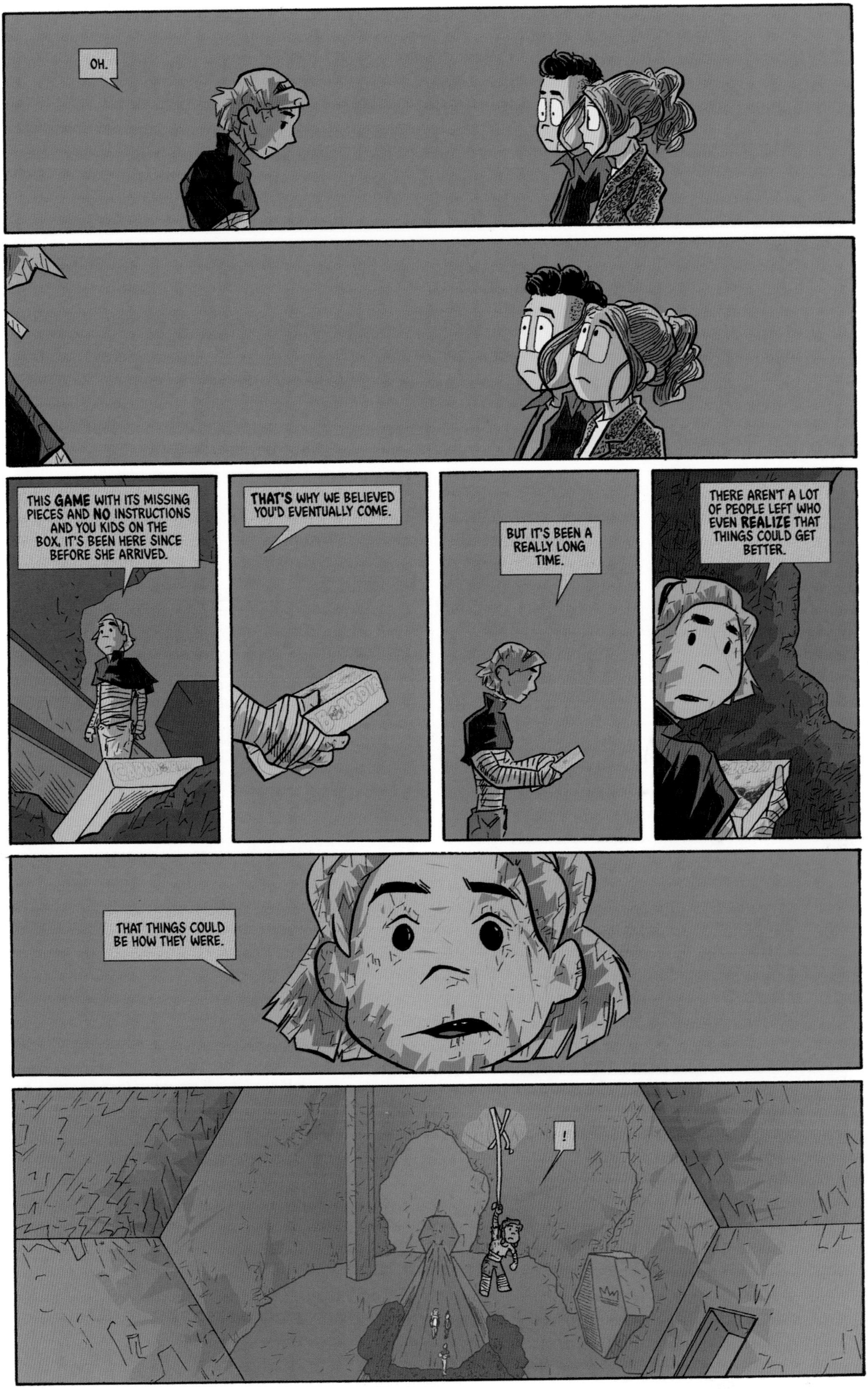
OH.
THIS **GAME** WITH ITS MISSING PIECES AND **NO** INSTRUCTIONS AND YOU KIDS ON THE BOX, IT'S BEEN HERE SINCE BEFORE SHE ARRIVED.
THAT'S WHY WE BELIEVED YOU'D EVENTUALLY COME.
BUT IT'S BEEN A REALLY LONG TIME.
THERE AREN'T A LOT OF PEOPLE LEFT WHO EVEN **REALIZE** THAT THINGS COULD GET BETTER.
THAT THINGS COULD BE HOW THEY WERE.
!

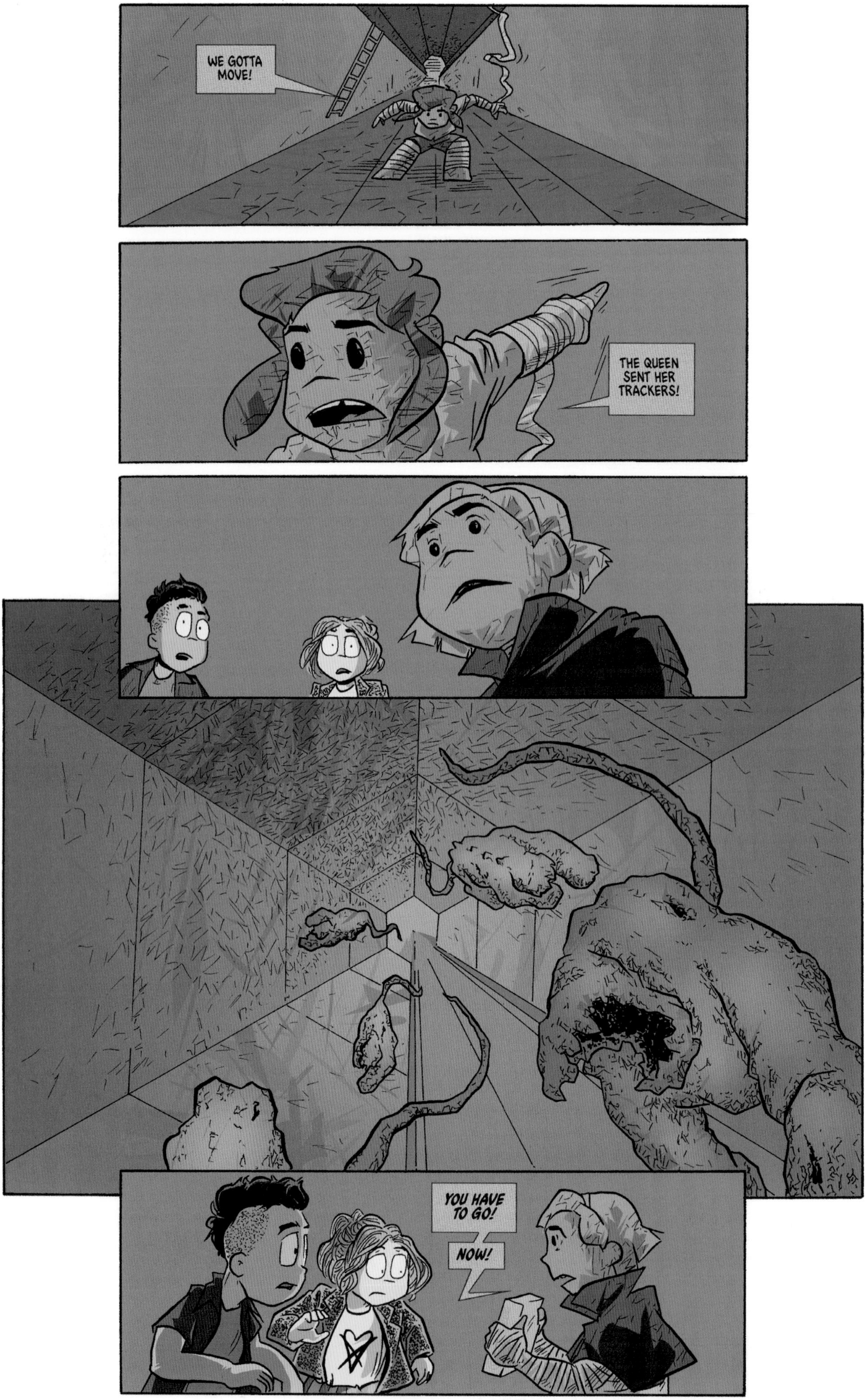
WE GOTTA MOVE!
THE QUEEN SENT HER TRACKERS!
YOU HAVE TO GO!
NOW!

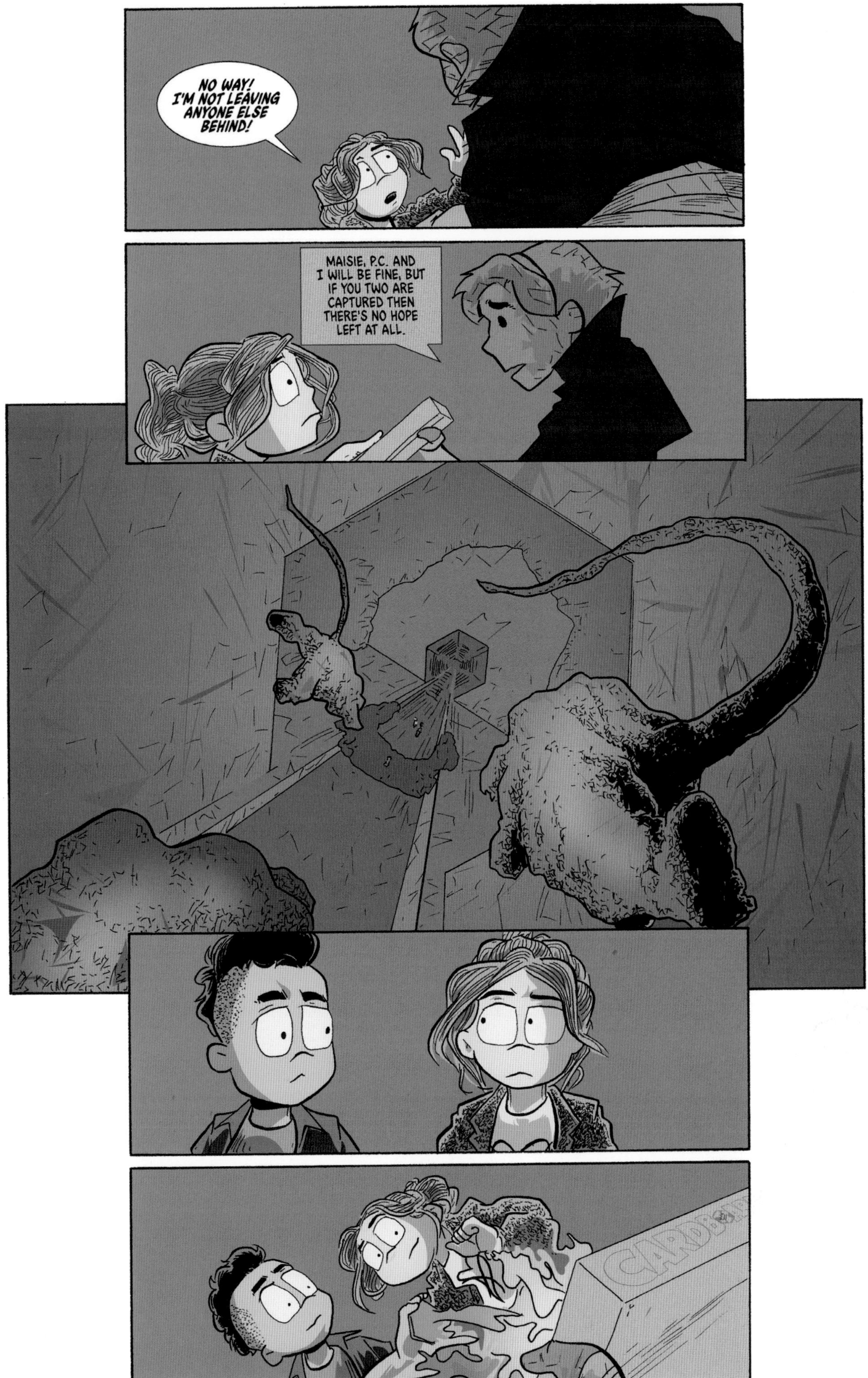
NO WAY! I'M NOT LEAVING ANYONE ELSE BEHIND!
MAISIE, P.C. AND I WILL BE FINE, BUT IF YOU TWO ARE CAPTURED THEN THERE'S NO HOPE LEFT AT ALL.

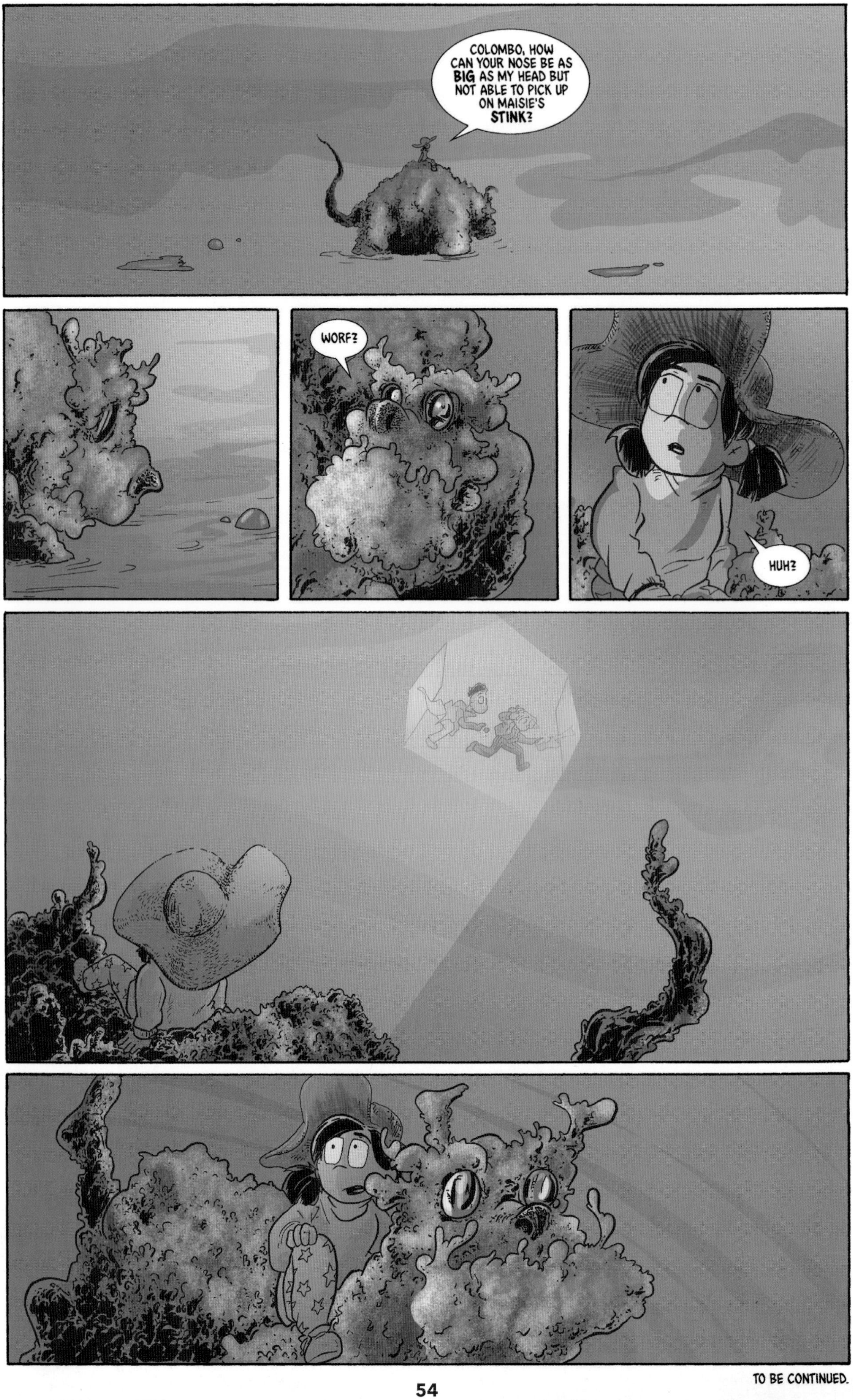
COLOMBO, HOW CAN YOUR NOSE BE AS BIG AS MY HEAD BUT NOT ABLE TO PICK UP ON MAISIE'S STINK?
WORF?
HUH?

TO BE CONTINUED.

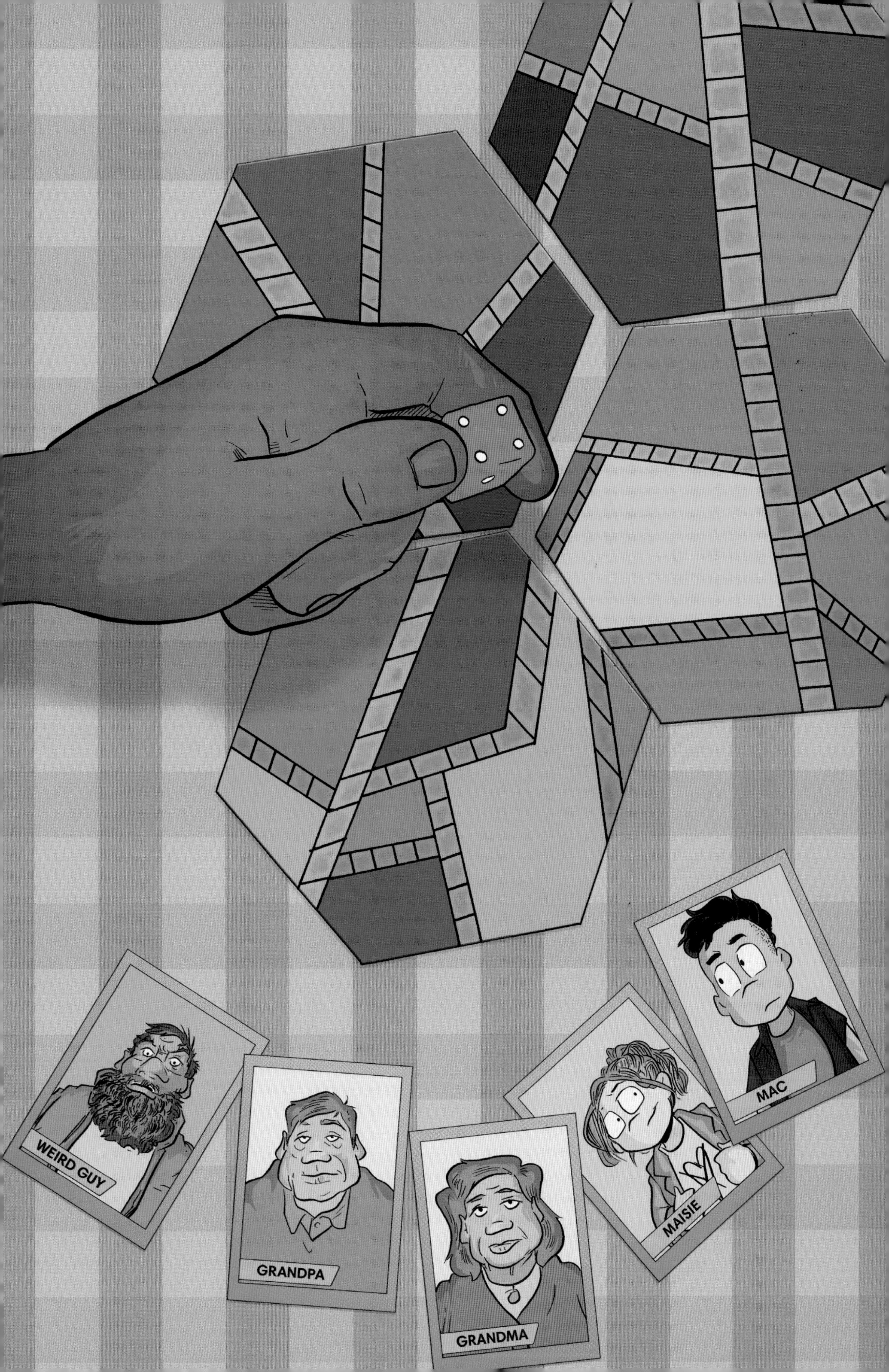
WEIRD GUY
GRANDPA
GRANDMA
MAISIE
MAC

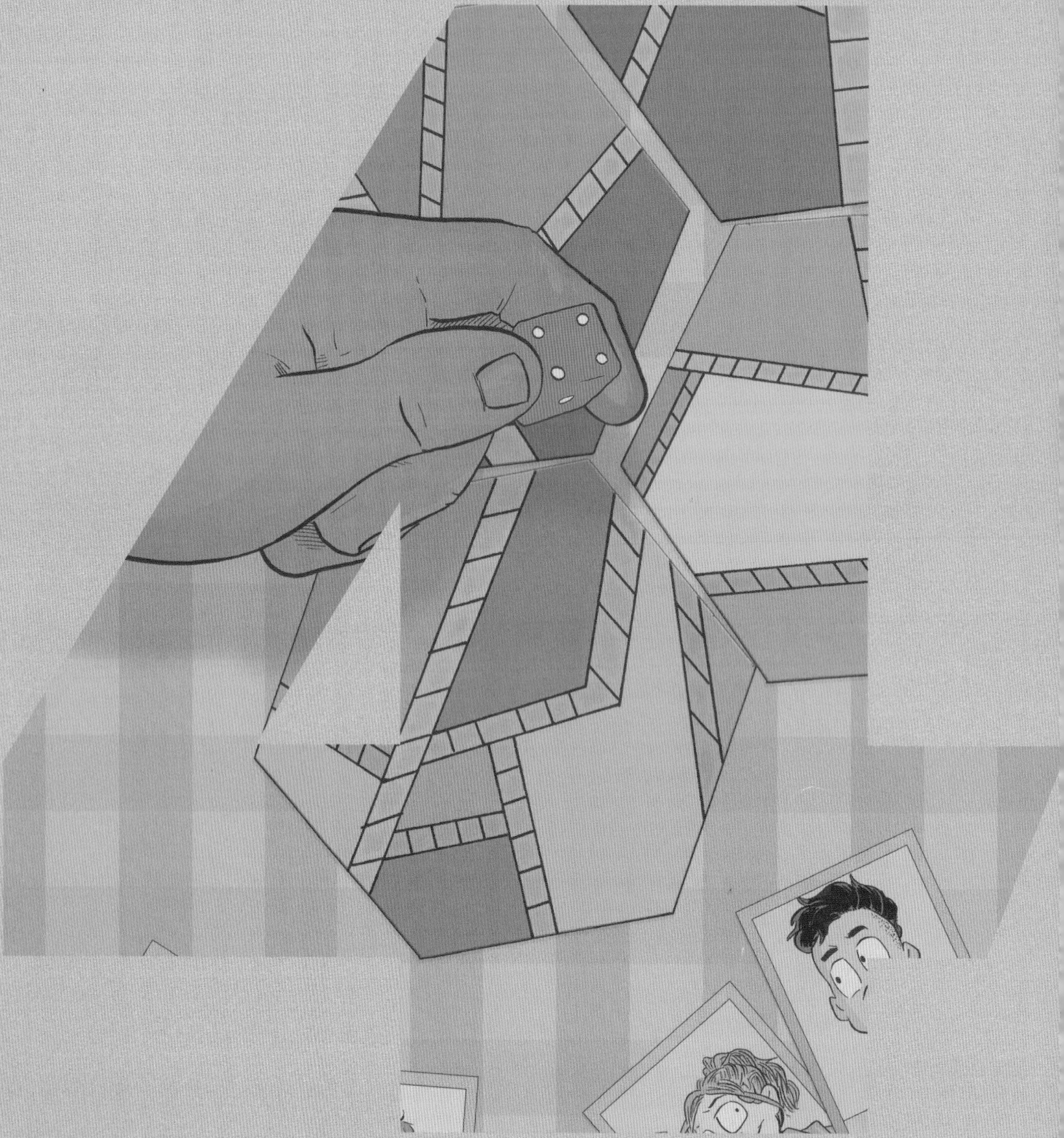

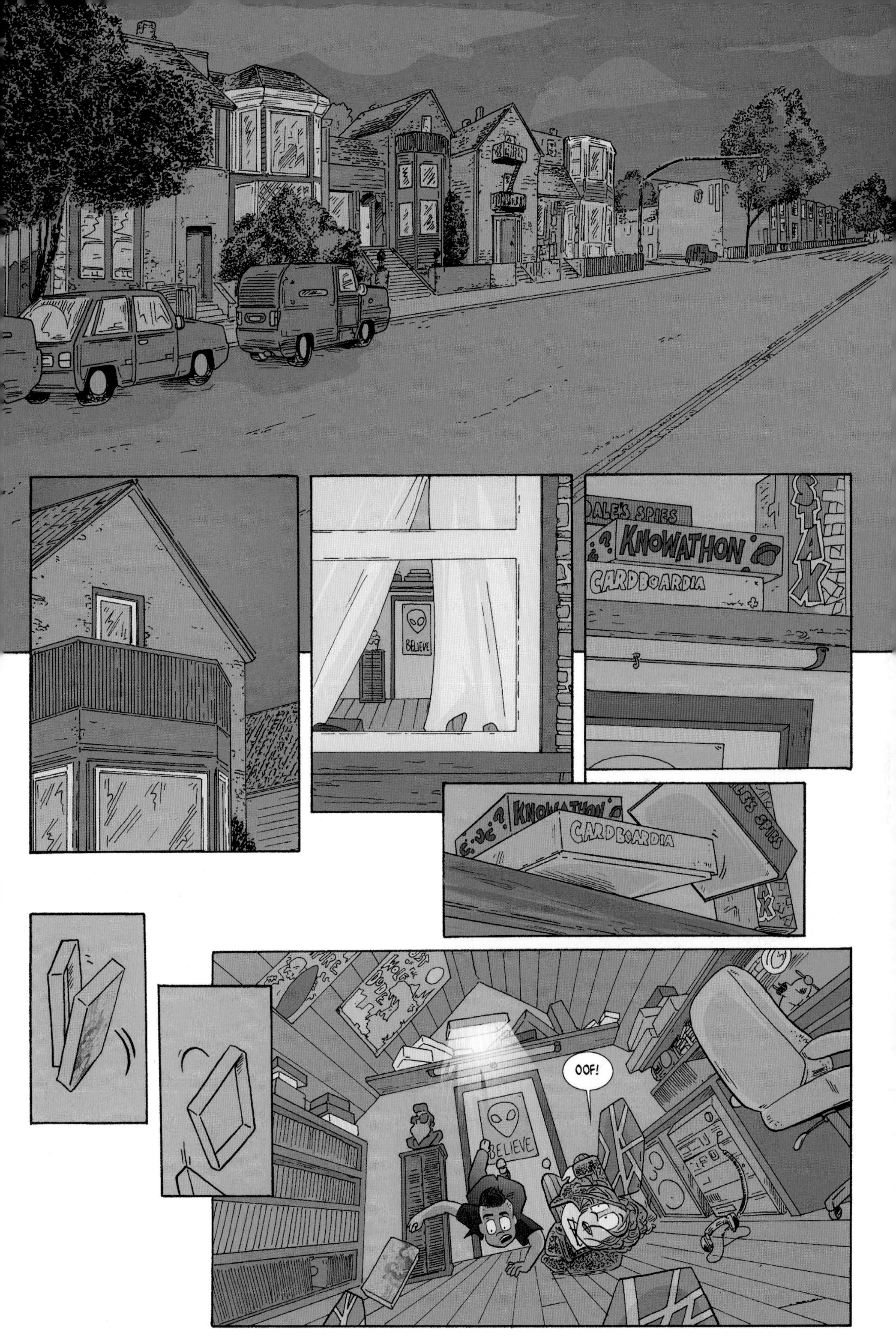

BELIEVE
DALE'S SPIES
KNOWATHON
CARDBOARDIA
STAX
KNOWATHON
CARDBOARDIA
OOF!
BELIEVE

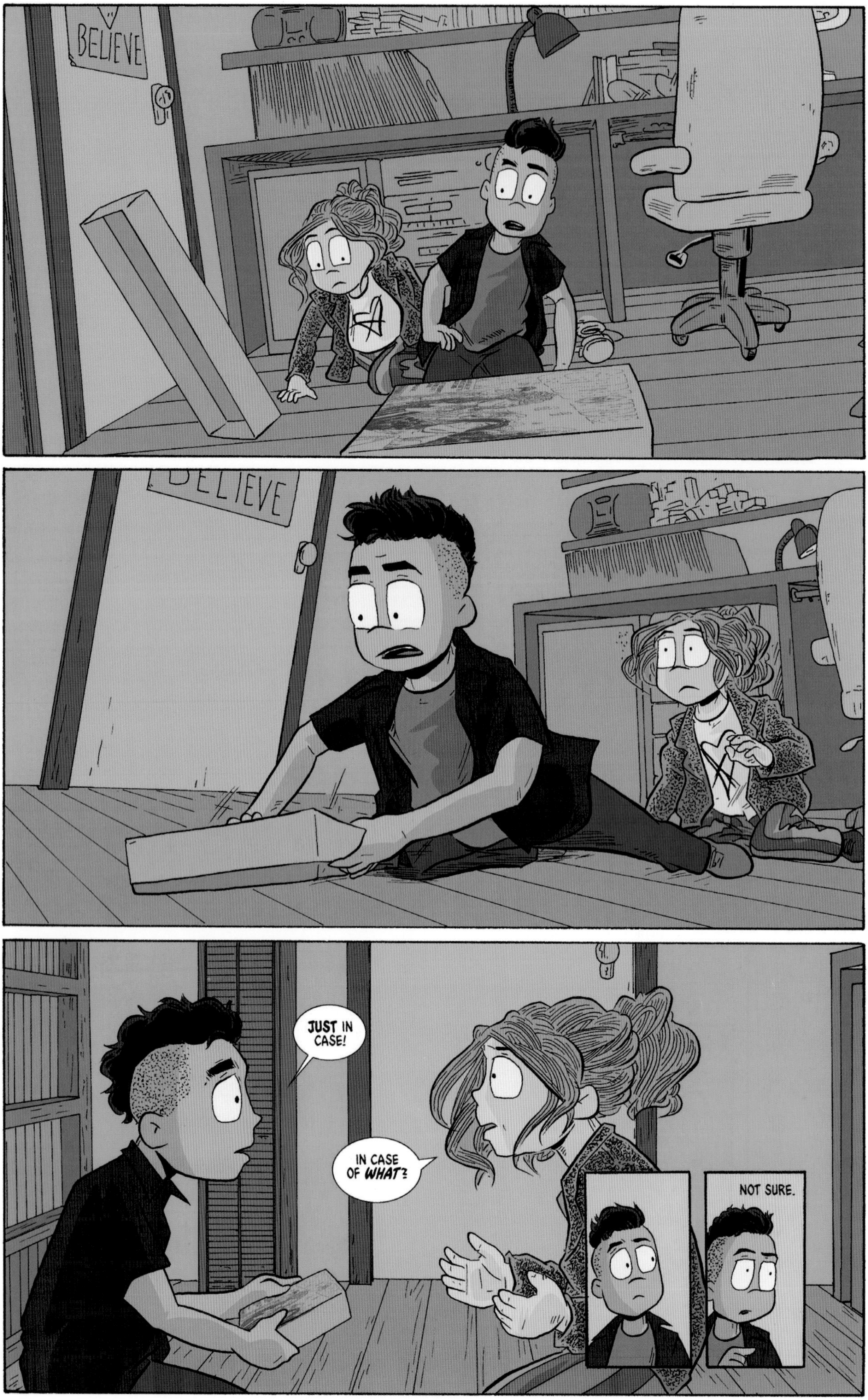
BELIEVE
BELIEVE
JUST IN CASE!
IN CASE OF WHAT?
NOT SURE.

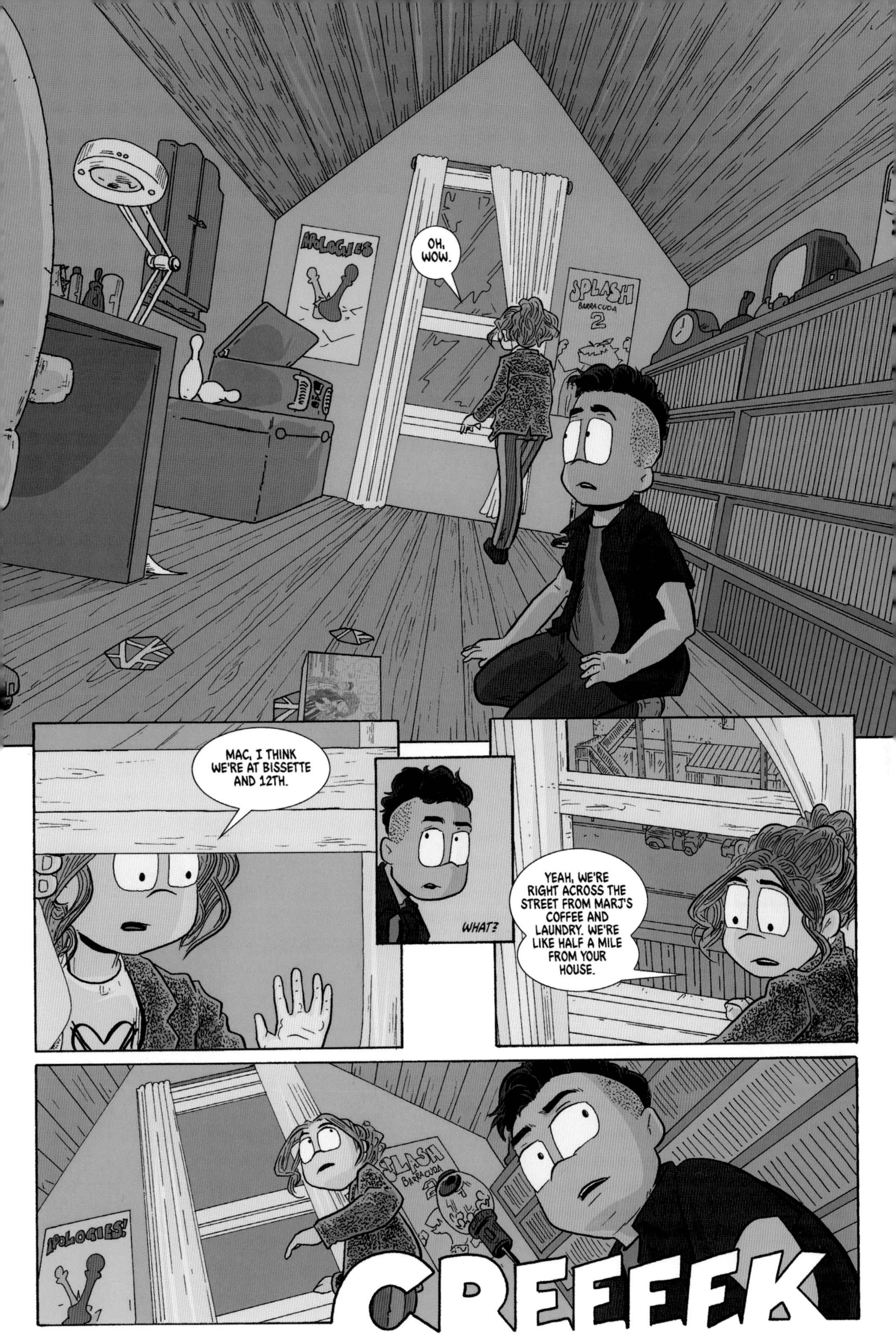
SPLASH BARRACUDA 2
OH, WOW.
MAC, I THINK WE'RE AT BISSETTE AND 12TH.
WHAT?
YEAH, WE'RE RIGHT ACROSS THE STREET FROM MARJ'S COFFEE AND LAUNDRY. WE'RE LIKE HALF A MILE FROM YOUR HOUSE.
CREEEK

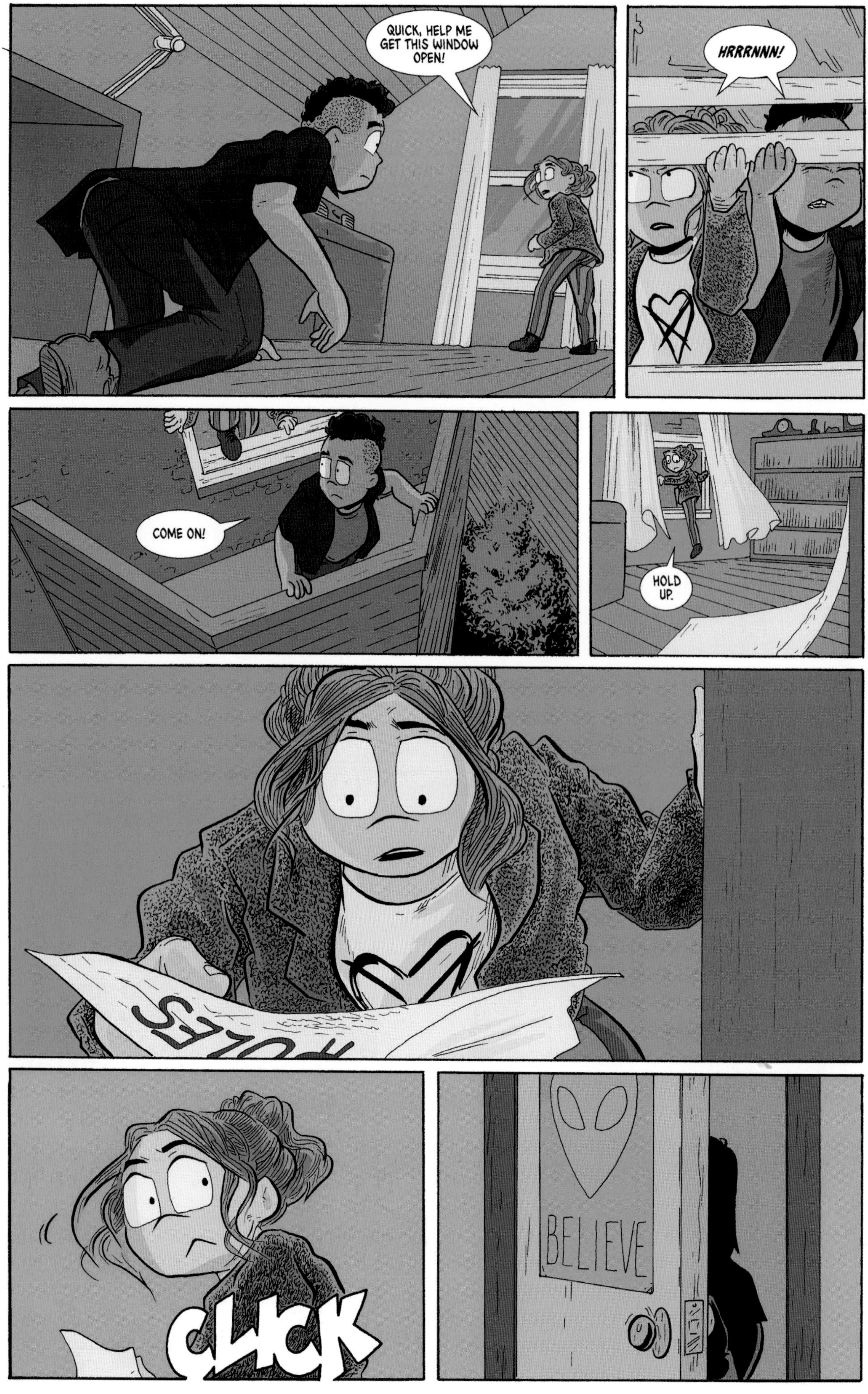
QUICK, HELP ME GET THIS WINDOW OPEN!
HRRRNNN!
COME ON!
HOLD UP.
RULES
BELIEVE
CLICK

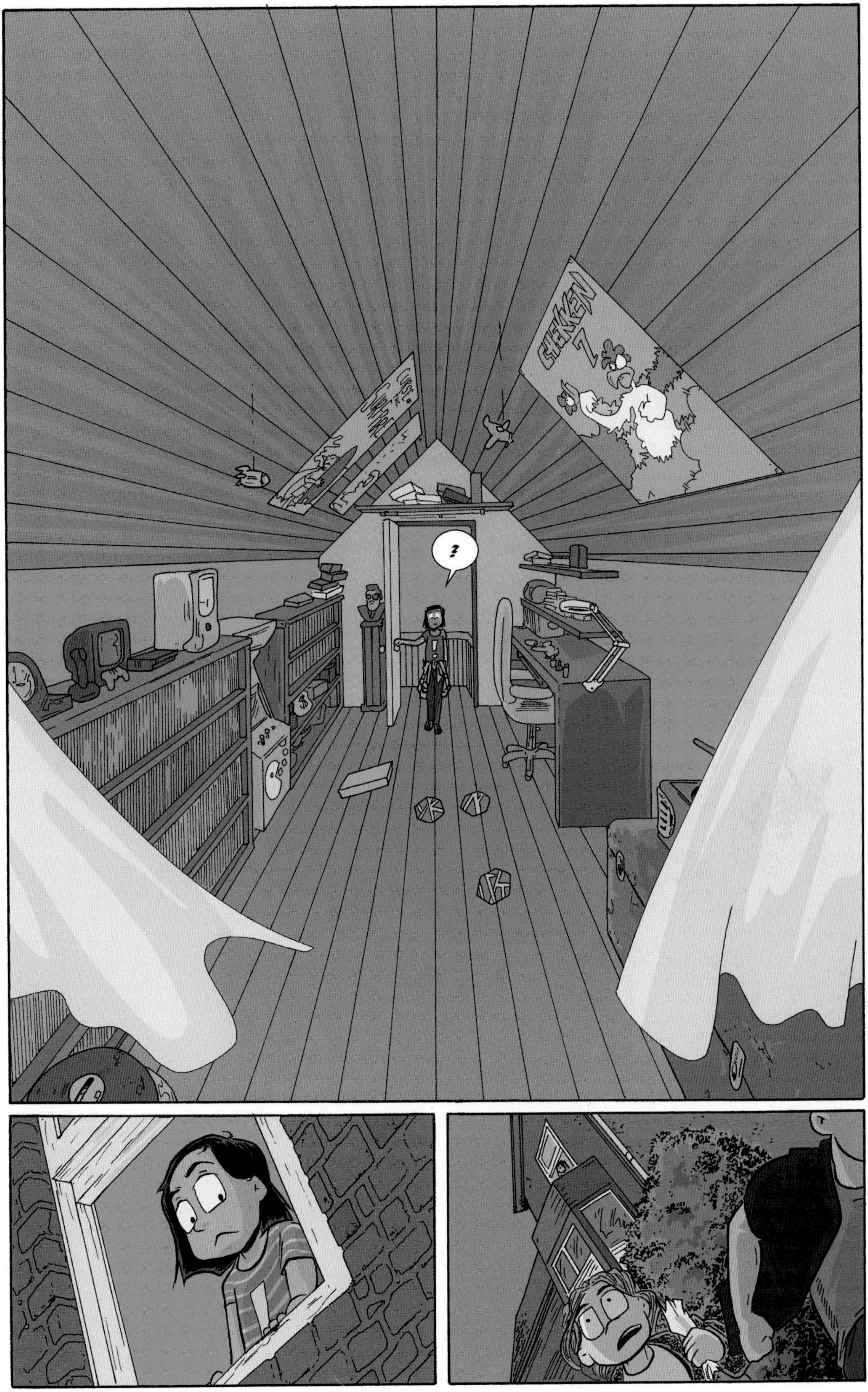
CHICKEN Z
?

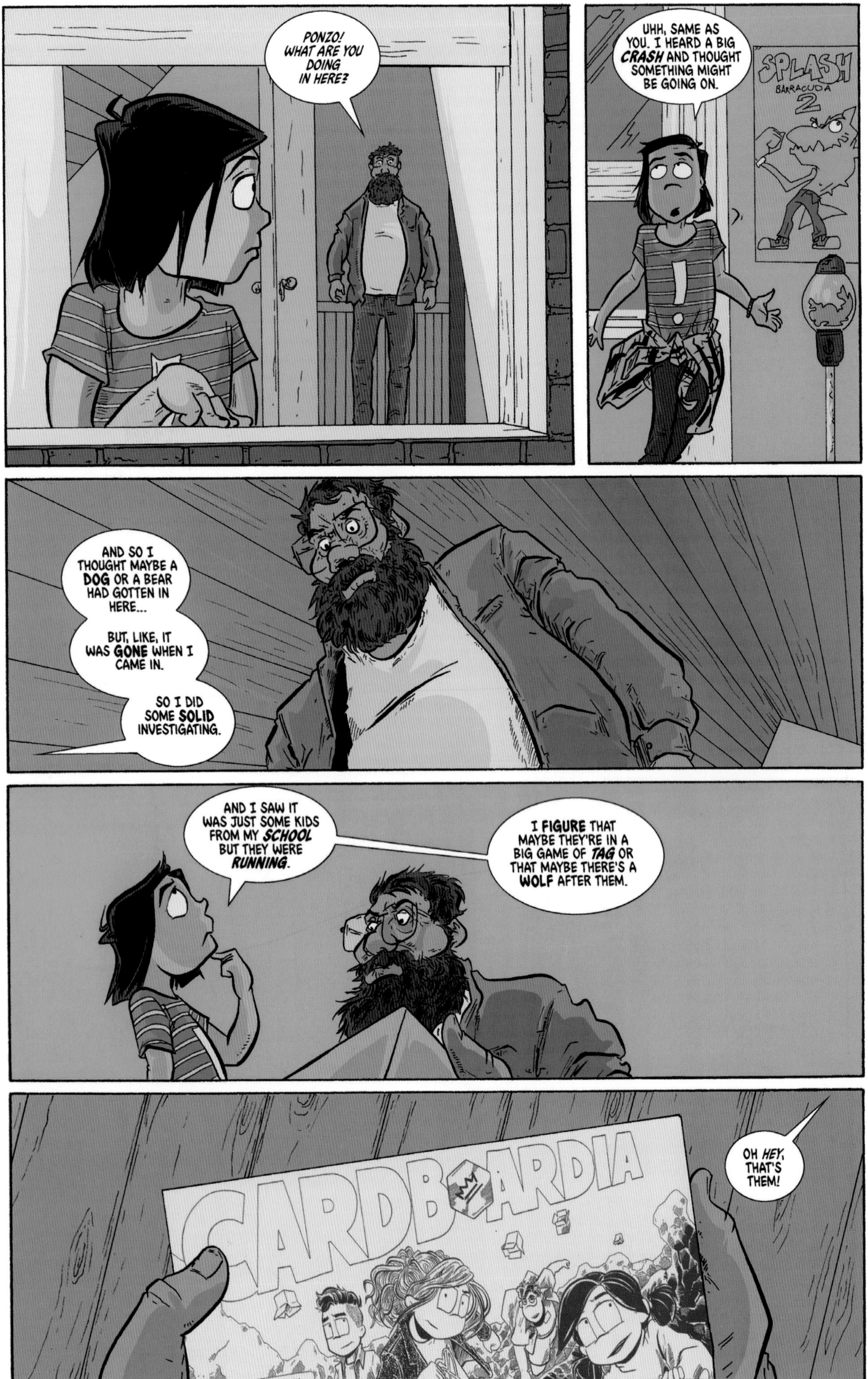
PONZO! WHAT ARE YOU DOING IN HERE?
UHH, SAME AS YOU. I HEARD A BIG CRASH AND THOUGHT SOMETHING MIGHT BE GOING ON.
SPLASH
BARRACUDA
2
AND SO I THOUGHT MAYBE A DOG OR A BEAR HAD GOTTEN IN HERE...
BUT, LIKE, IT WAS GONE WHEN I CAME IN.
SO I DID SOME SOLID INVESTIGATING.
AND I SAW IT WAS JUST SOME KIDS FROM MY SCHOOL BUT THEY WERE RUNNING.
I FIGURE THAT MAYBE THEY'RE IN A BIG GAME OF TAG OR THAT MAYBE THERE'S A WOLF AFTER THEM.
CARDBOARDIA
OH HEY, THAT'S THEM!

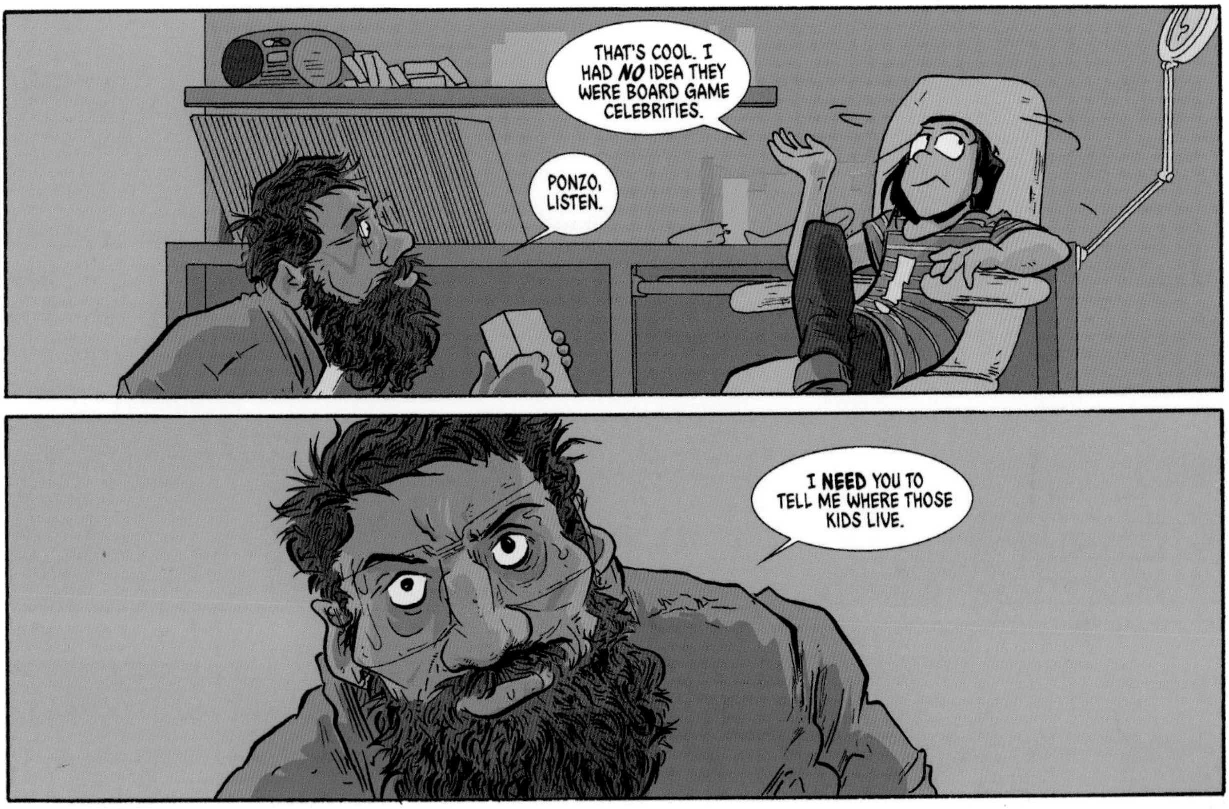
THAT'S COOL. I HAD NO IDEA THEY WERE BOARD GAME CELEBRITIES.
PONZO, LISTEN.
I NEED YOU TO TELL ME WHERE THOSE KIDS LIVE.

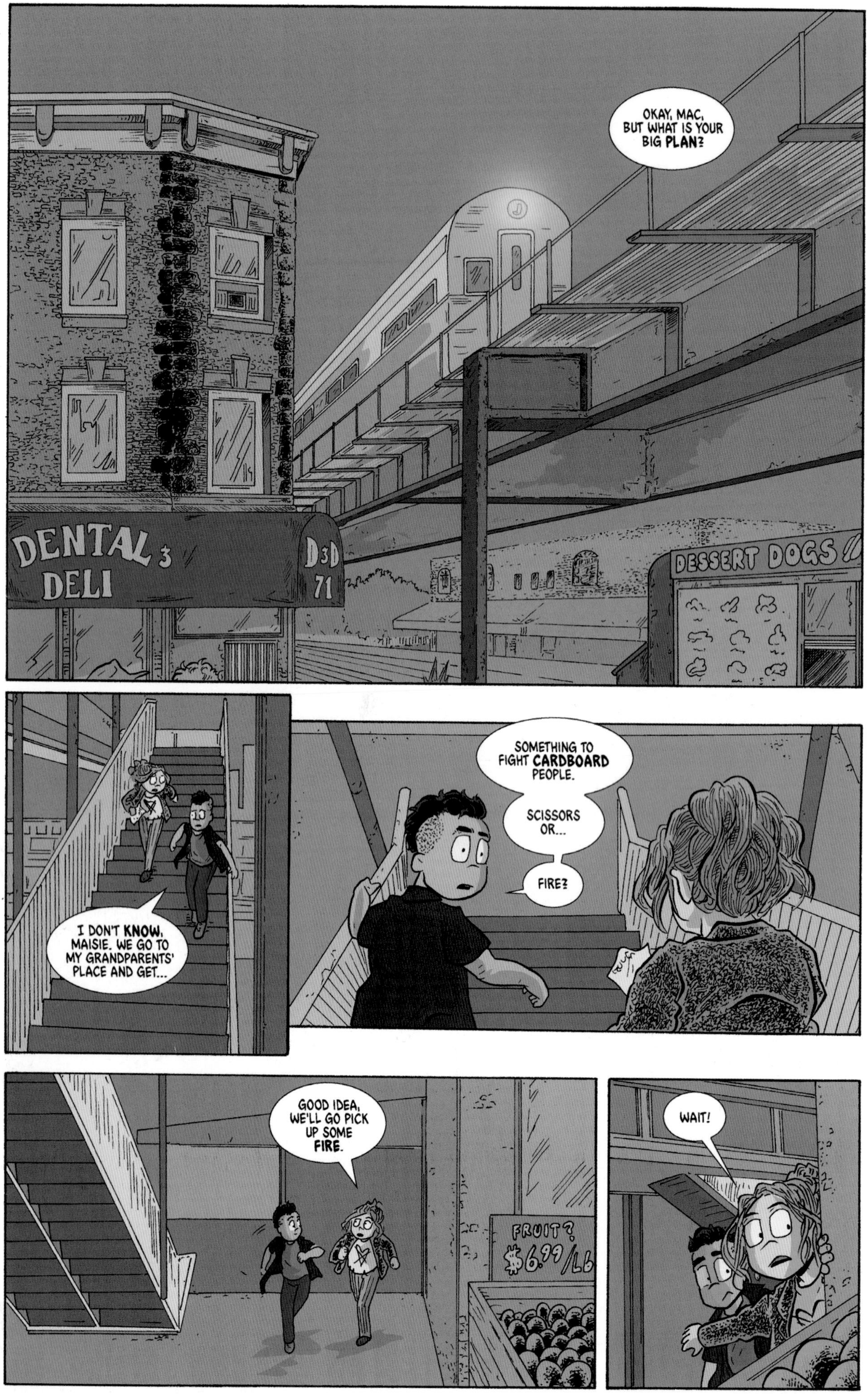
DENTAL 3 DELI
D3D 71
DESSERT DOGS
OKAY, MAC, BUT WHAT IS YOUR BIG PLAN?
I DON'T KNOW, MAISIE. WE GO TO MY GRANDPARENTS' PLACE AND GET...
SOMETHING TO FIGHT CARDBOARD PEOPLE.
SCISSORS OR...
FIRE?
GOOD IDEA, WE'LL GO PICK UP SOME FIRE.
FRUIT? $6.99/Lb
WAIT!

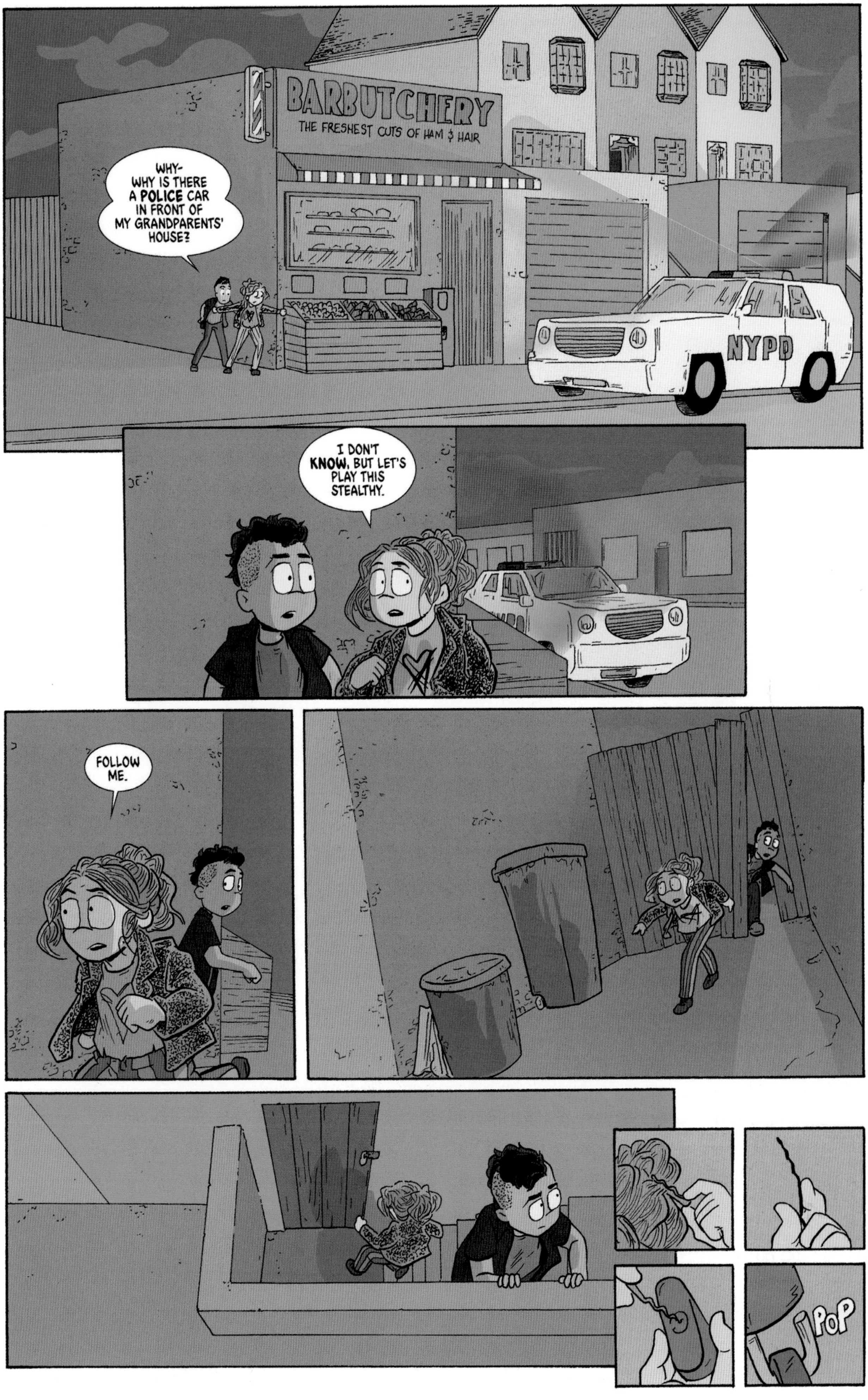
BARBUTCHERY
THE FRESHEST CUTS OF HAM & HAIR
WHY- WHY IS THERE A POLICE CAR IN FRONT OF MY GRANDPARENTS' HOUSE?
NYPD
I DON'T KNOW, BUT LET'S PLAY THIS STEALTHY.
FOLLOW ME.
POP

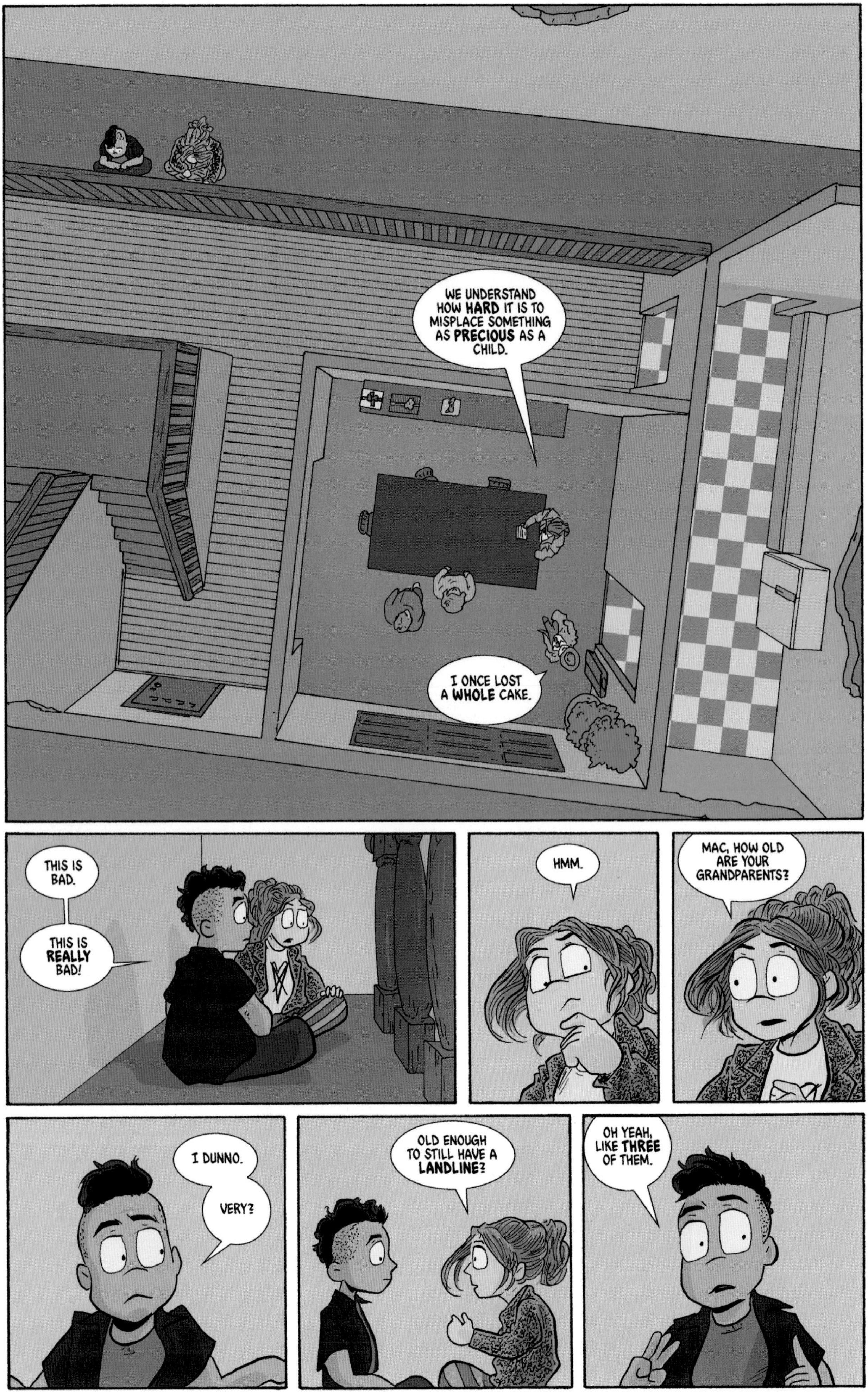
WE UNDERSTAND HOW HARD IT IS TO MISPLACE SOMETHING AS PRECIOUS AS A CHILD.
I ONCE LOST A WHOLE CAKE.
THIS IS BAD.
THIS IS REALLY BAD!
HMM.
MAC, HOW OLD ARE YOUR GRANDPARENTS?
I DUNNO.
VERY?
OLD ENOUGH TO STILL HAVE A LANDLINE?
OH YEAH, LIKE THREE OF THEM.

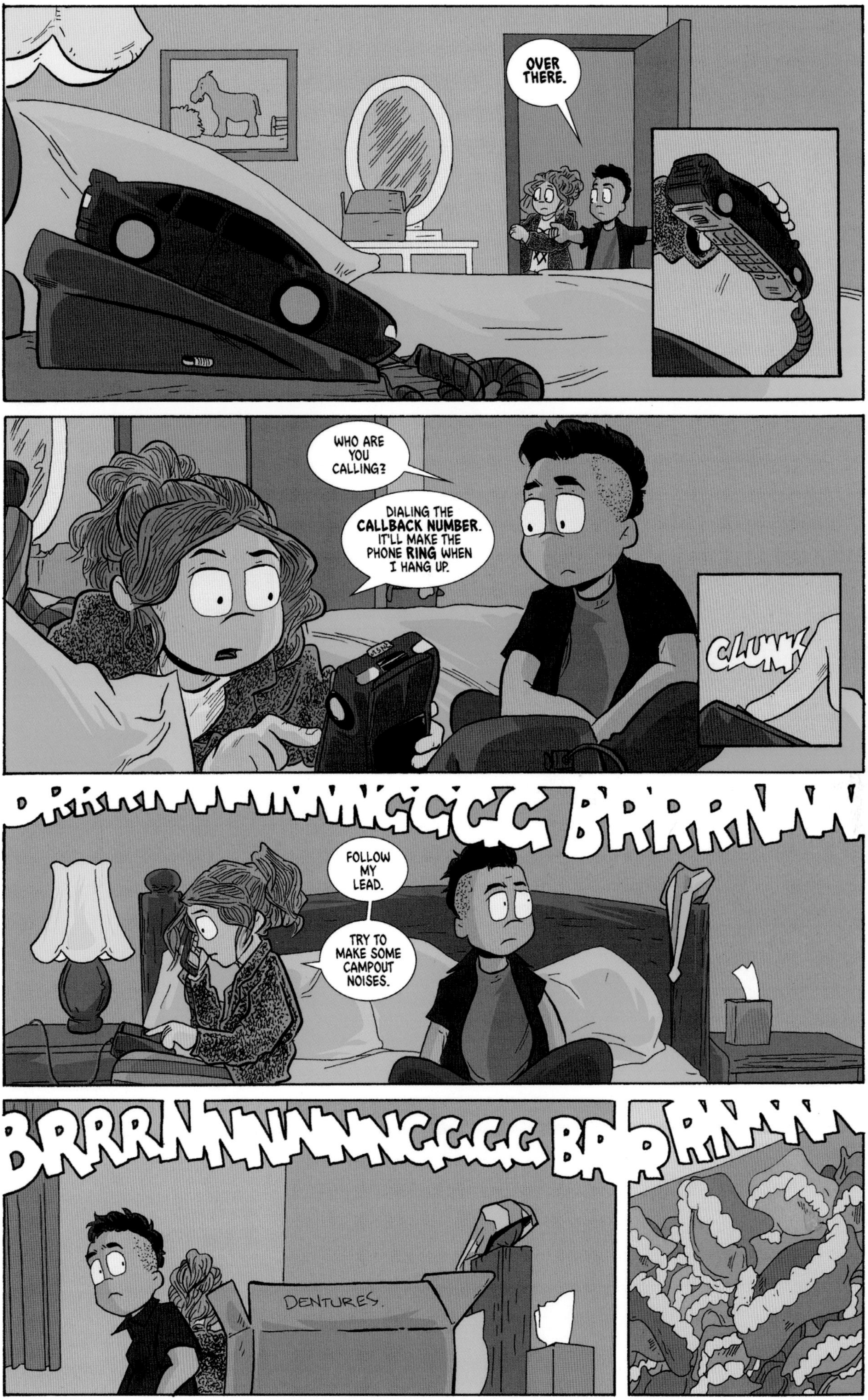

OVER THERE.
WHO ARE YOU CALLING?
DIALING THE **CALLBACK NUMBER**. IT'LL MAKE THE PHONE **RING** WHEN I HANG UP.
CLUNK
BRRRNNNNNNGGGG BRRRNNN
FOLLOW MY LEAD.
TRY TO MAKE SOME CAMPOUT NOISES.
BRRRNNNNNNGGGG BRRRNNN
DENTURES.

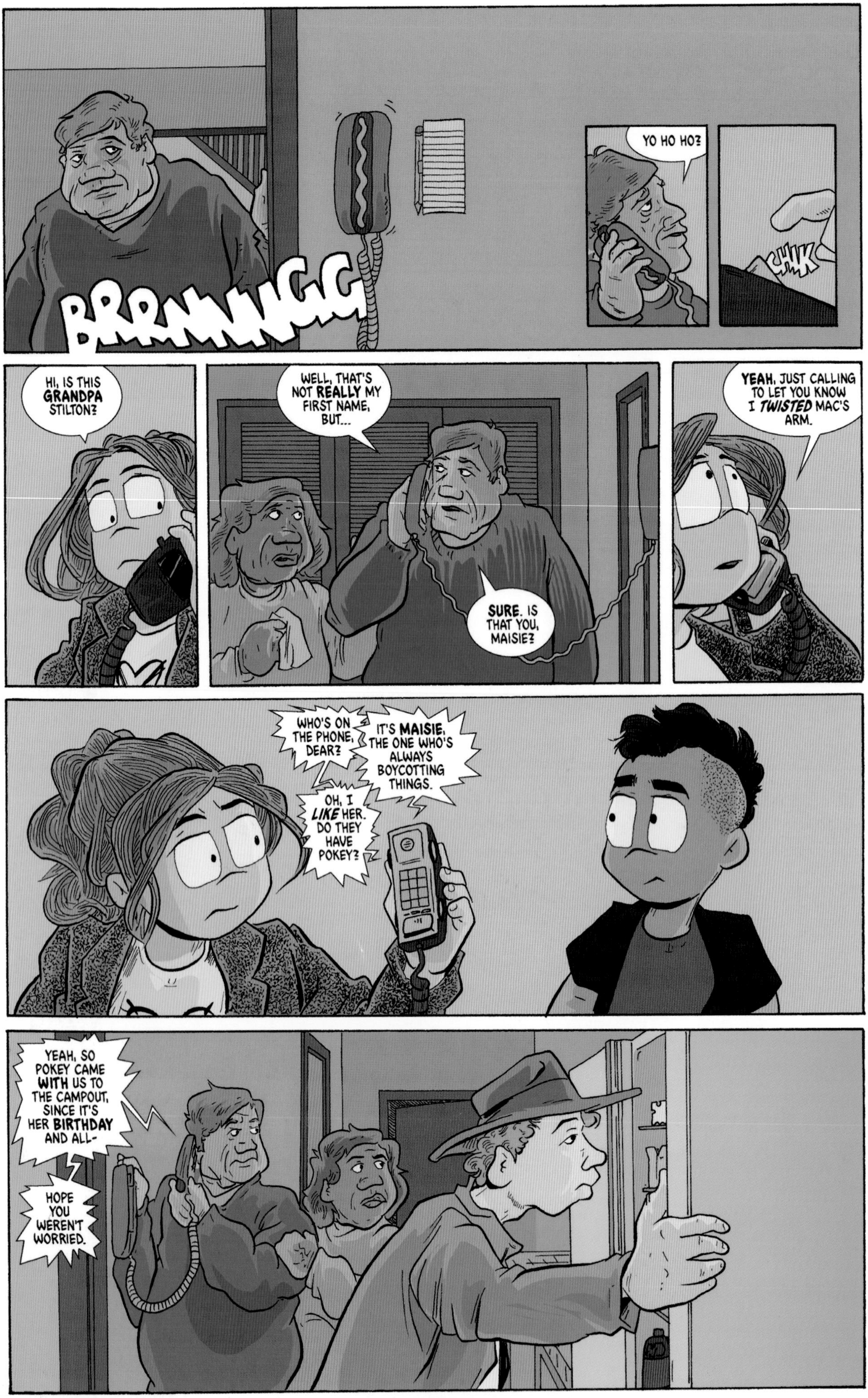
BRRNNNGG
YO HO HO?
CHIK
HI, IS THIS GRANDPA STILTON?
WELL, THAT'S NOT REALLY MY FIRST NAME, BUT...
SURE. IS THAT YOU, MAISIE?
YEAH, JUST CALLING TO LET YOU KNOW I TWISTED MAC'S ARM.
WHO'S ON THE PHONE, DEAR?
IT'S MAISIE, THE ONE WHO'S ALWAYS BOYCOTTING THINGS.
OH, I LIKE HER. DO THEY HAVE POKEY?
YEAH, SO POKEY CAME WITH US TO THE CAMPOUT, SINCE IT'S HER BIRTHDAY AND ALL-
HOPE YOU WEREN'T WORRIED.

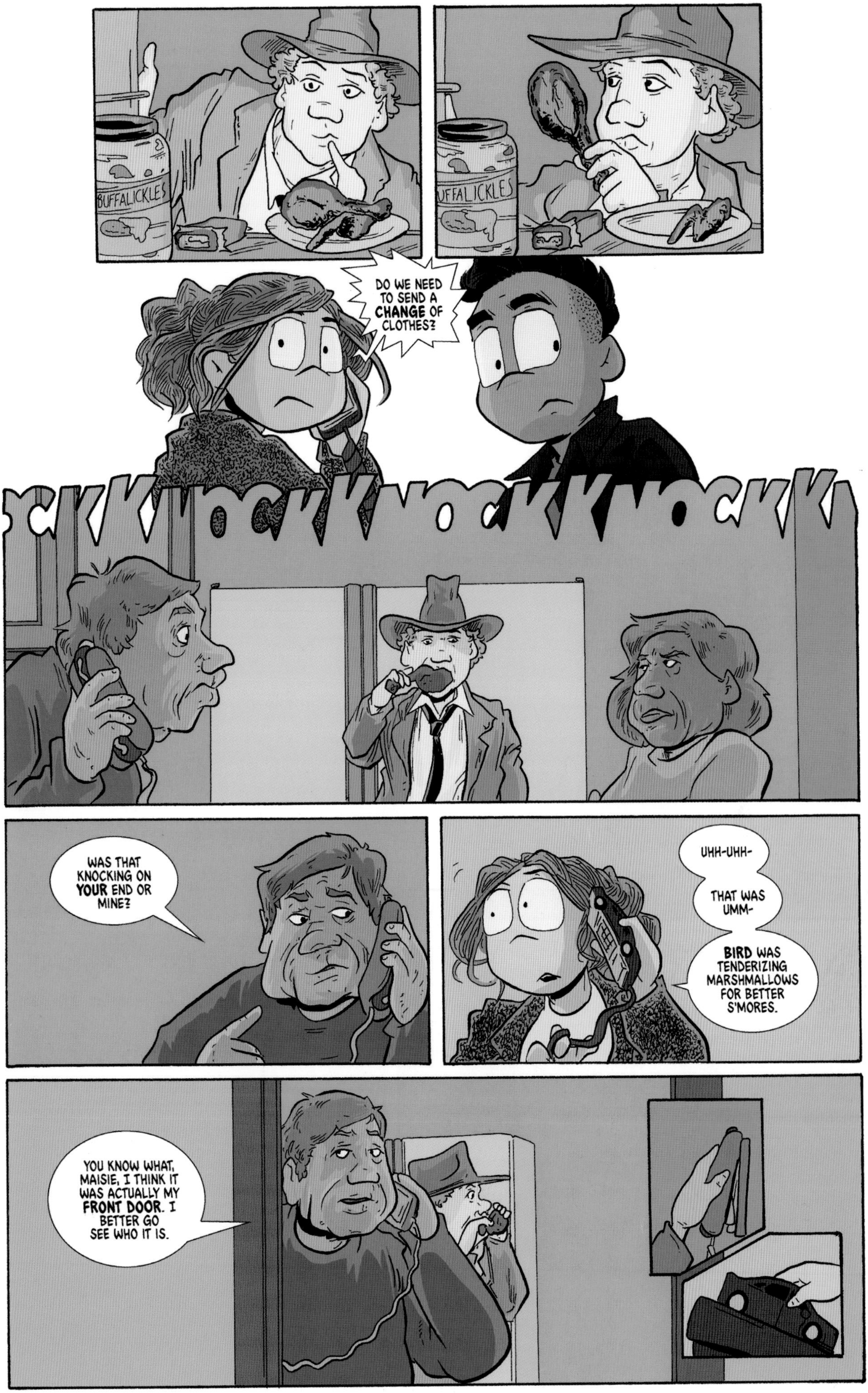
BUFFALICKLES
BUFFALICKLES
DO WE NEED TO SEND A CHANGE OF CLOTHES?
CKKNOCKKNOCKKNOCKK
WAS THAT KNOCKING ON YOUR END OR MINE?
UHH-UHH-
THAT WAS UMM-
BIRD WAS TENDERIZING MARSHMALLOWS FOR BETTER S'MORES.
YOU KNOW WHAT, MAISIE, I THINK IT WAS ACTUALLY MY FRONT DOOR. I BETTER GO SEE WHO IT IS.

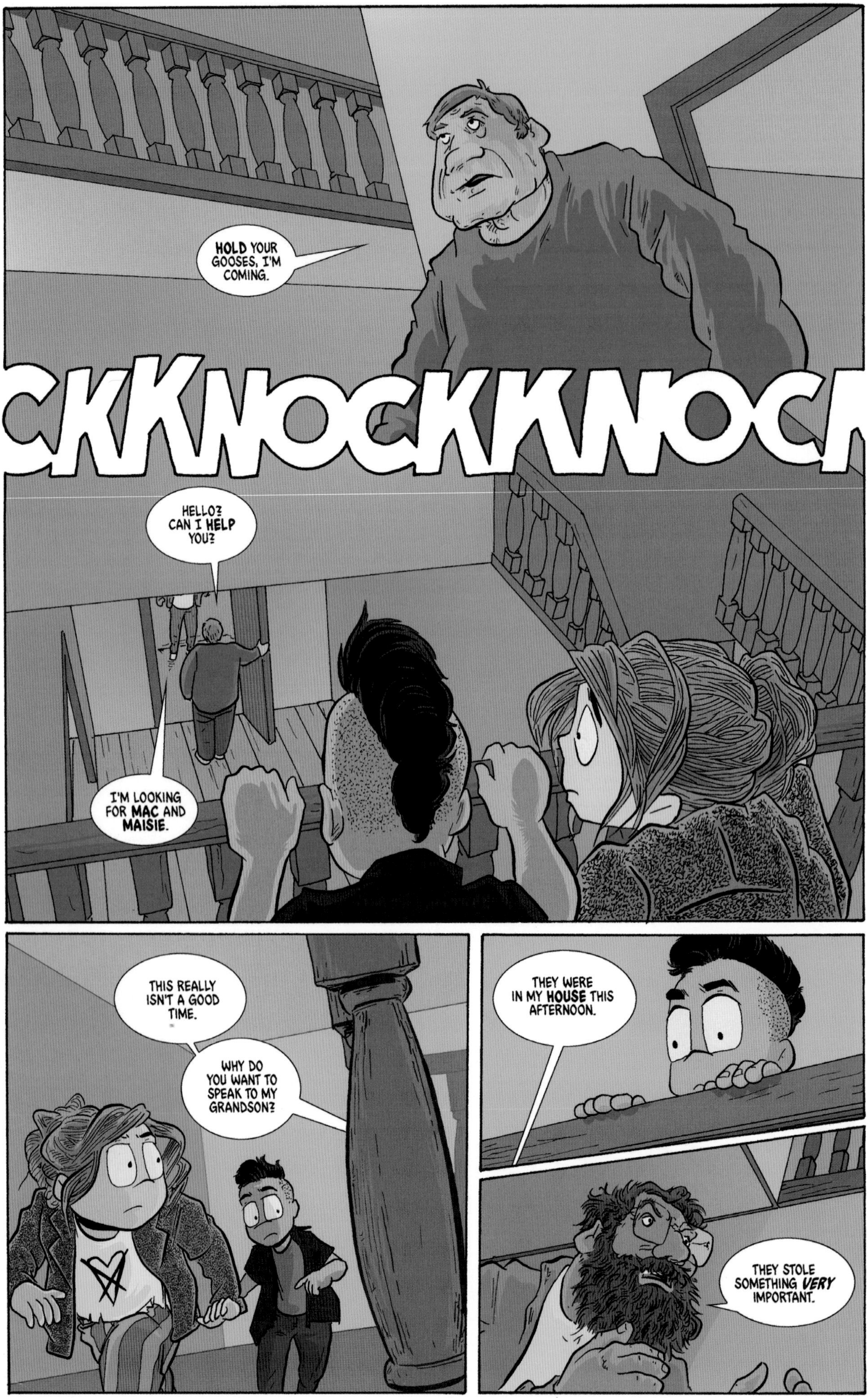
HOLD YOUR GOOSES, I'M COMING.
CKKNOCKKNOCK
HELLO? CAN I HELP YOU?
I'M LOOKING FOR MAC AND MAISIE.
THIS REALLY ISN'T A GOOD TIME.
WHY DO YOU WANT TO SPEAK TO MY GRANDSON?
THEY WERE IN MY HOUSE THIS AFTERNOON.
THEY STOLE SOMETHING VERY IMPORTANT.

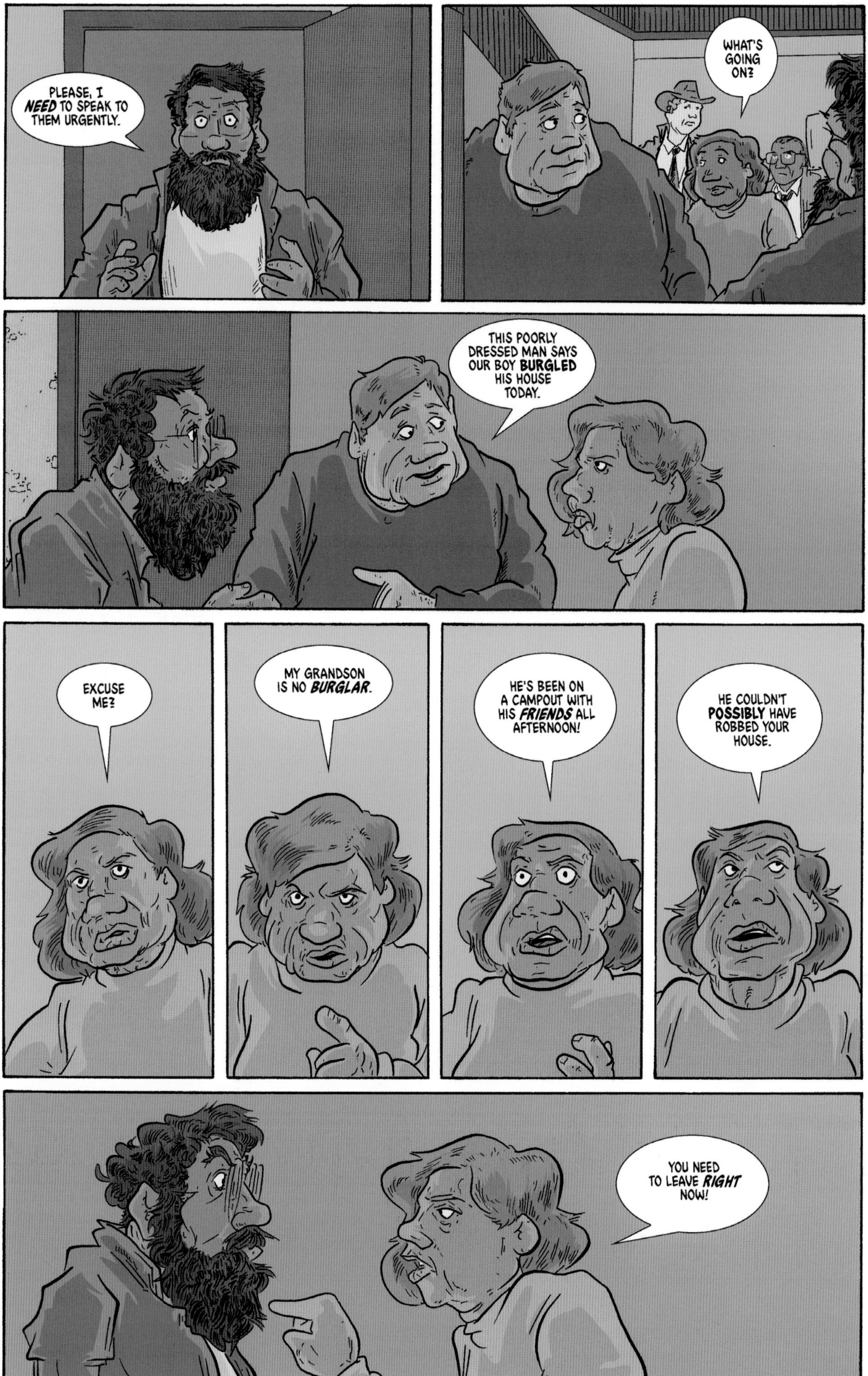
PLEASE, I *NEED* TO SPEAK TO THEM URGENTLY.
WHAT'S GOING ON?
THIS POORLY DRESSED MAN SAYS OUR BOY **BURGLED** HIS HOUSE TODAY.
EXCUSE ME?
MY GRANDSON IS NO *BURGLAR*.
HE'S BEEN ON A CAMPOUT WITH HIS *FRIENDS* ALL AFTERNOON!
HE COULDN'T **POSSIBLY** HAVE ROBBED YOUR HOUSE.
YOU NEED TO LEAVE *RIGHT* NOW!

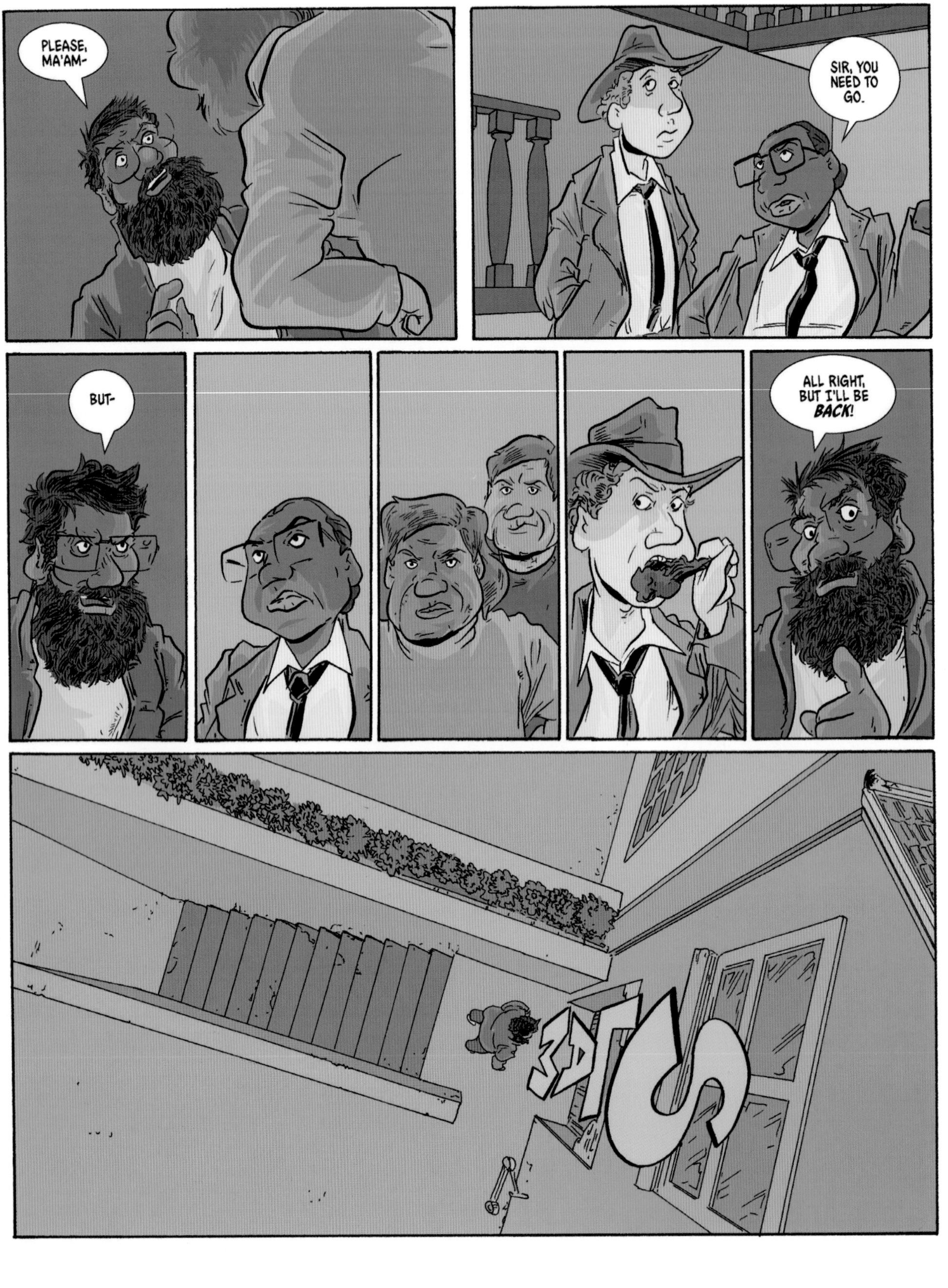
PLEASE, MA'AM-
SIR, YOU NEED TO GO.
BUT-
ALL RIGHT, BUT I'LL BE *BACK*!

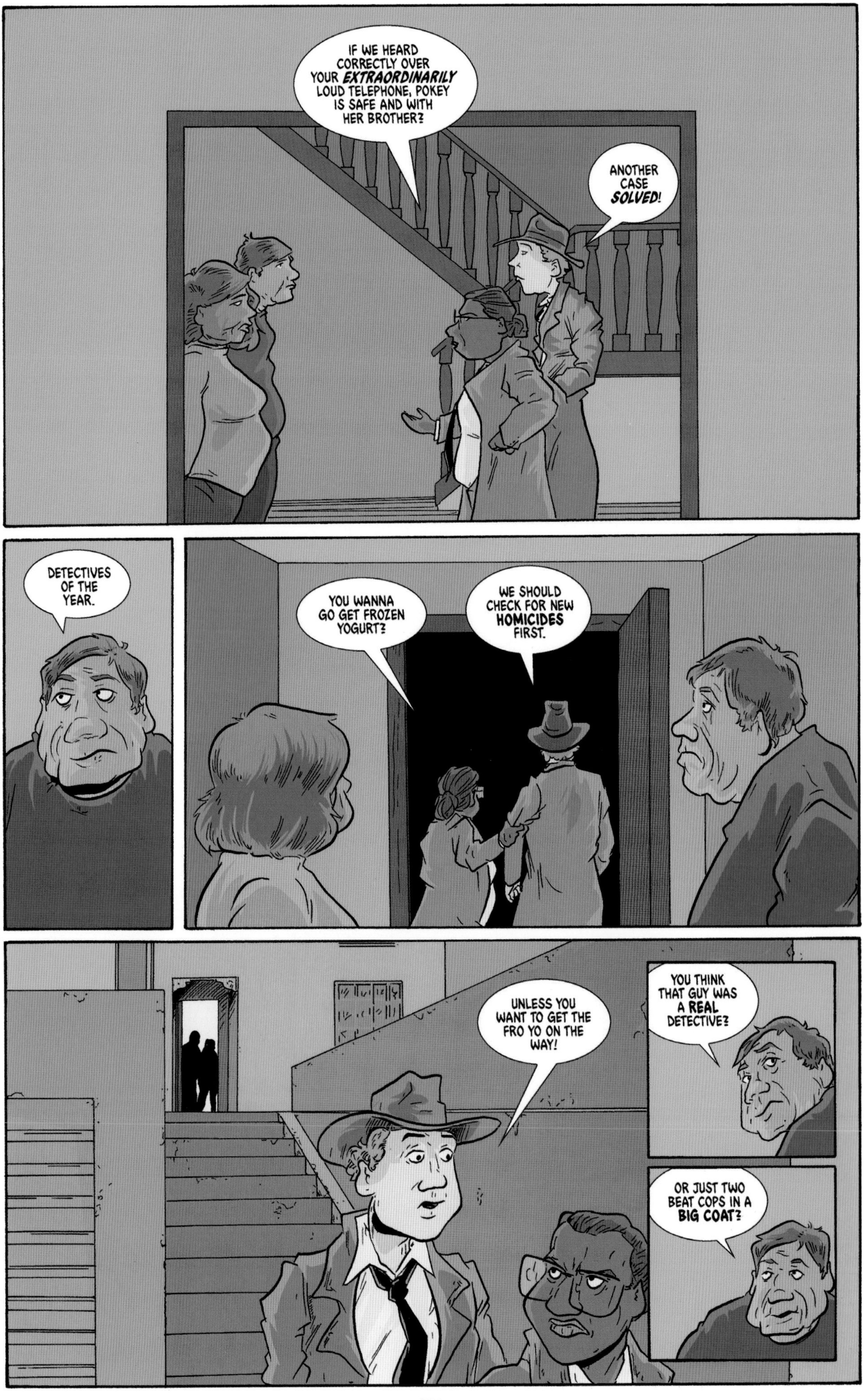
IF WE HEARD CORRECTLY OVER YOUR EXTRAORDINARILY LOUD TELEPHONE, POKEY IS SAFE AND WITH HER BROTHER?
ANOTHER CASE SOLVED!
DETECTIVES OF THE YEAR.
YOU WANNA GO GET FROZEN YOGURT?
WE SHOULD CHECK FOR NEW HOMICIDES FIRST.
UNLESS YOU WANT TO GET THE FRO YO ON THE WAY!
YOU THINK THAT GUY WAS A REAL DETECTIVE?
OR JUST TWO BEAT COPS IN A BIG COAT?

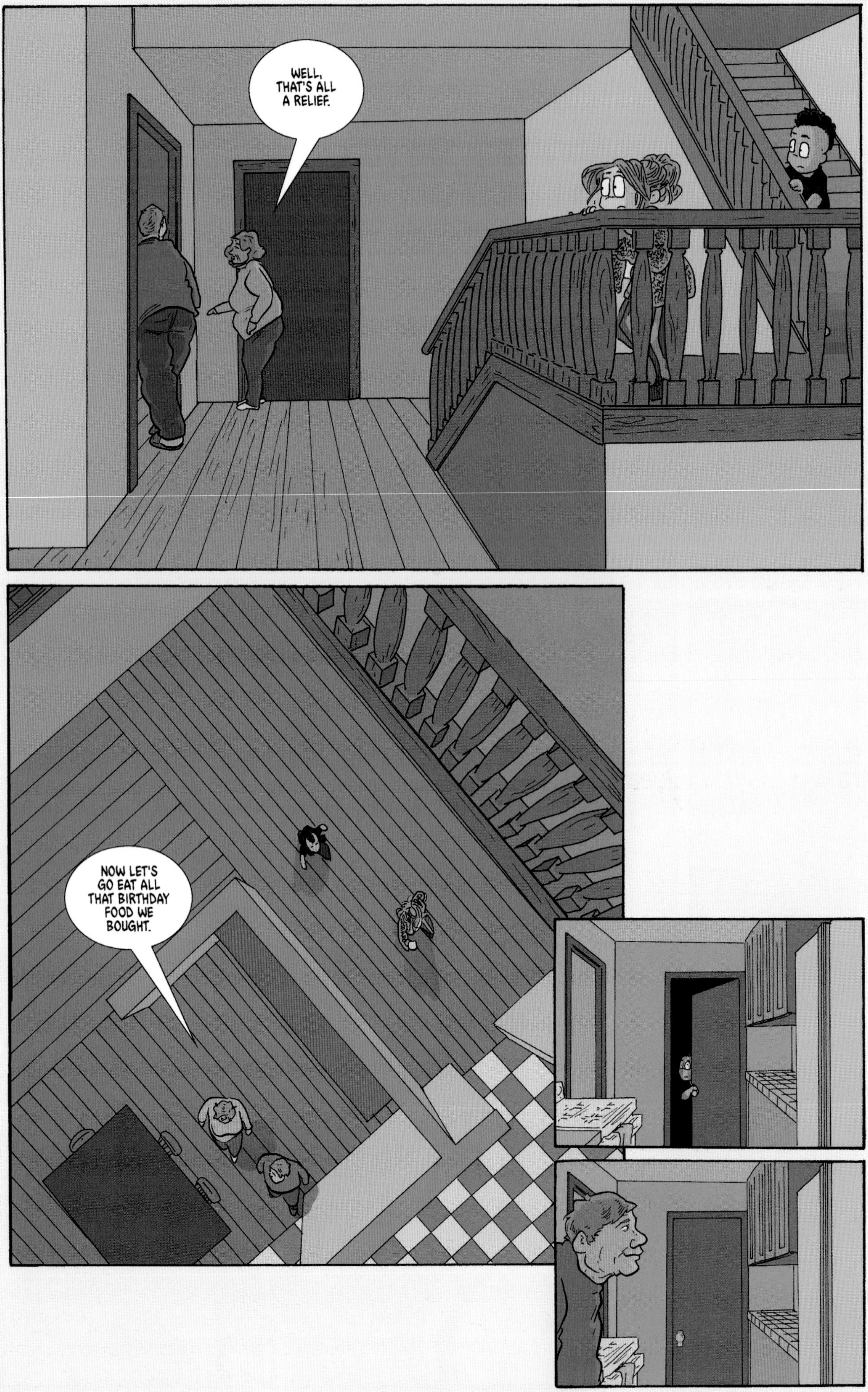
WELL, THAT'S ALL A RELIEF.
NOW LET'S GO EAT ALL THAT BIRTHDAY FOOD WE BOUGHT.

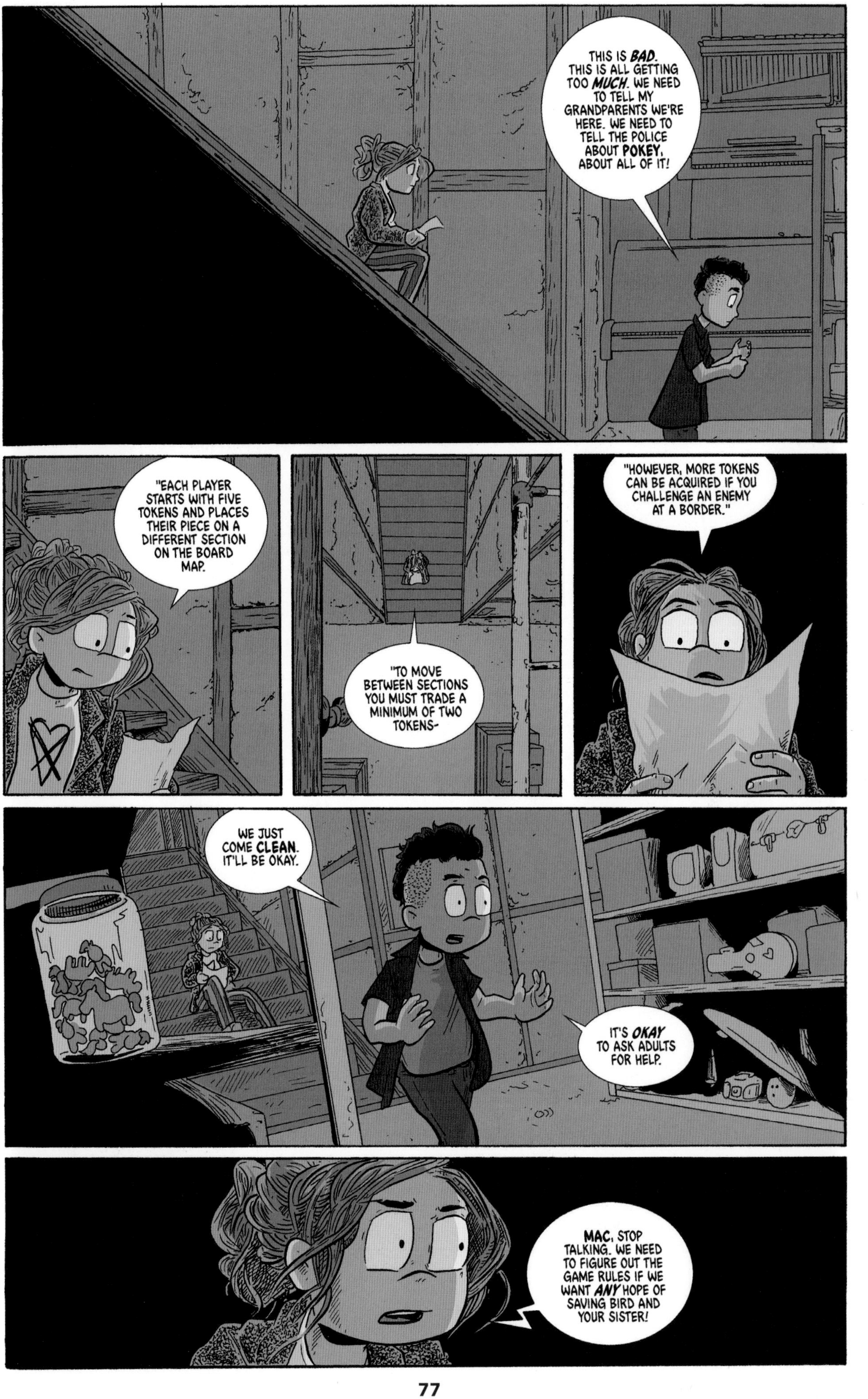
THIS IS BAD. THIS IS ALL GETTING TOO MUCH. WE NEED TO TELL MY GRANDPARENTS WE'RE HERE. WE NEED TO TELL THE POLICE ABOUT POKEY, ABOUT ALL OF IT!
"EACH PLAYER STARTS WITH FIVE TOKENS AND PLACES THEIR PIECE ON A DIFFERENT SECTION ON THE BOARD MAP.
"TO MOVE BETWEEN SECTIONS YOU MUST TRADE A MINIMUM OF TWO TOKENS-
"HOWEVER, MORE TOKENS CAN BE ACQUIRED IF YOU CHALLENGE AN ENEMY AT A BORDER."
WE JUST COME CLEAN. IT'LL BE OKAY.
IT'S OKAY TO ASK ADULTS FOR HELP.
MAC, STOP TALKING. WE NEED TO FIGURE OUT THE GAME RULES IF WE WANT ANY HOPE OF SAVING BIRD AND YOUR SISTER!

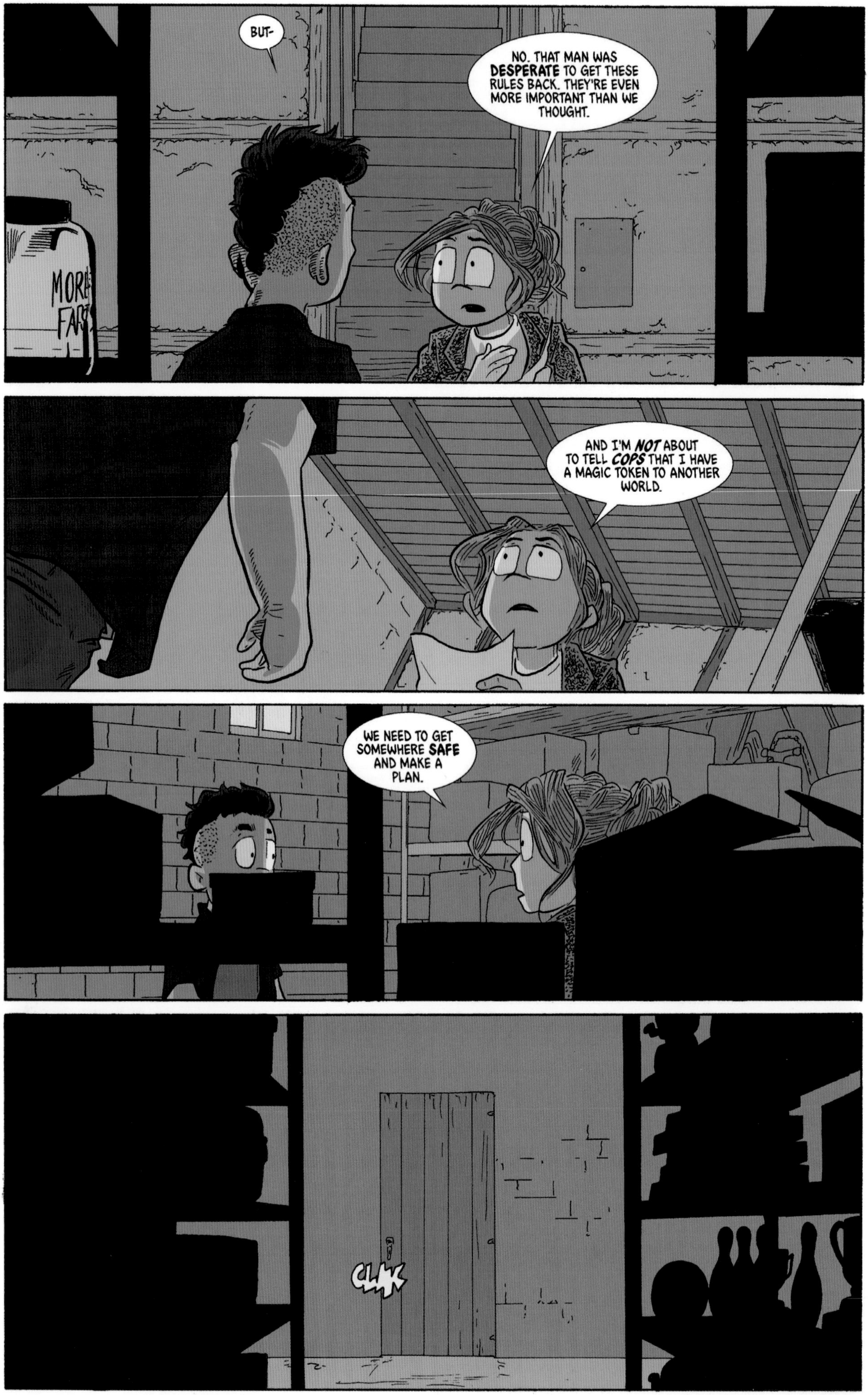
BUT-
NO. THAT MAN WAS DESPERATE TO GET THESE RULES BACK. THEY'RE EVEN MORE IMPORTANT THAN WE THOUGHT.
AND I'M NOT ABOUT TO TELL COPS THAT I HAVE A MAGIC TOKEN TO ANOTHER WORLD.
WE NEED TO GET SOMEWHERE SAFE AND MAKE A PLAN.
CLAK

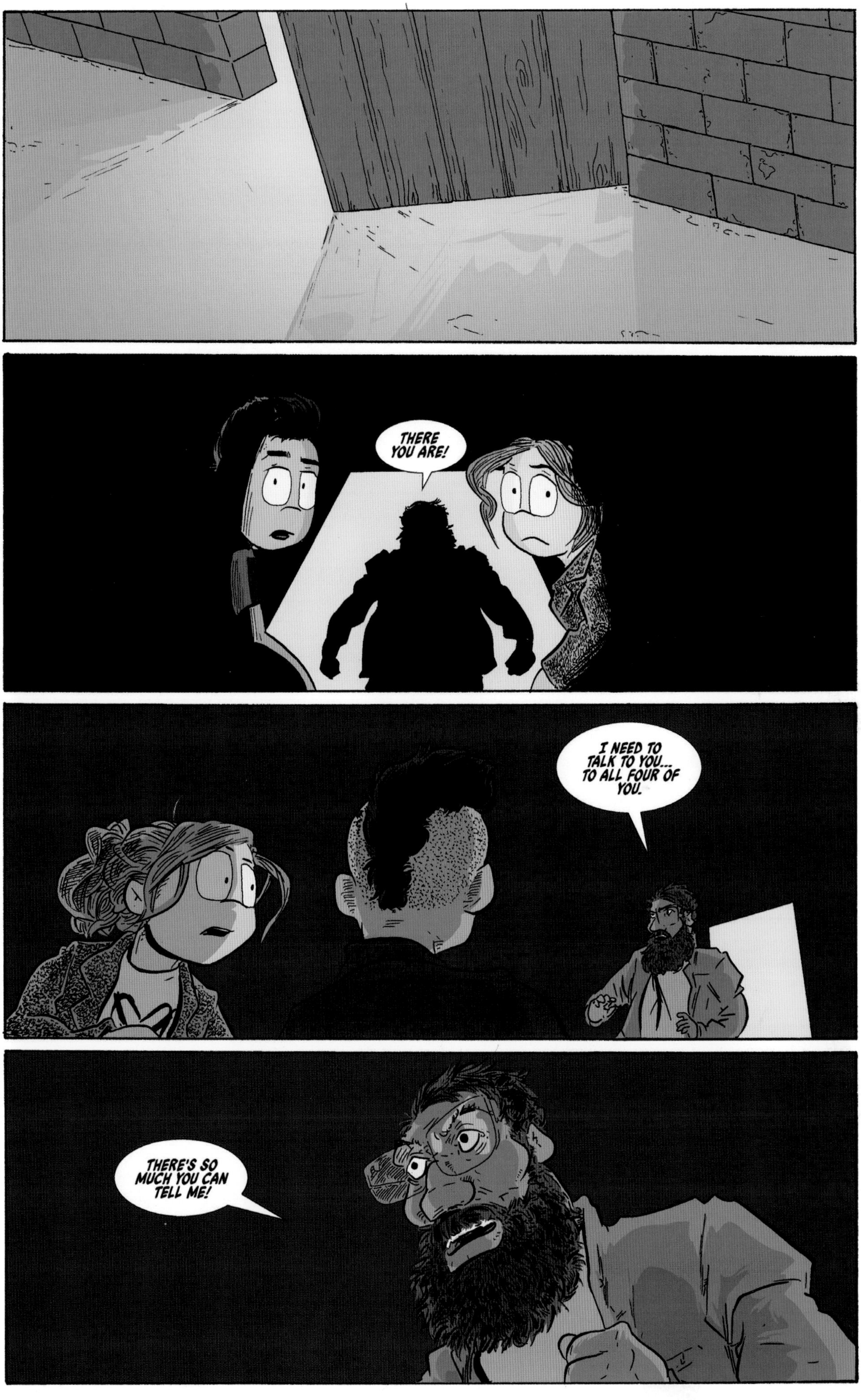
THERE YOU ARE!
I NEED TO TALK TO YOU... TO ALL FOUR OF YOU.
THERE'S SO MUCH YOU CAN TELL ME!

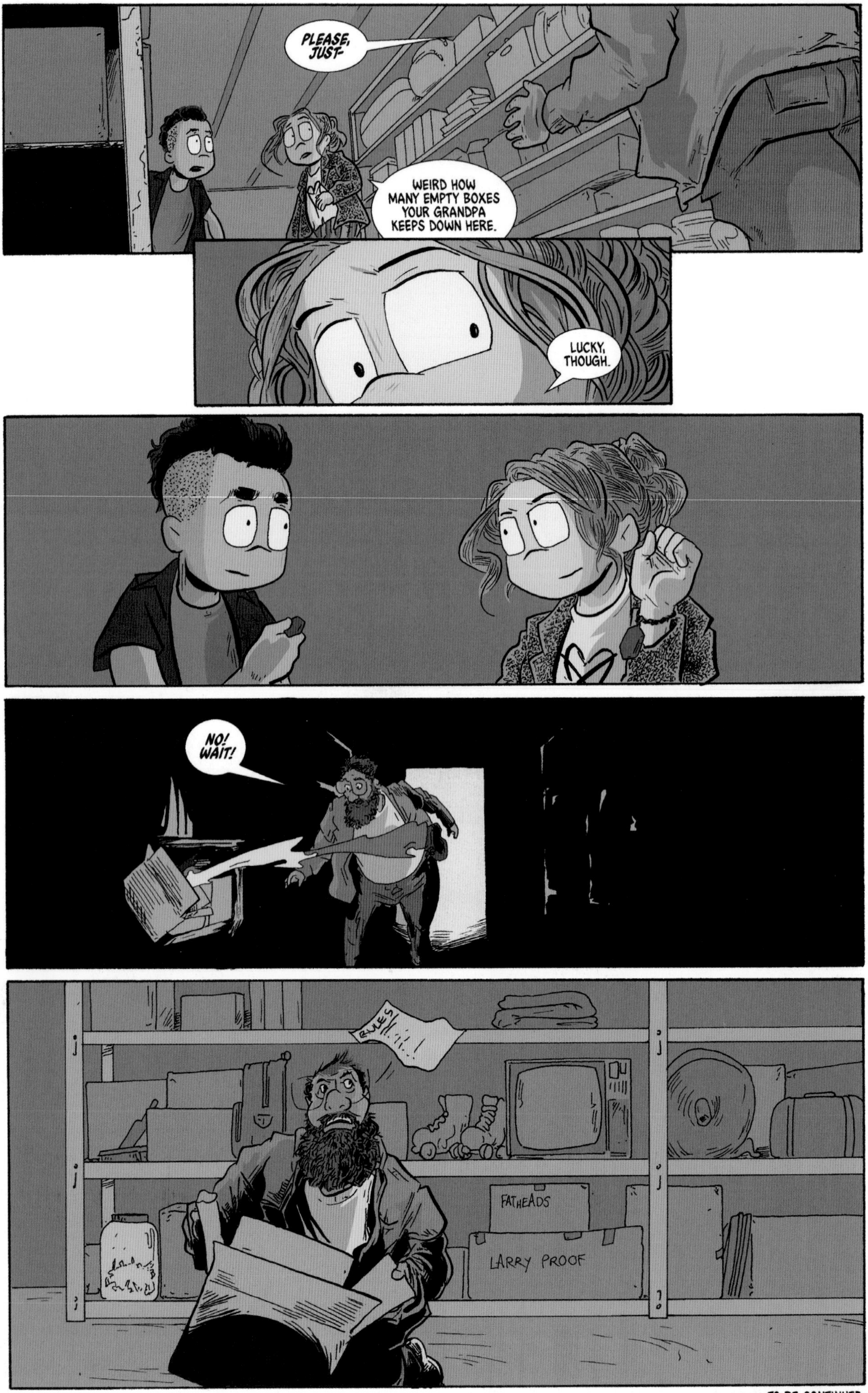
PLEASE, JUST-
WEIRD HOW MANY EMPTY BOXES YOUR GRANDPA KEEPS DOWN HERE.
LUCKY, THOUGH.
NO! WAIT!
RULES
FATHEADS
LARRY PROOF

TO BE CONTINUED.

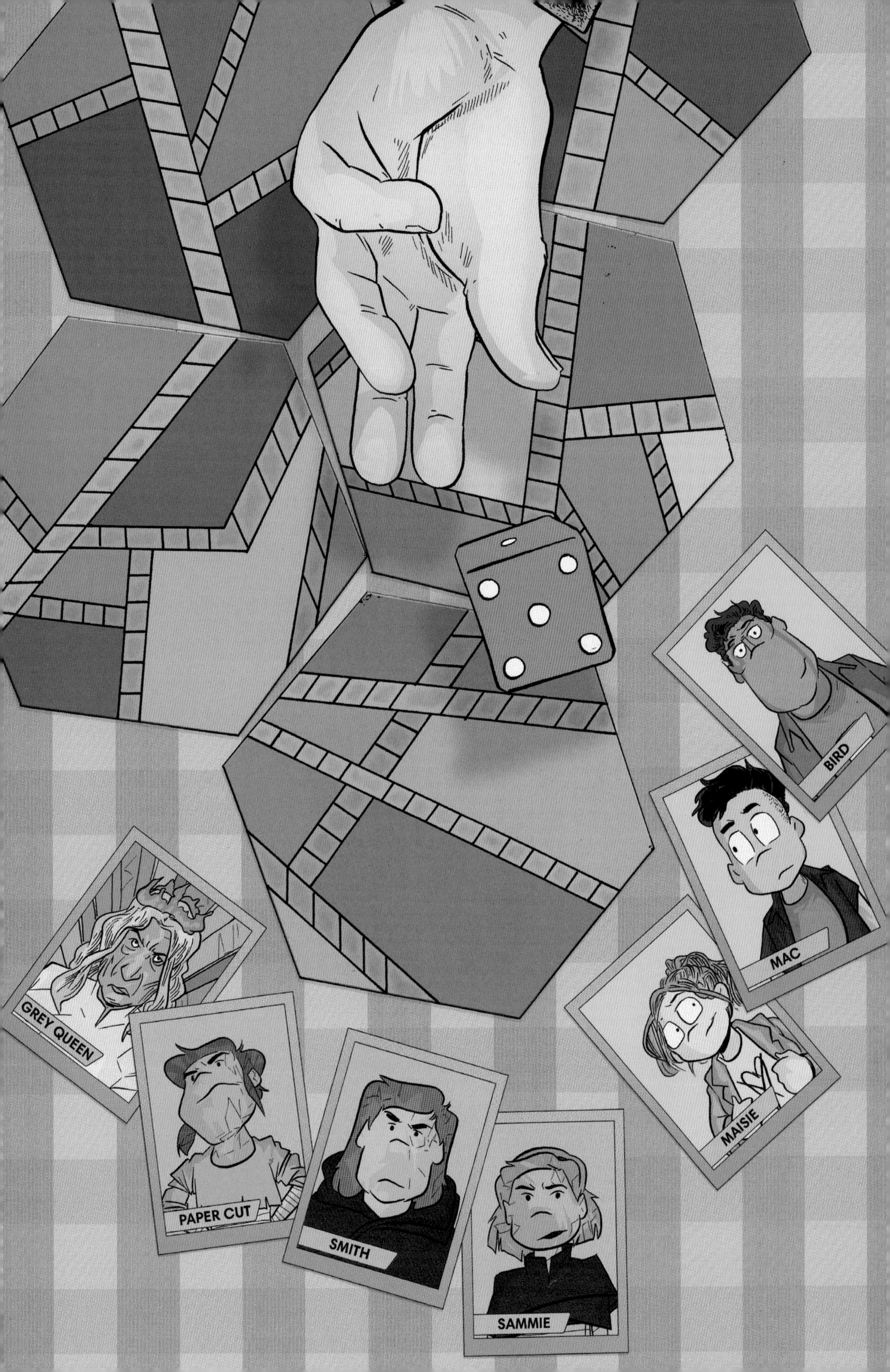
BIRD
MAC
MAISIE
GREY QUEEN
PAPER CUT
SMITH
SAMMIE

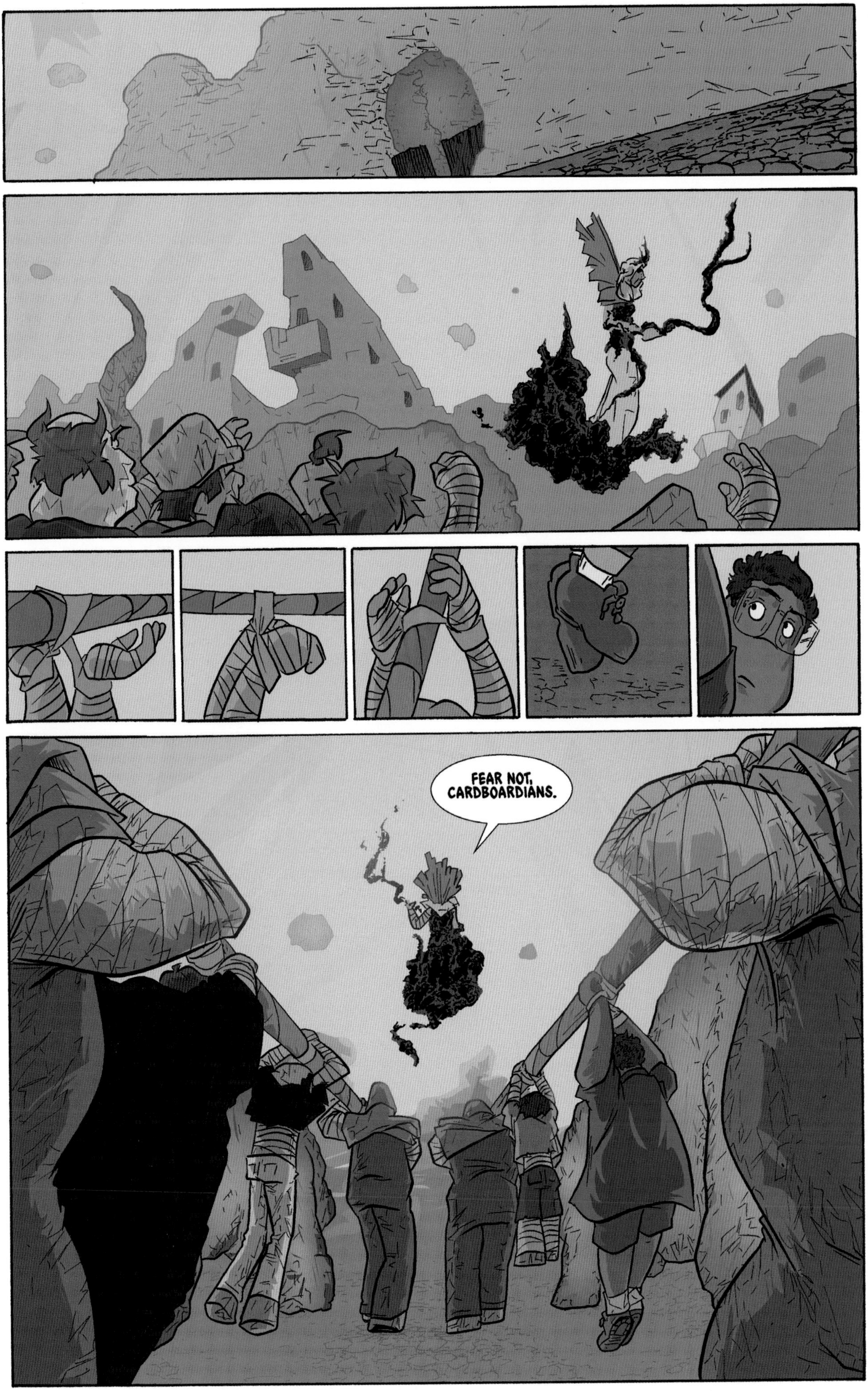
FEAR NOT, CARDBOARDIANS.

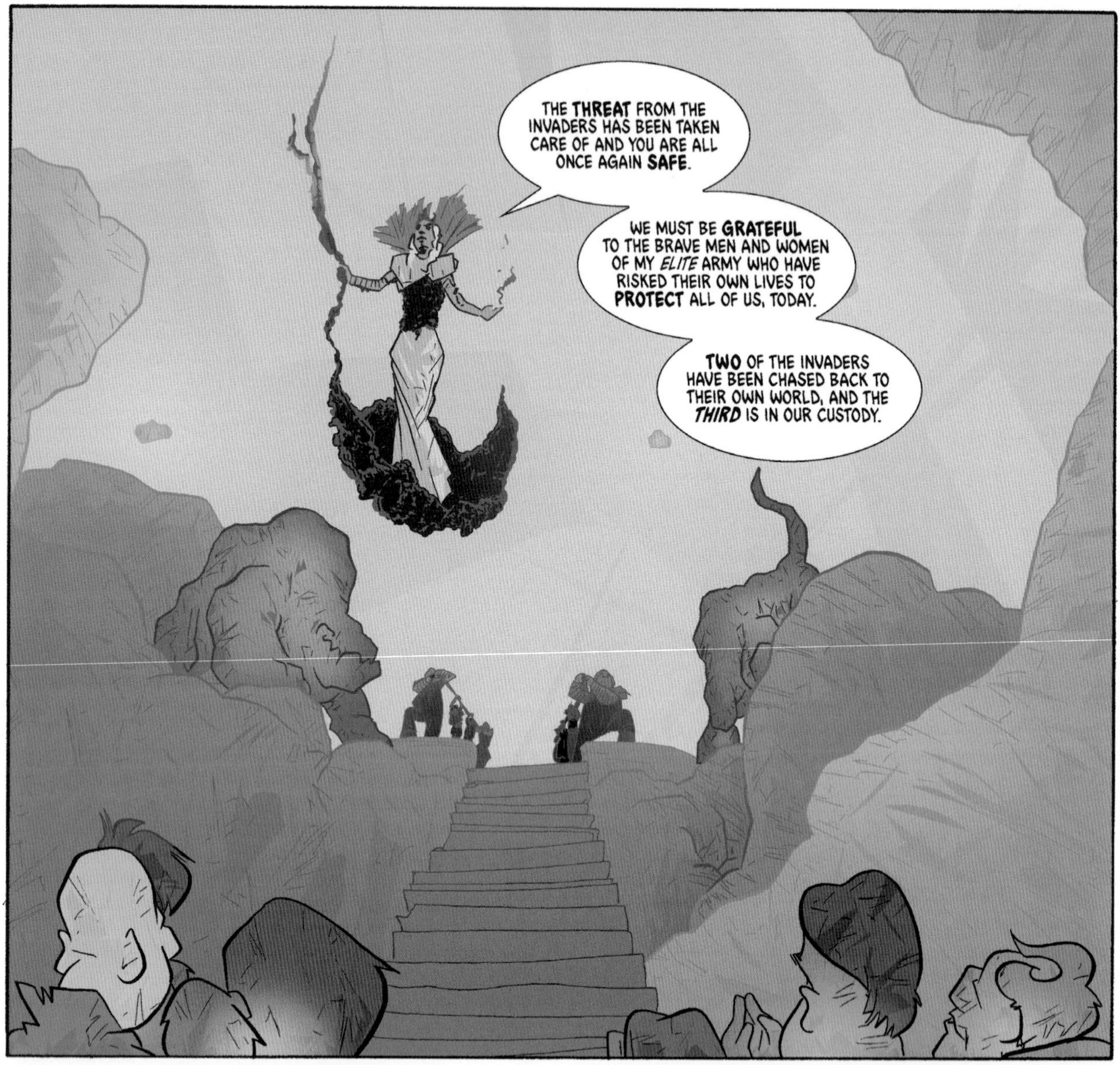
THE **THREAT** FROM THE INVADERS HAS BEEN TAKEN CARE OF AND YOU ARE ALL ONCE AGAIN **SAFE**.
WE MUST BE **GRATEFUL** TO THE BRAVE MEN AND WOMEN OF MY *ELITE* ARMY WHO HAVE RISKED THEIR OWN LIVES TO **PROTECT** ALL OF US, TODAY.
TWO OF THE INVADERS HAVE BEEN CHASED BACK TO THEIR OWN WORLD, AND THE ***THIRD*** IS IN OUR CUSTODY.

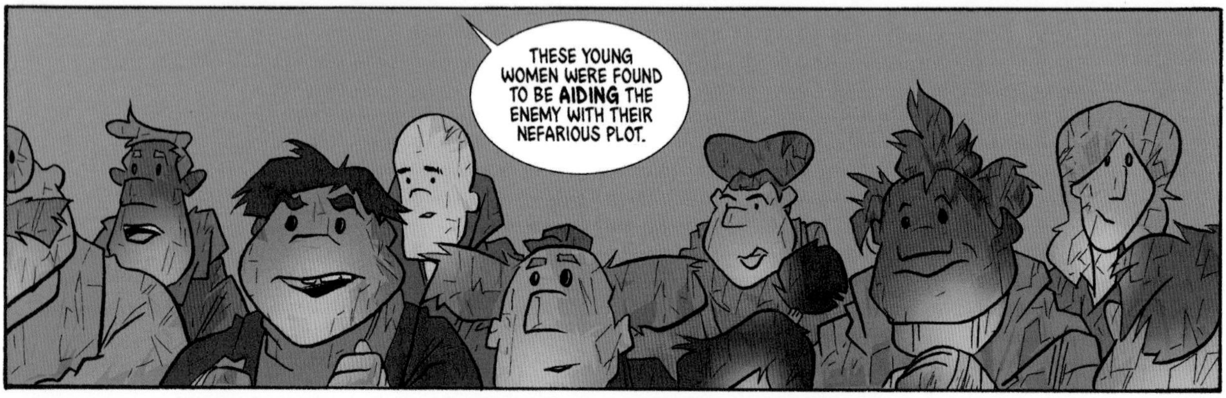
THESE YOUNG WOMEN WERE FOUND TO BE **AIDING** THE ENEMY WITH THEIR NEFARIOUS PLOT.

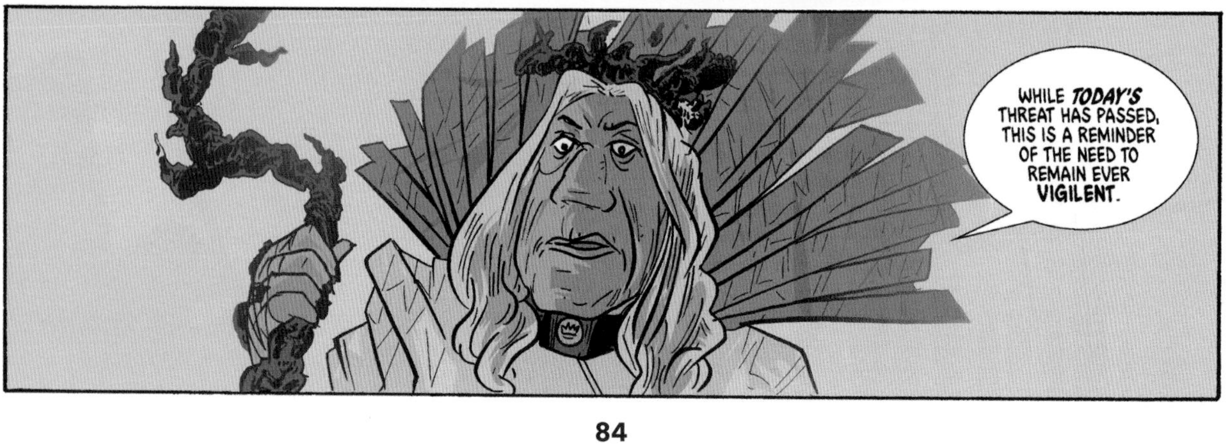
WHILE ***TODAY'S*** THREAT HAS PASSED, THIS IS A REMINDER OF THE NEED TO REMAIN EVER **VIGILENT**.

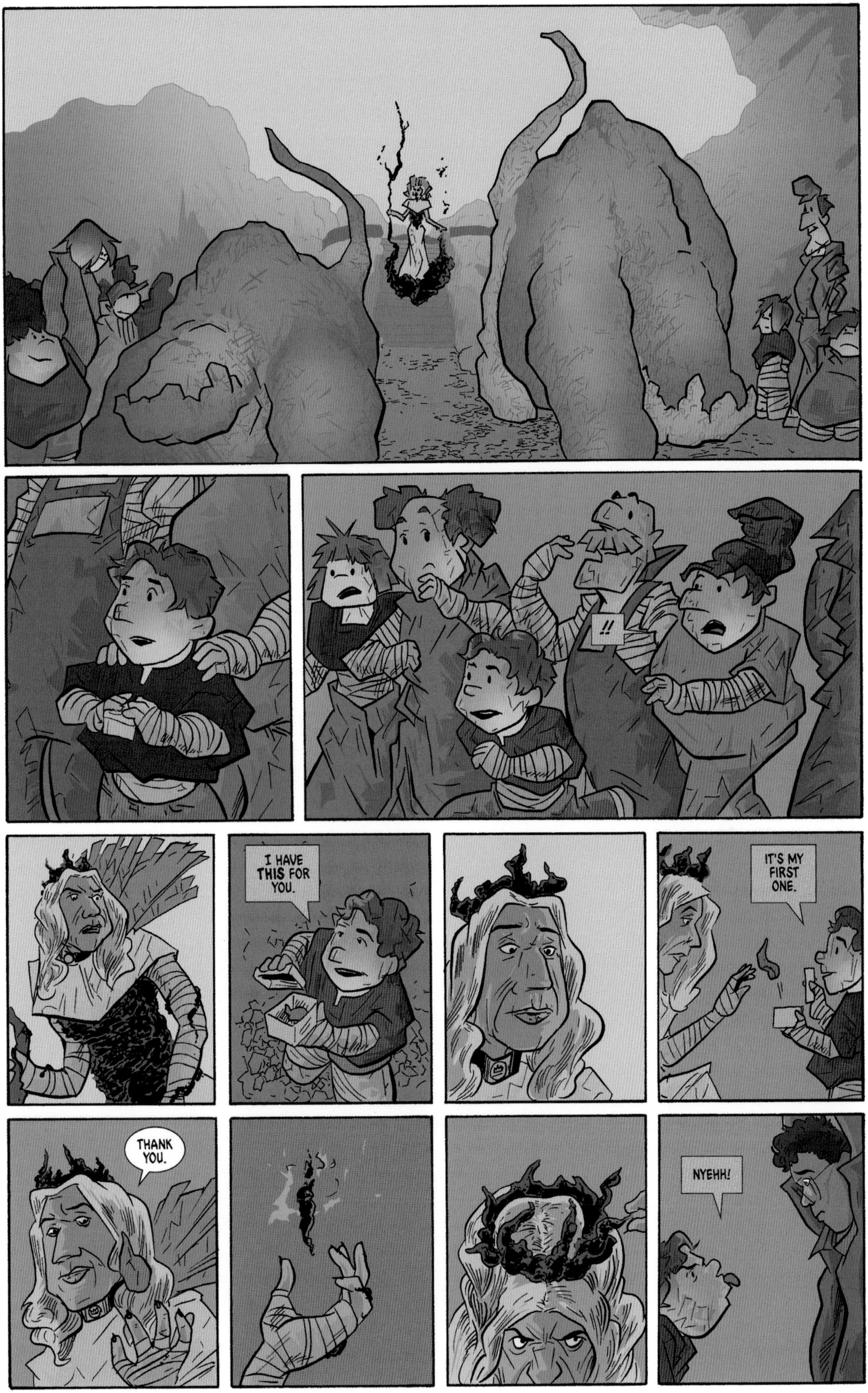
!!
I HAVE THIS FOR YOU.
IT'S MY FIRST ONE.
THANK YOU.
NYEHH!

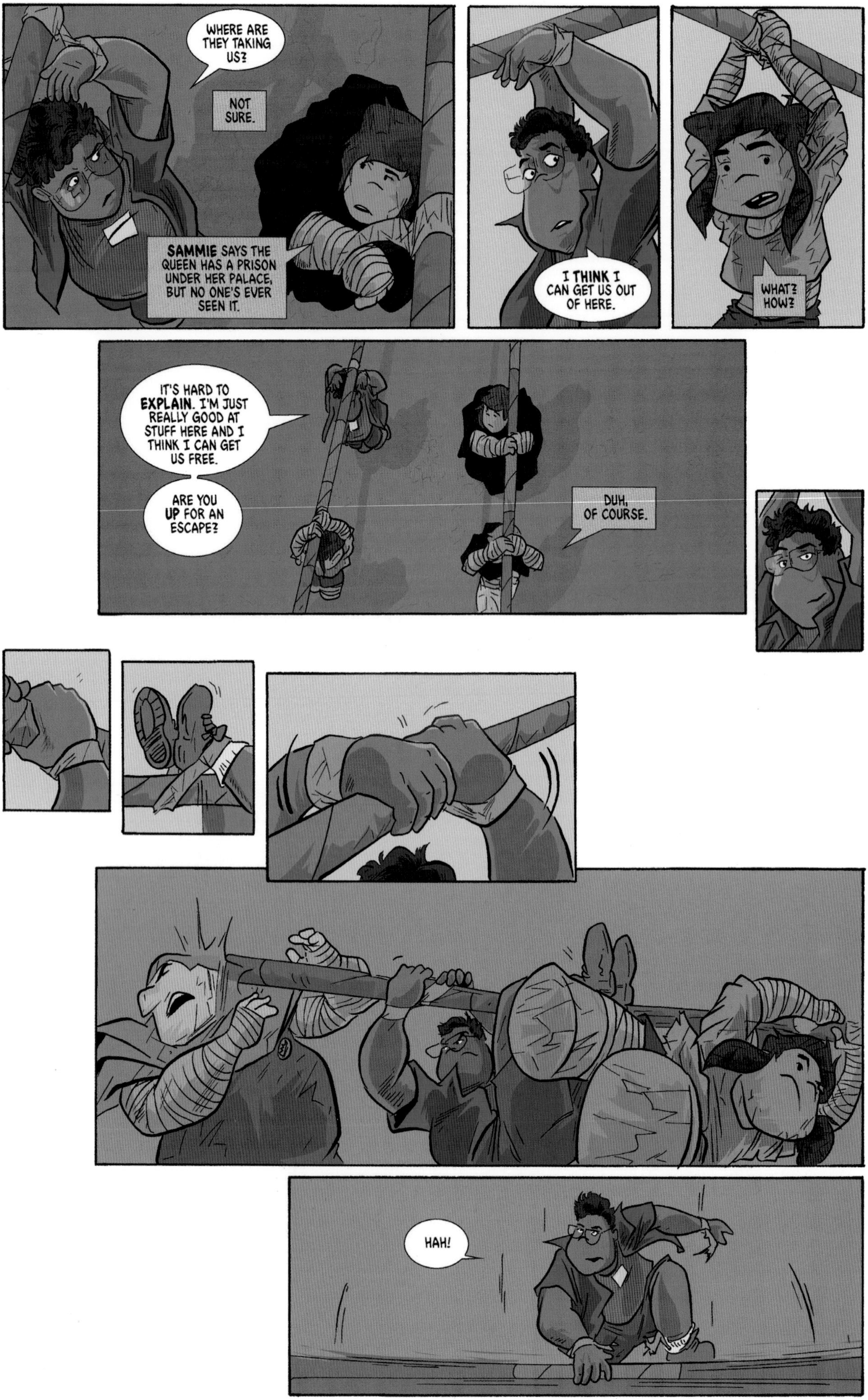
WHERE ARE THEY TAKING US?
NOT SURE.
SAMMIE SAYS THE QUEEN HAS A PRISON UNDER HER PALACE, BUT NO ONE'S EVER SEEN IT.
I THINK I CAN GET US OUT OF HERE.
WHAT? HOW?
IT'S HARD TO EXPLAIN. I'M JUST REALLY GOOD AT STUFF HERE AND I THINK I CAN GET US FREE.
ARE YOU UP FOR AN ESCAPE?
DUH, OF COURSE.
HAH!

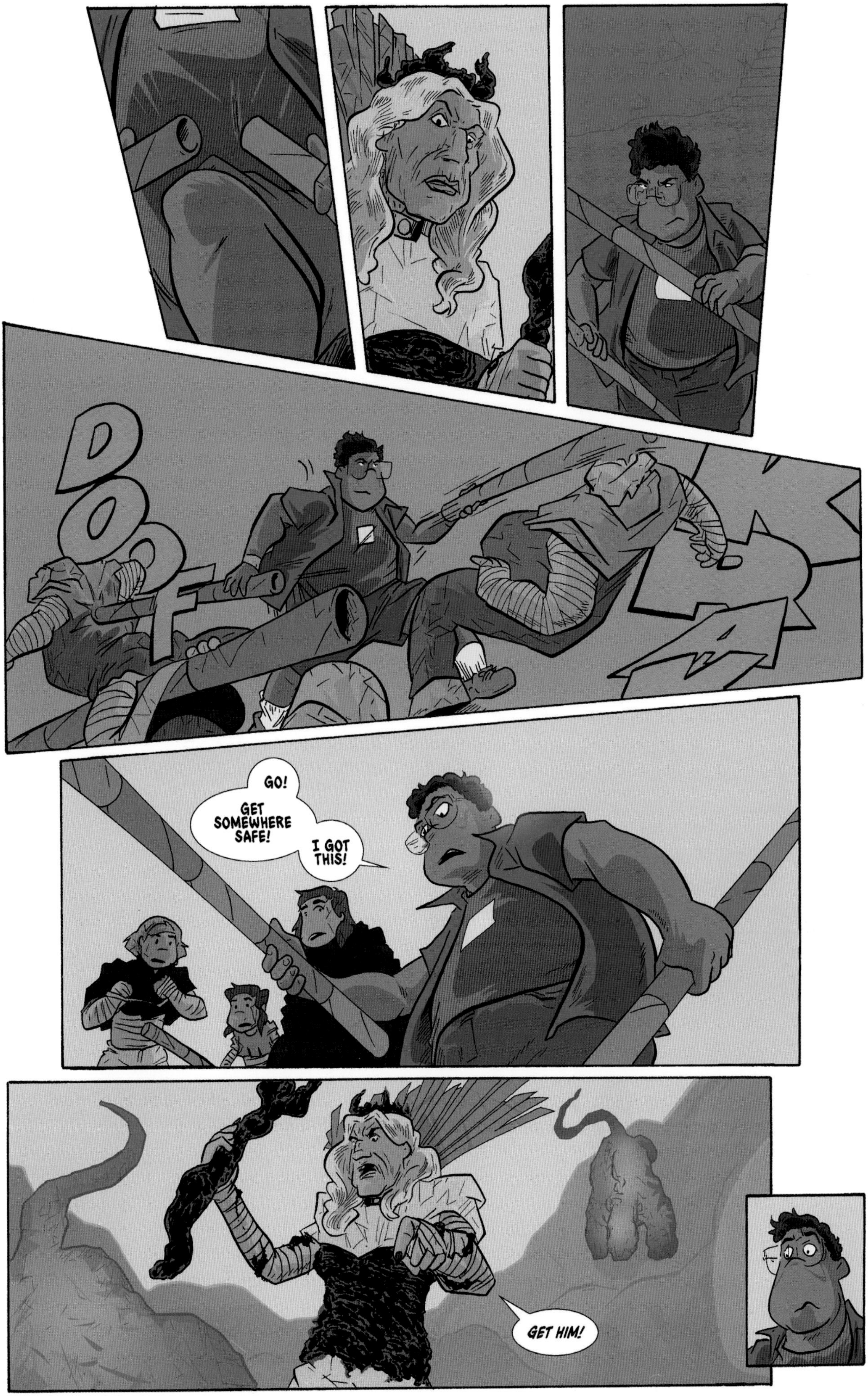
DOOF
GO!
GET SOMEWHERE SAFE!
I GOT THIS!
GET HIM!

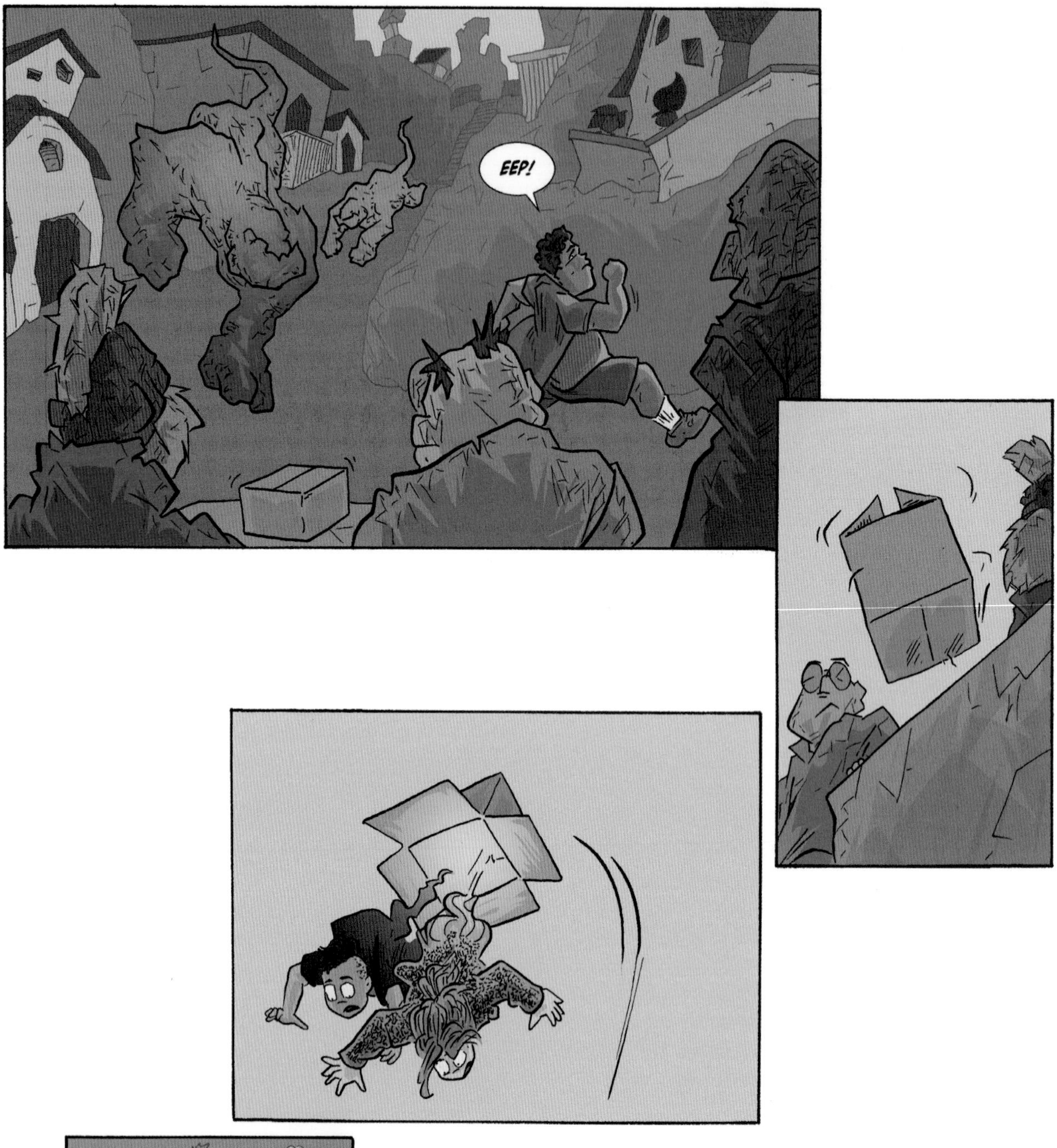
EEP!
GET THE BOX!
!

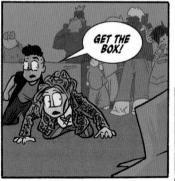

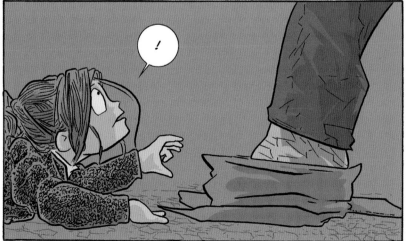

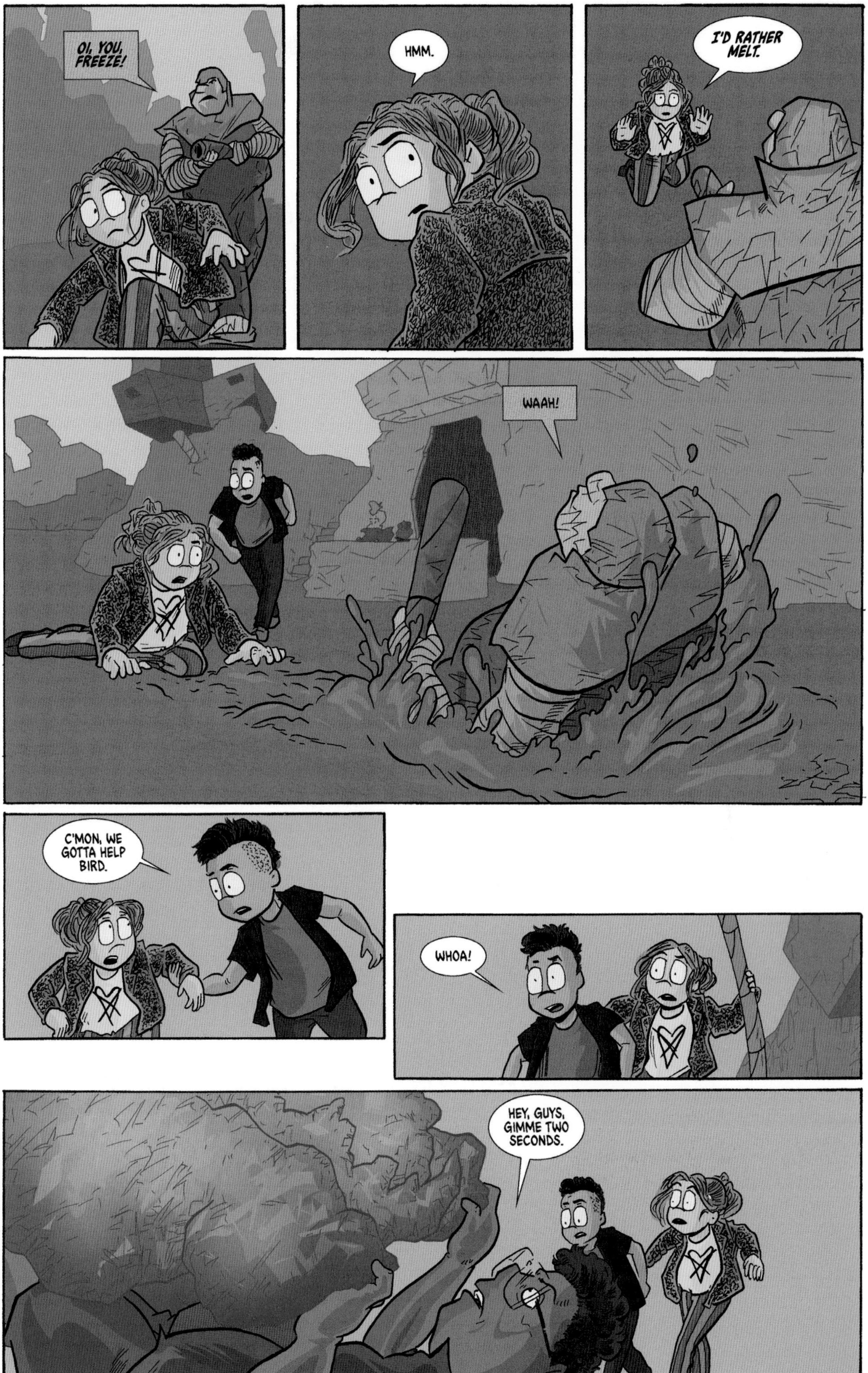

OI, YOU, FREEZE!
HMM.
I'D RATHER MELT.
WAAH!
C'MON, WE GOTTA HELP BIRD.
WHOA!
HEY, GUYS, GIMME TWO SECONDS.

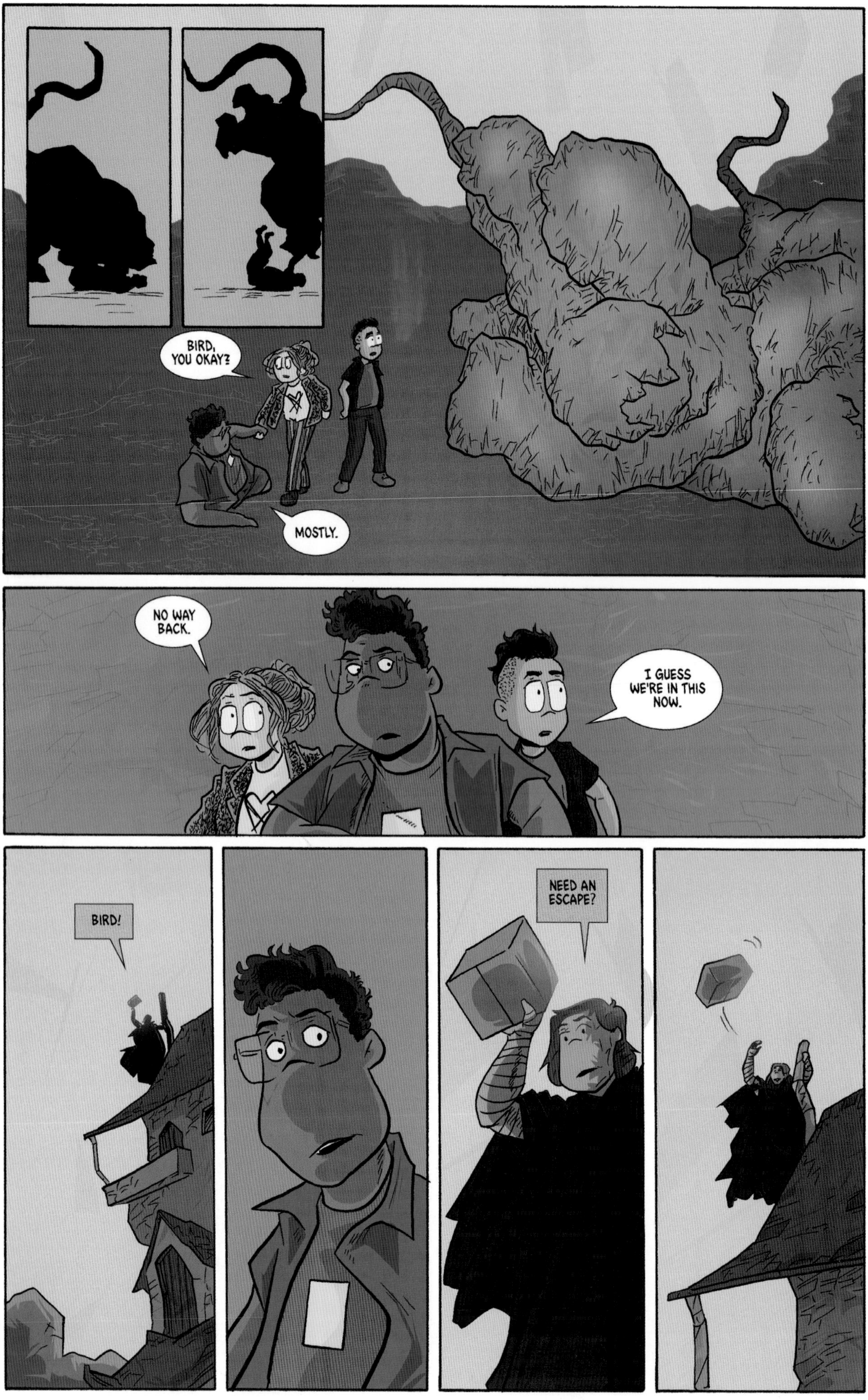
BIRD, YOU OKAY?
MOSTLY.
NO WAY BACK.
I GUESS WE'RE IN THIS NOW.
BIRD!
NEED AN ESCAPE?

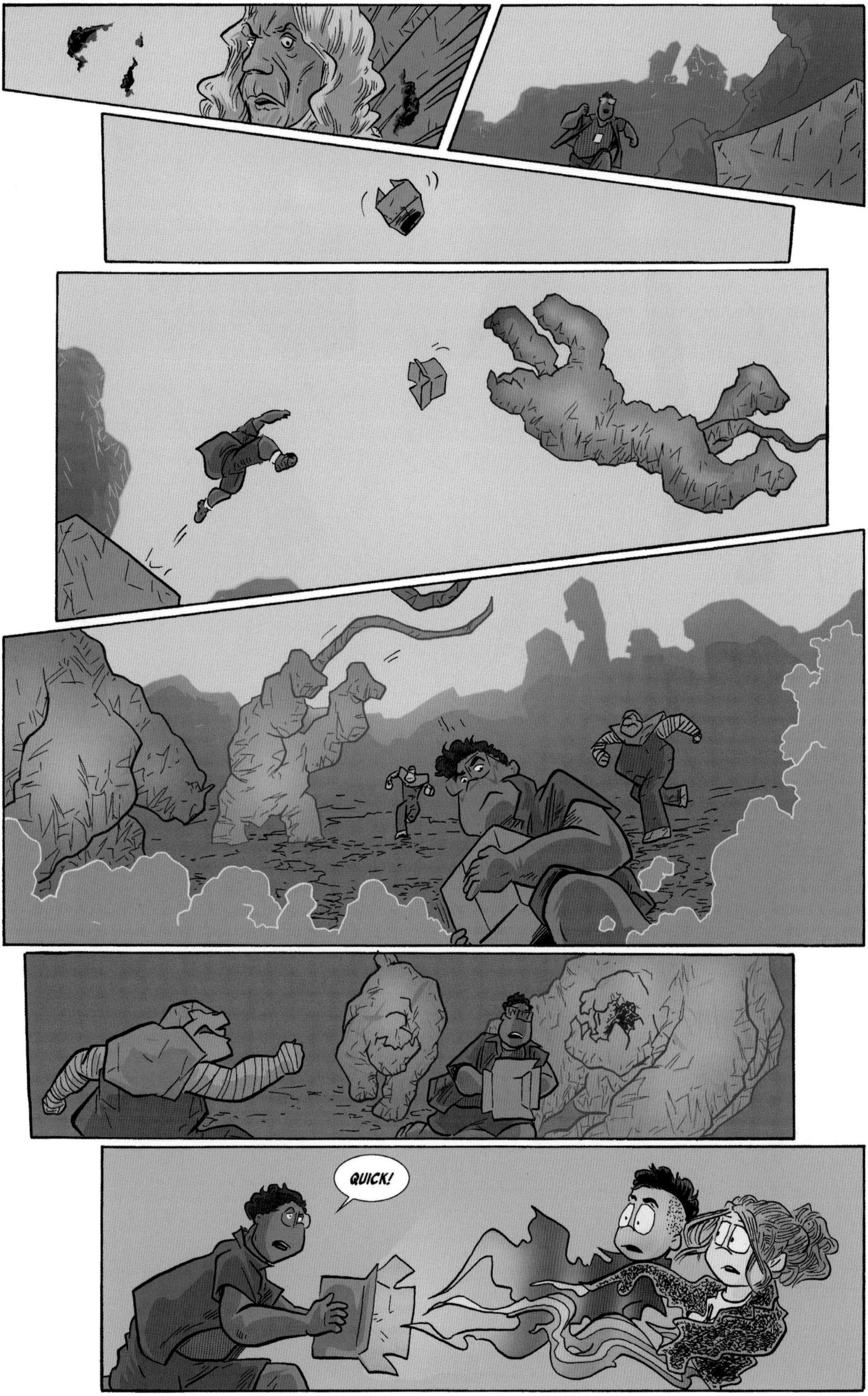
QUICK!

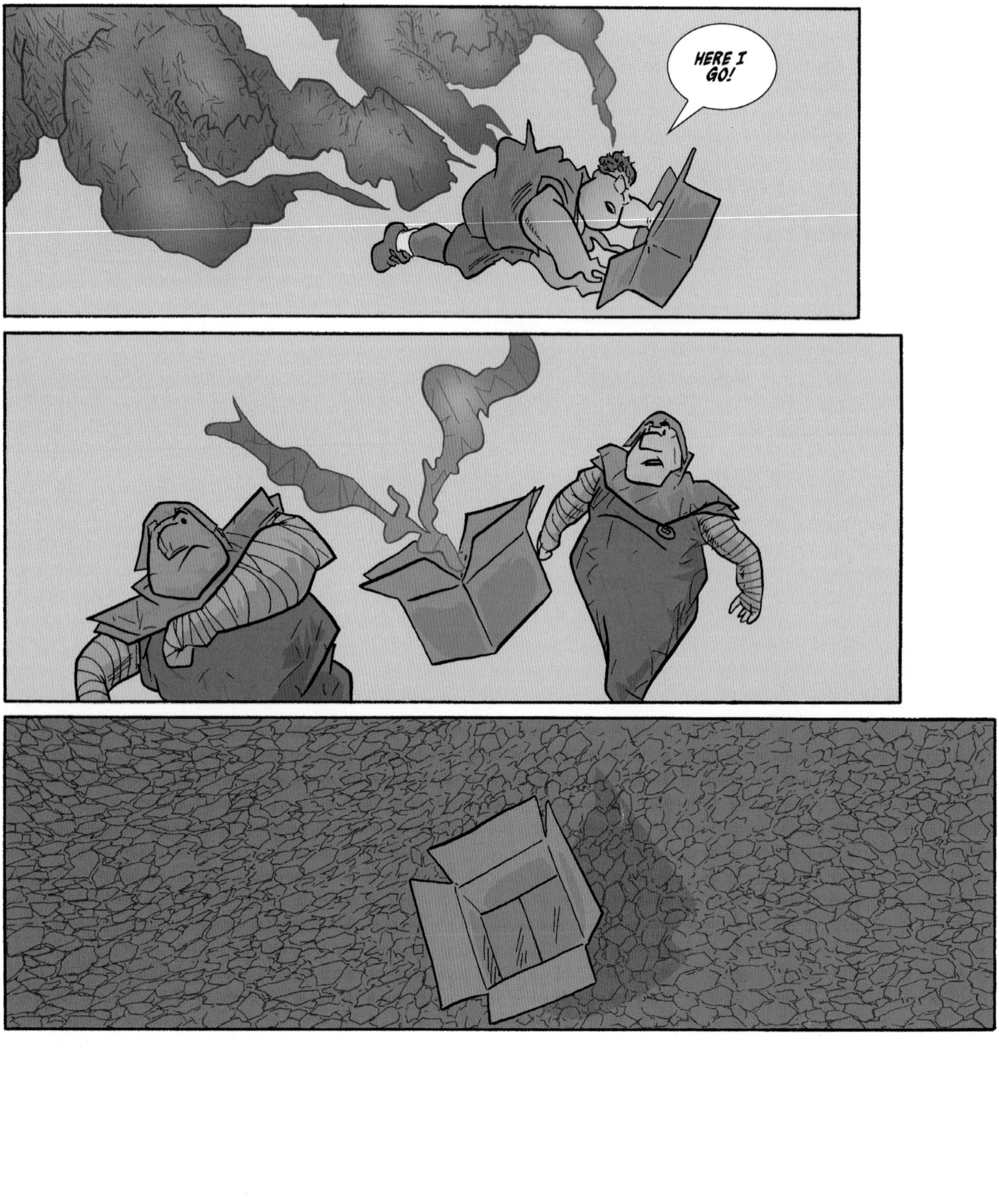
HERE I GO!

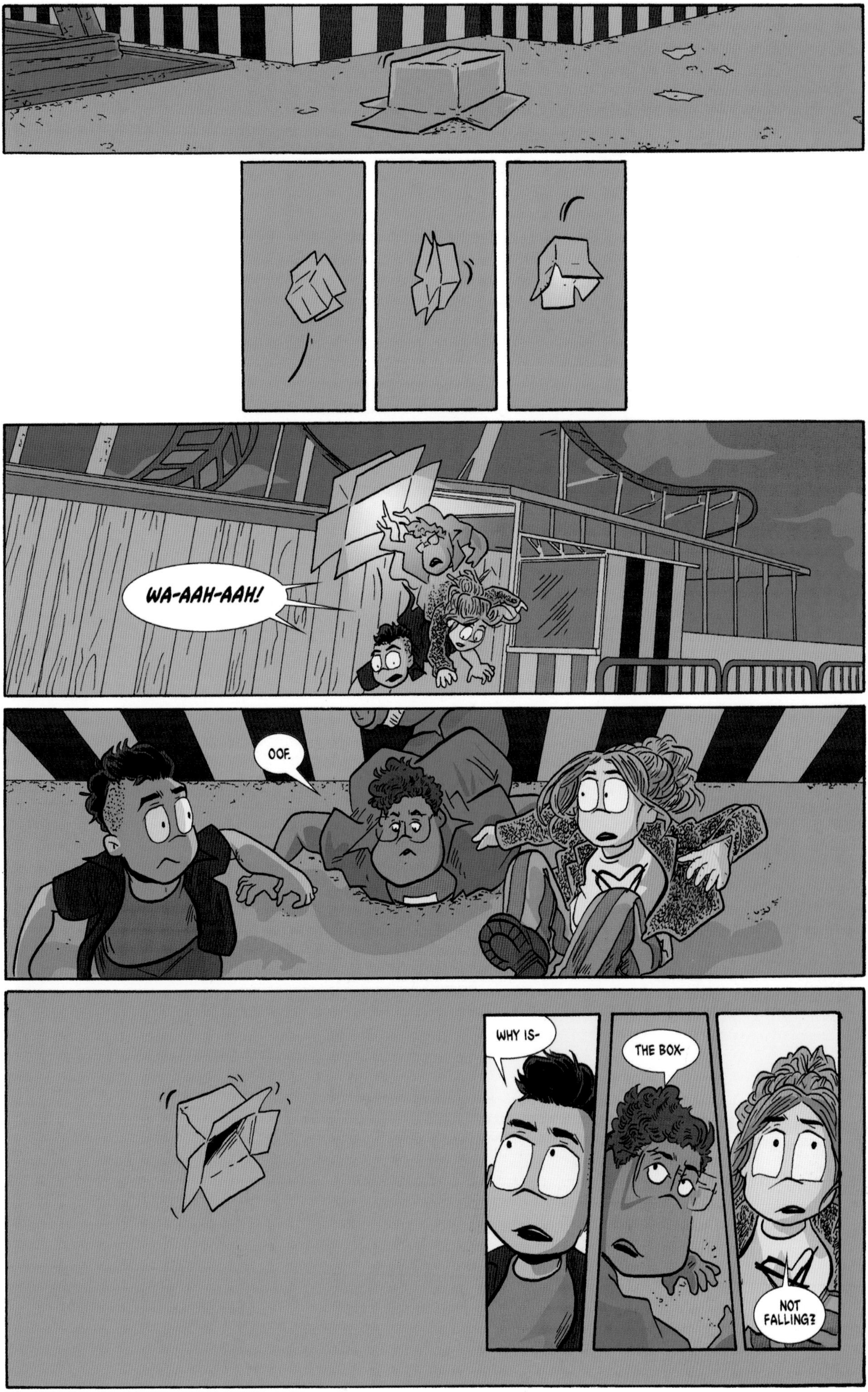
WA-AAH-AAH!
OOF.
WHY IS-
THE BOX-
NOT FALLING?

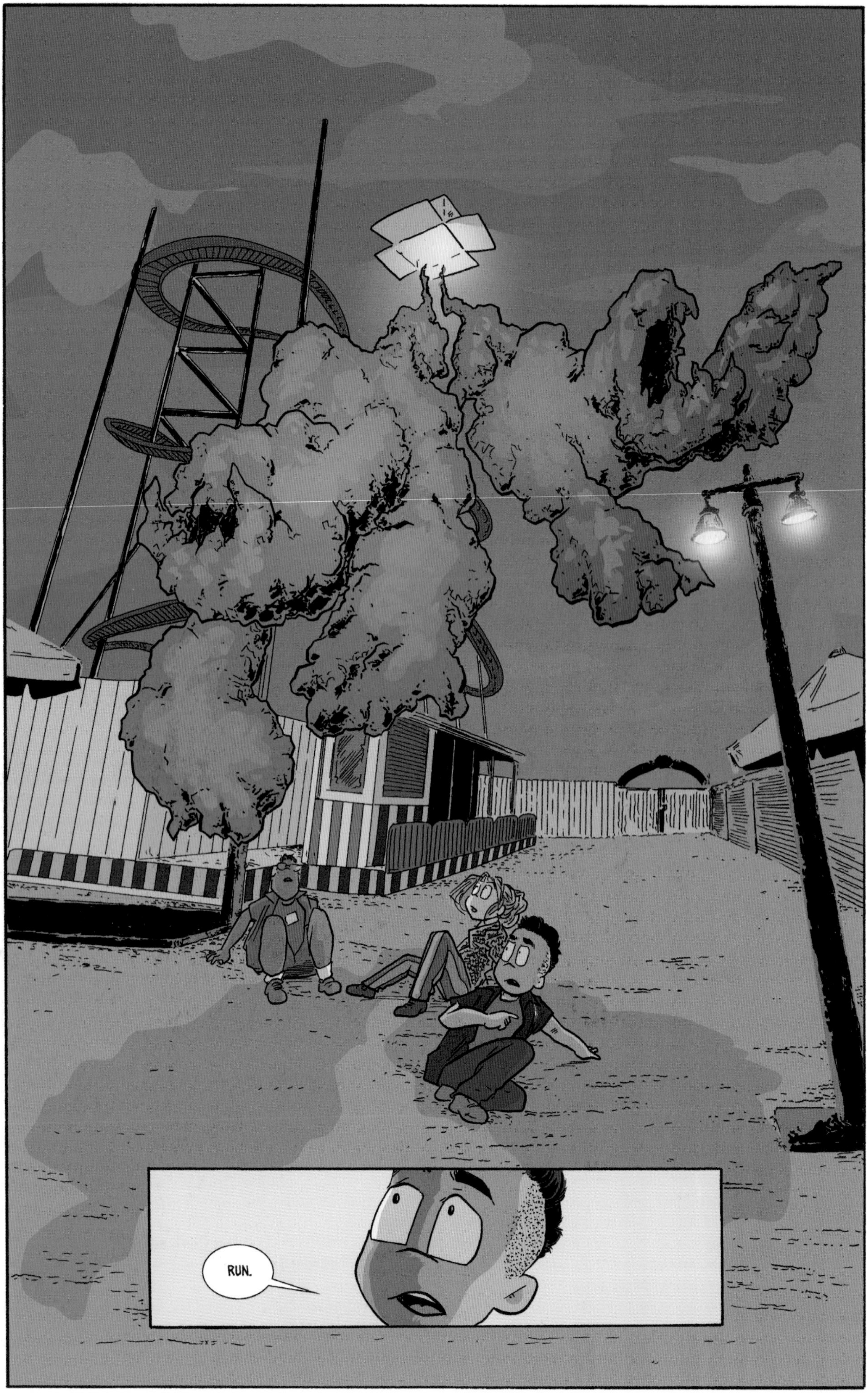
RUN.

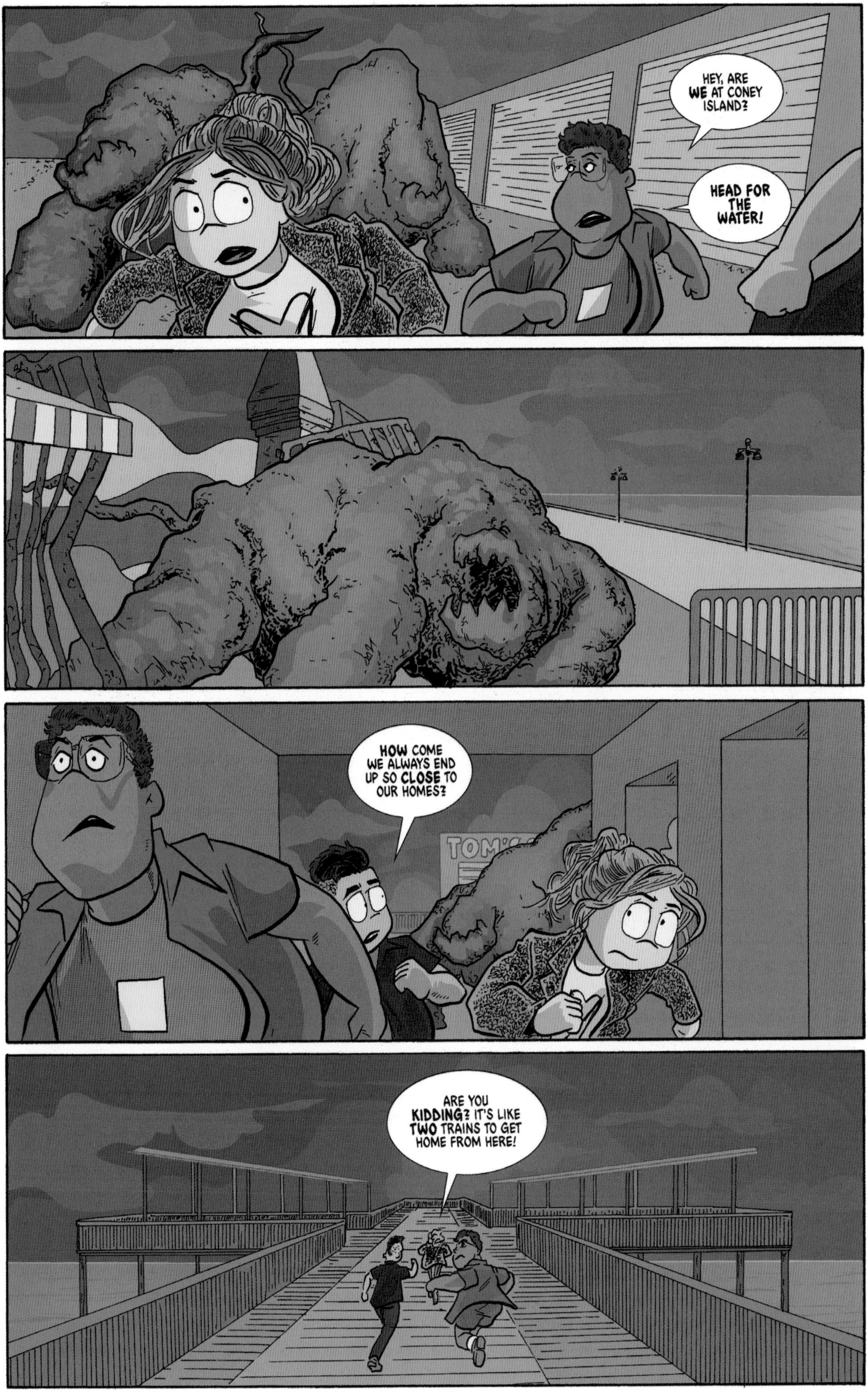
HEY, ARE WE AT CONEY ISLAND?
HEAD FOR THE WATER!
HOW COME WE ALWAYS END UP SO CLOSE TO OUR HOMES?
ARE YOU KIDDING? IT'S LIKE TWO TRAINS TO GET HOME FROM HERE!

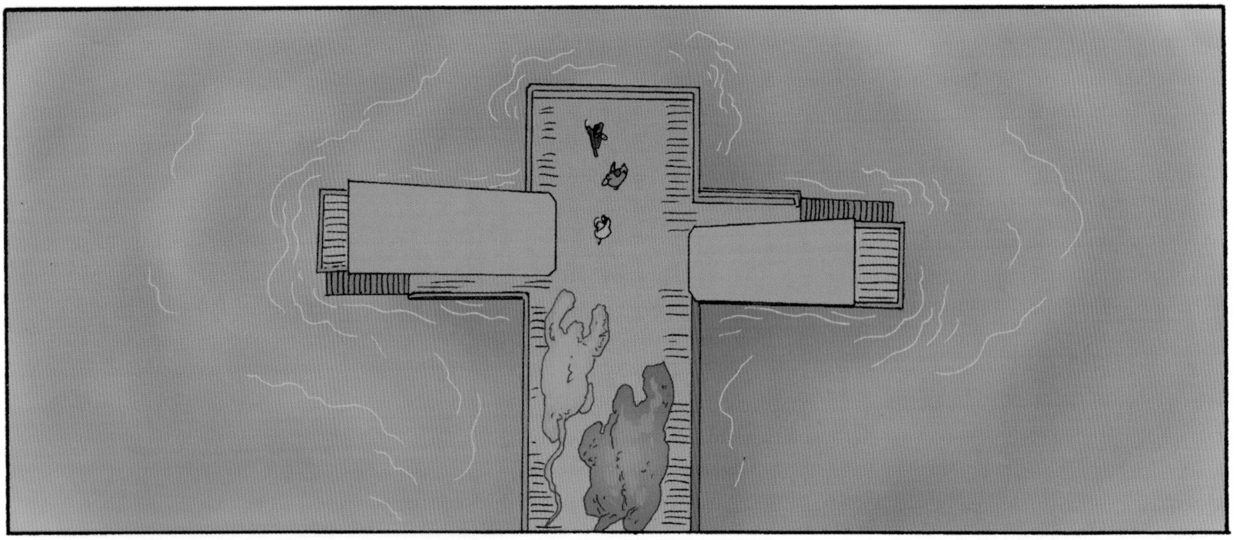

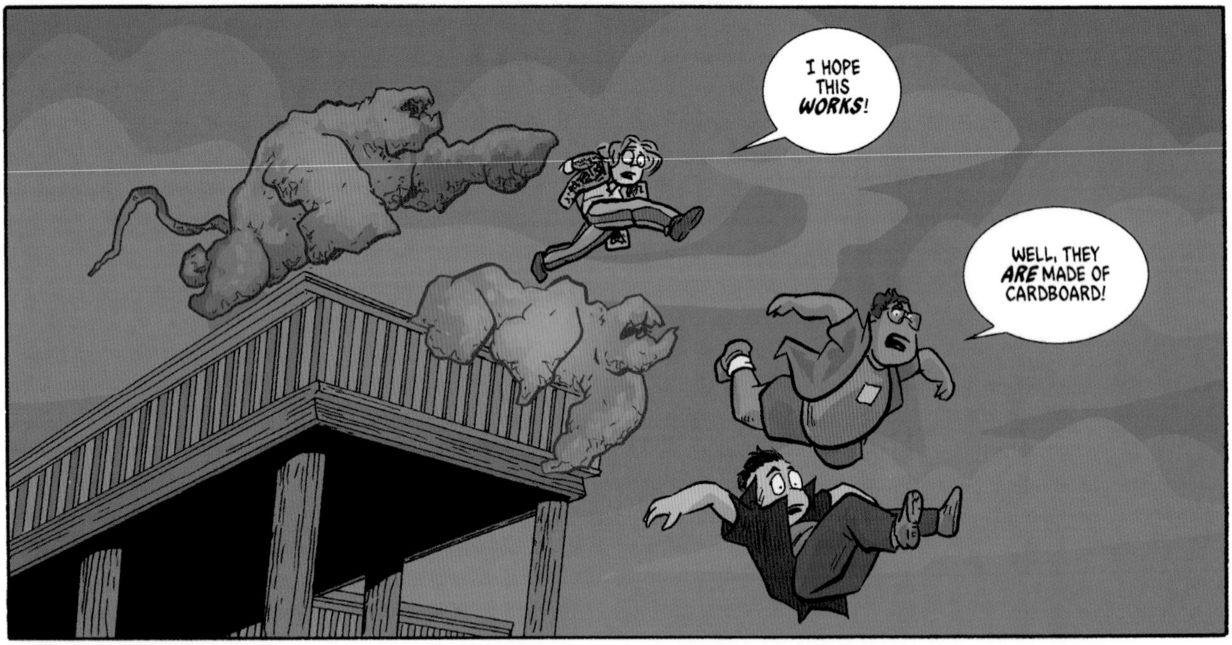
I HOPE THIS **WORKS**!
WELL, THEY **ARE** MADE OF CARDBOARD!

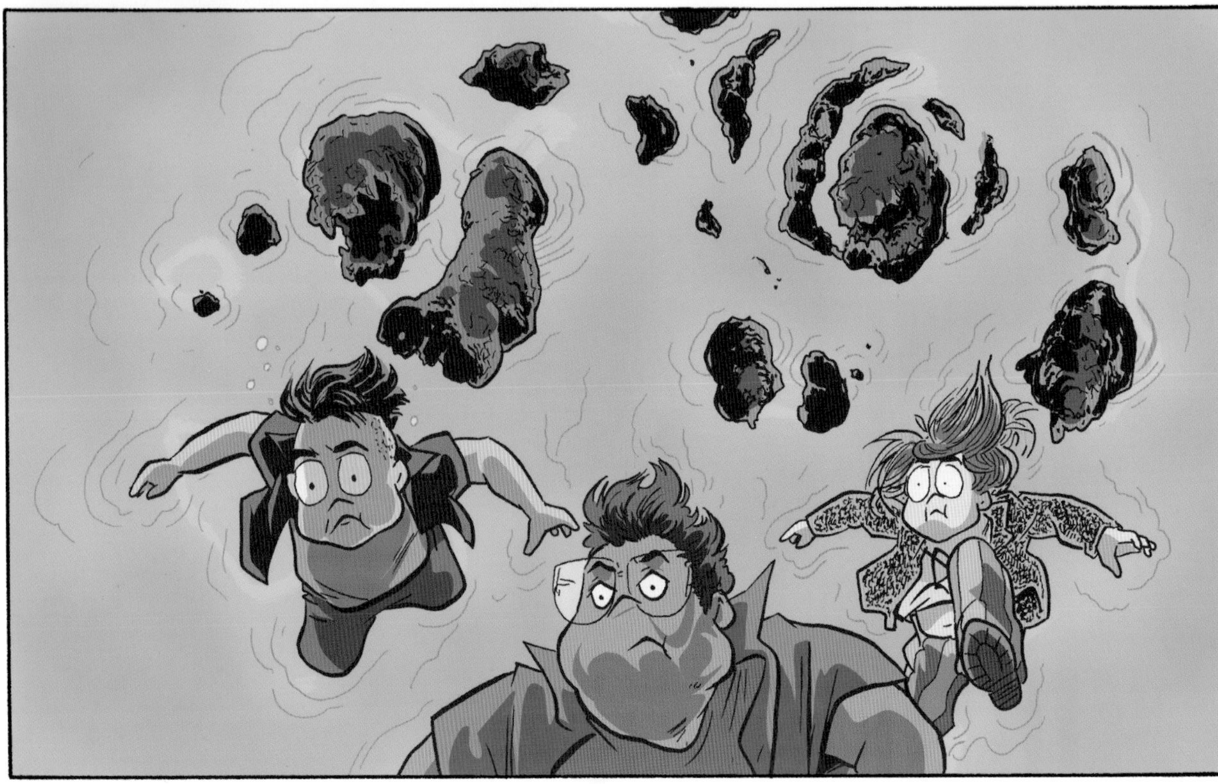

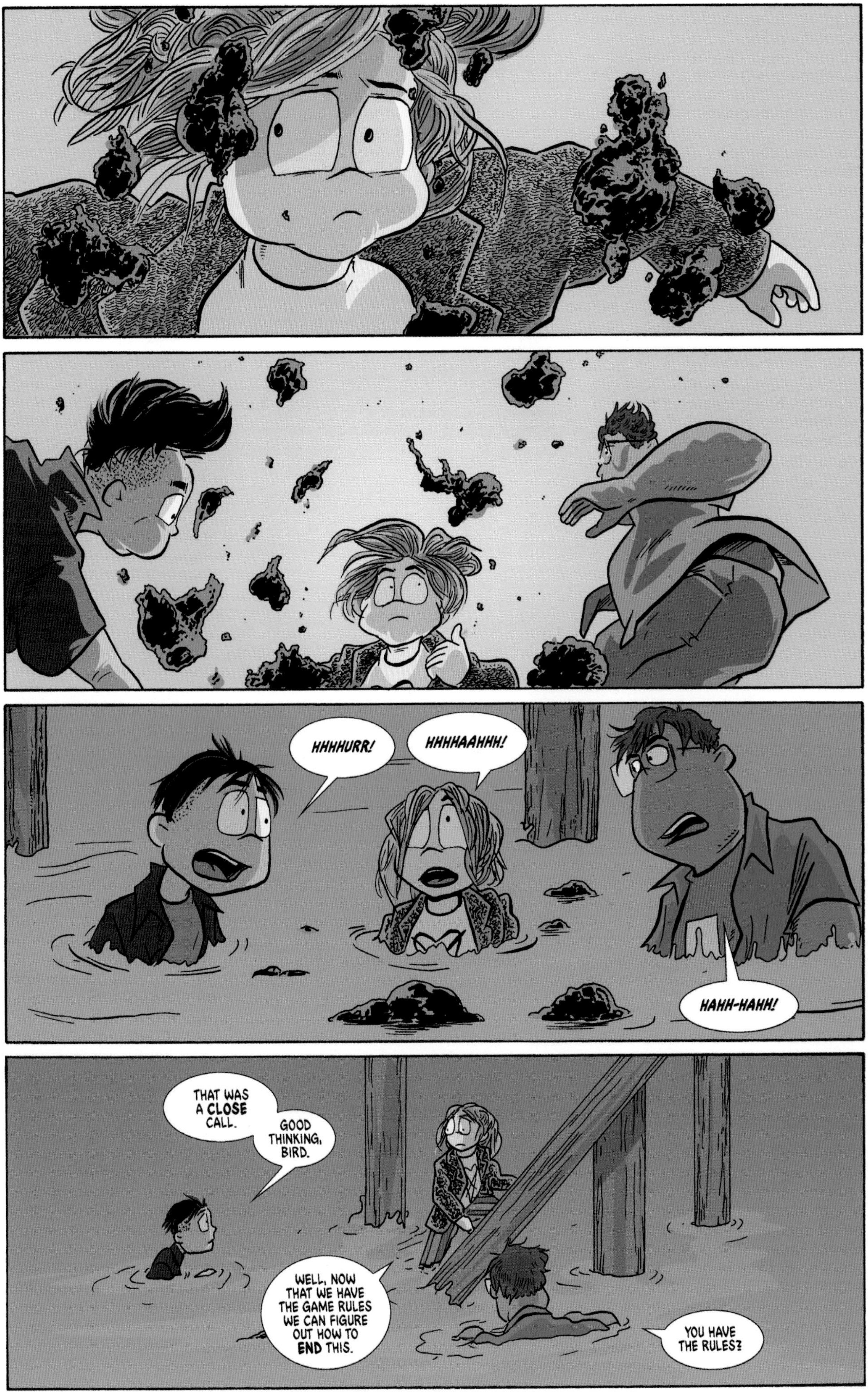
HHHHURR!
HHHHAAHHH!
HAHH-HAHH!
THAT WAS A CLOSE CALL.
GOOD THINKING, BIRD.
WELL, NOW THAT WE HAVE THE GAME RULES WE CAN FIGURE OUT HOW TO END THIS.
YOU HAVE THE RULES?

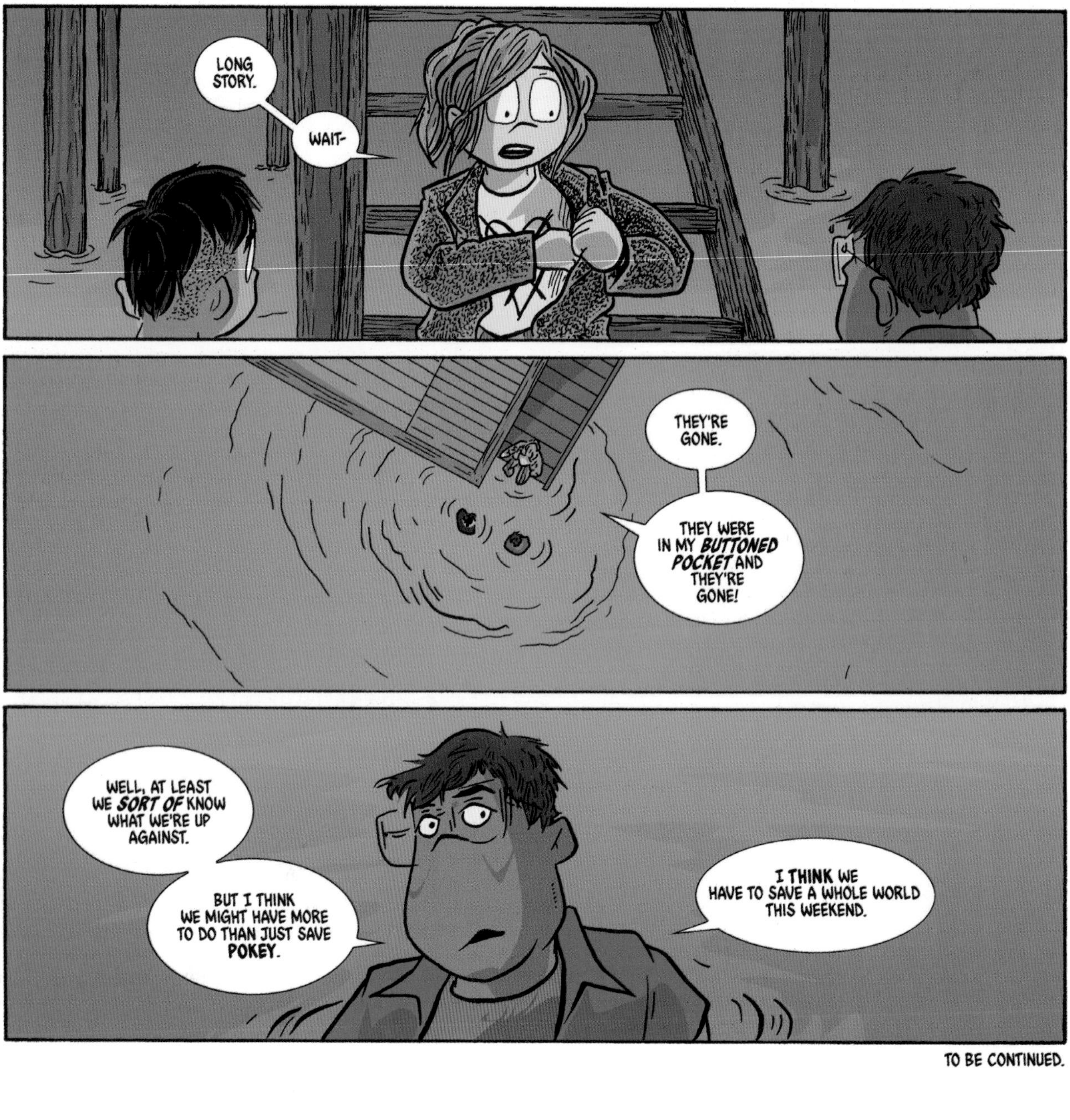
LONG STORY.
WAIT-
THEY'RE GONE.
THEY WERE IN MY *BUTTONED POCKET* AND THEY'RE GONE!
WELL, AT LEAST WE *SORT OF* KNOW WHAT WE'RE UP AGAINST.
BUT I THINK WE MIGHT HAVE MORE TO DO THAN JUST SAVE **POKEY**.
I THINK WE HAVE TO SAVE A WHOLE WORLD THIS WEEKEND.

TO BE CONTINUED.

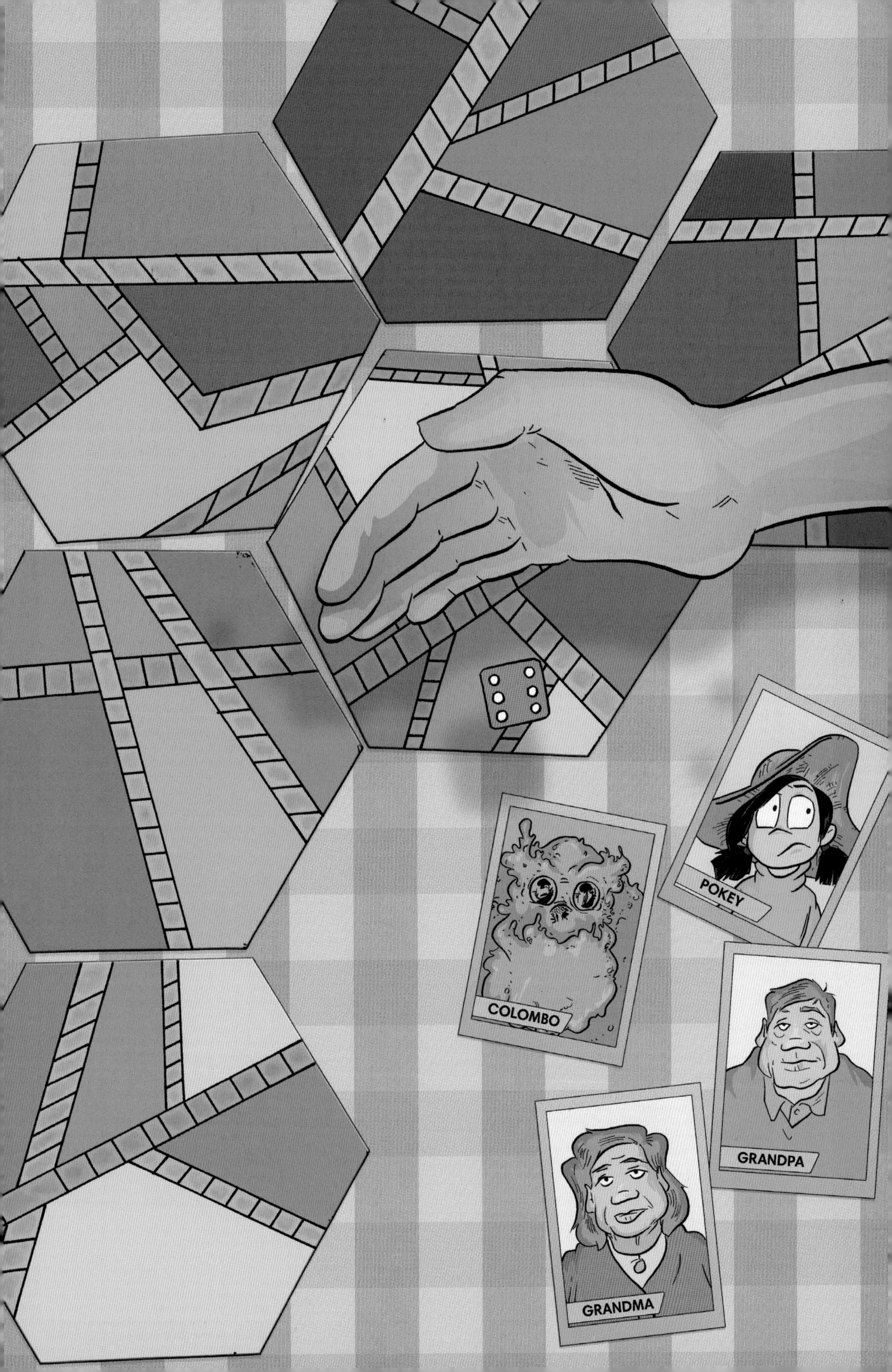
POKEY
COLOMBO
GRANDPA
GRANDMA

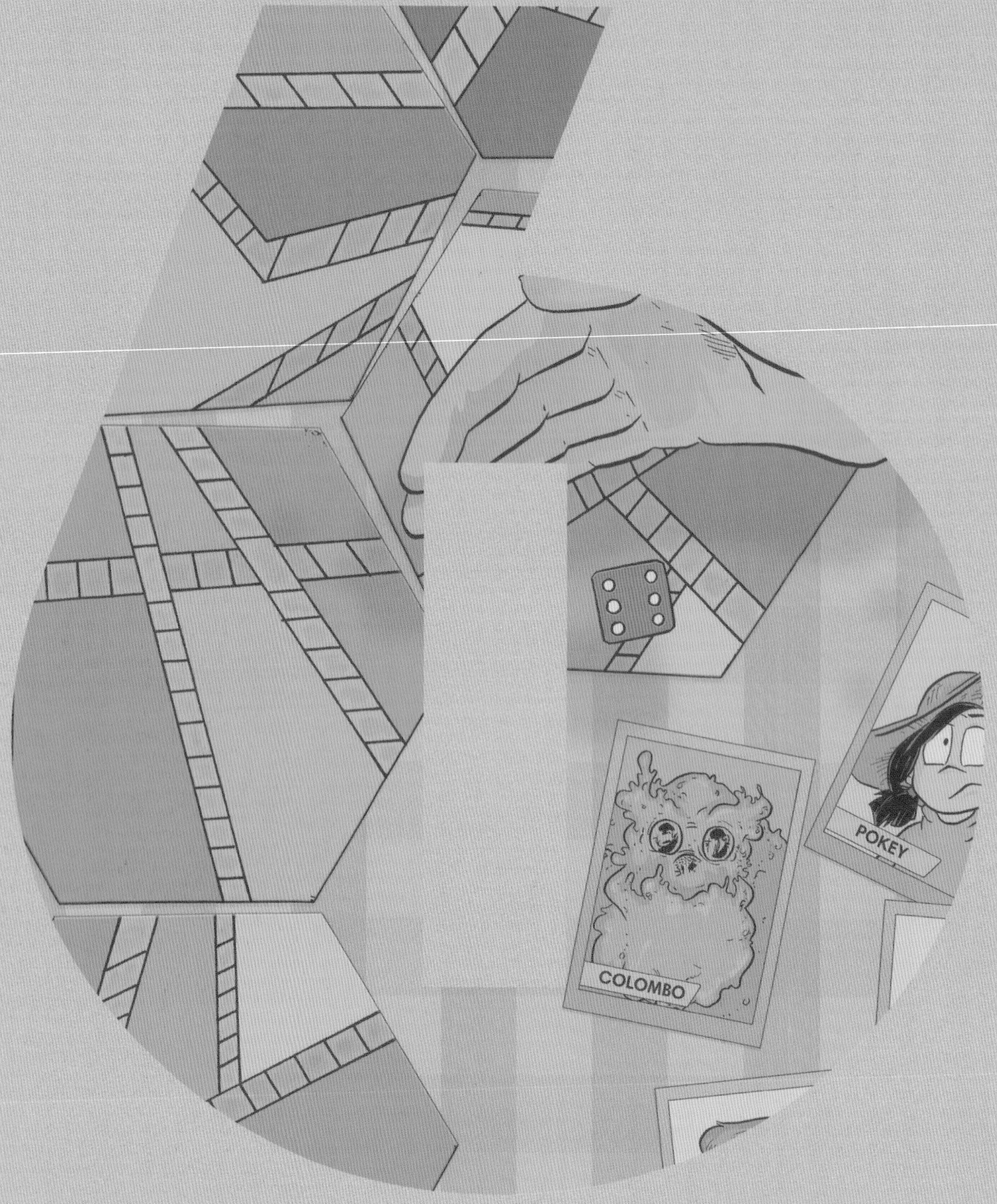
POKEY
COLOMBO

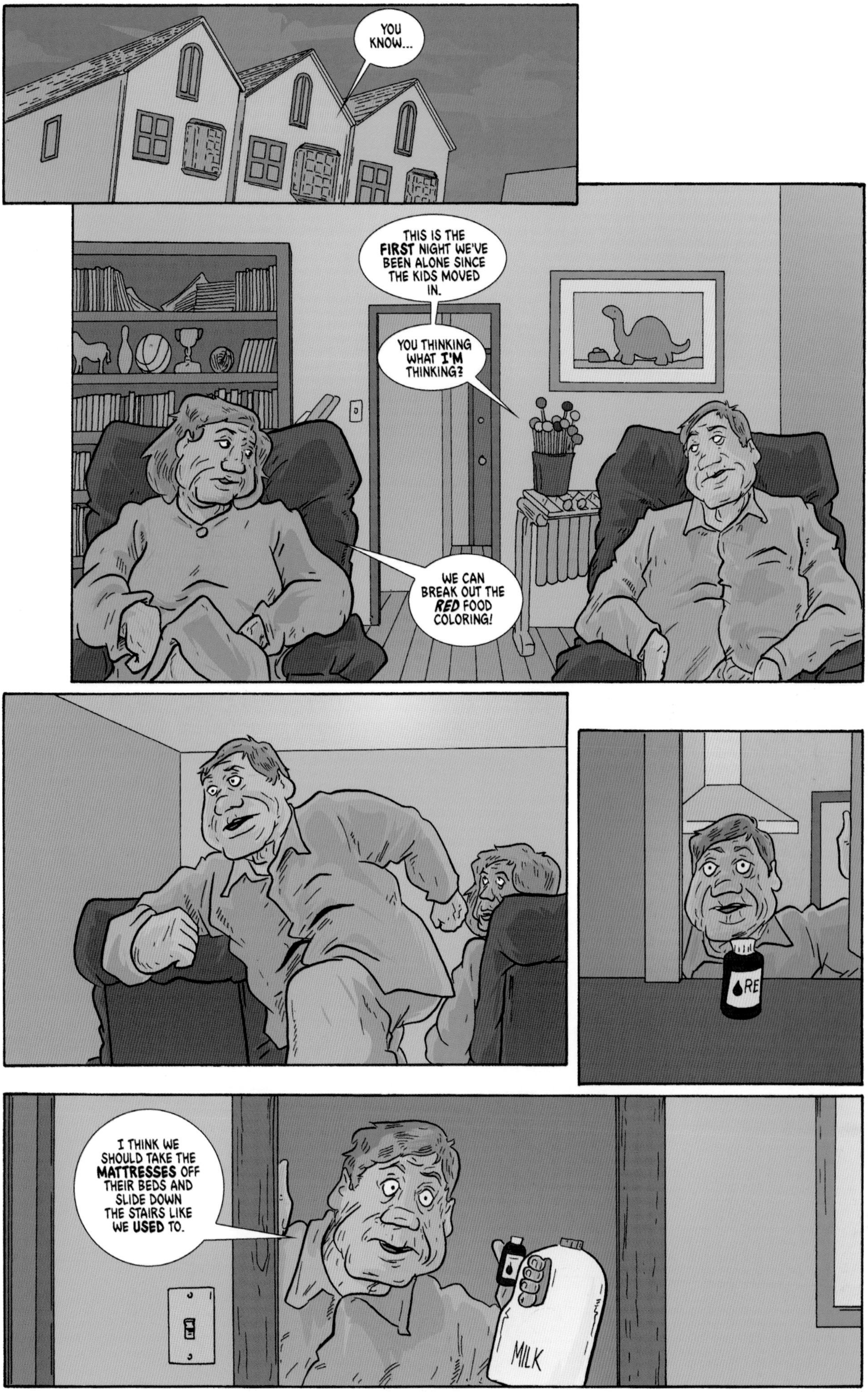
YOU KNOW...
THIS IS THE **FIRST** NIGHT WE'VE BEEN ALONE SINCE THE KIDS MOVED IN.
YOU THINKING WHAT **I'M** THINKING?
WE CAN BREAK OUT THE ***RED*** FOOD COLORING!
RE
I THINK WE SHOULD TAKE THE **MATTRESSES** OFF THEIR BEDS AND SLIDE DOWN THE STAIRS LIKE WE **USED** TO.
MILK

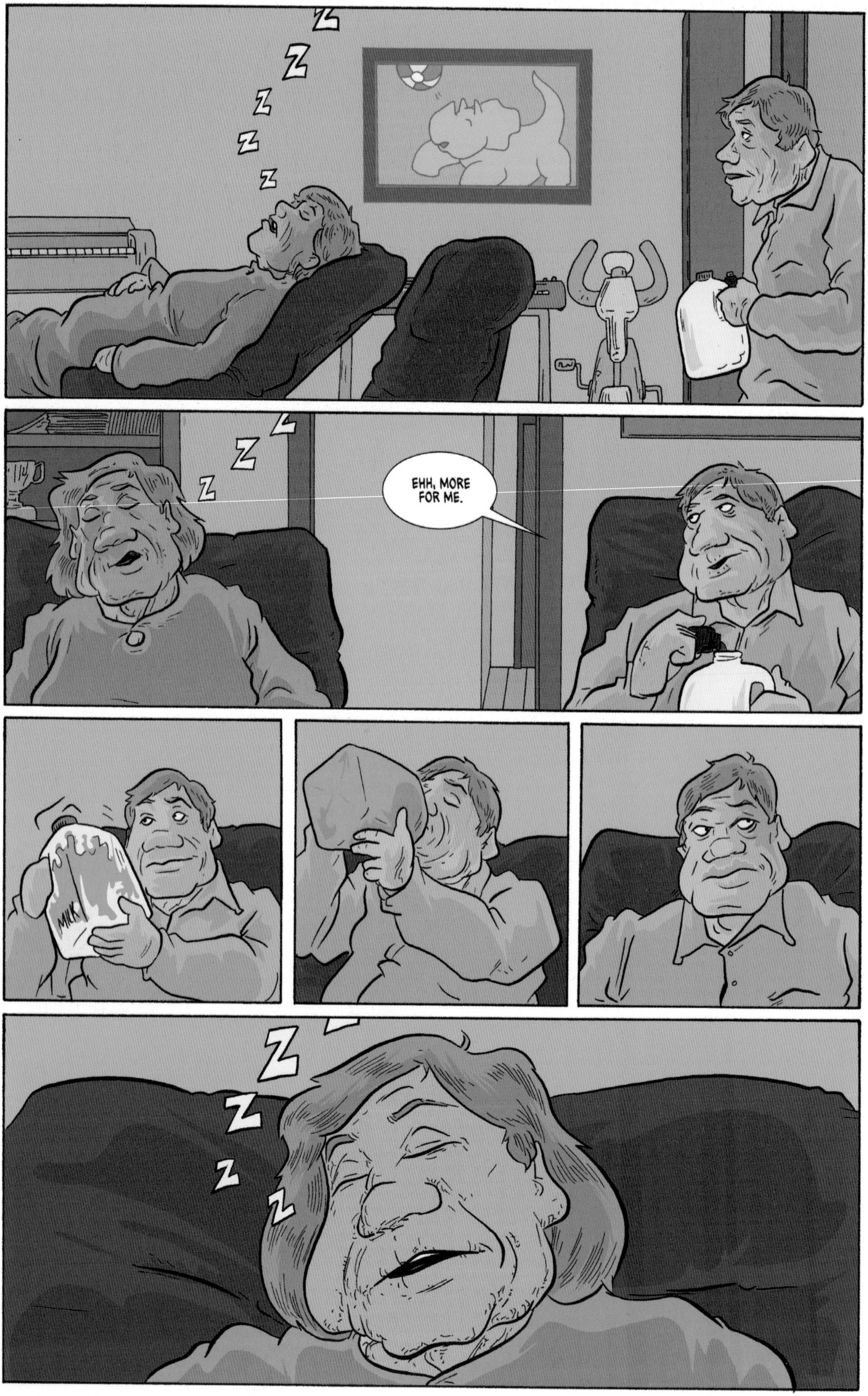
Z Z Z Z Z
Z Z Z
EHH, MORE FOR ME.
MILK
Z Z Z Z

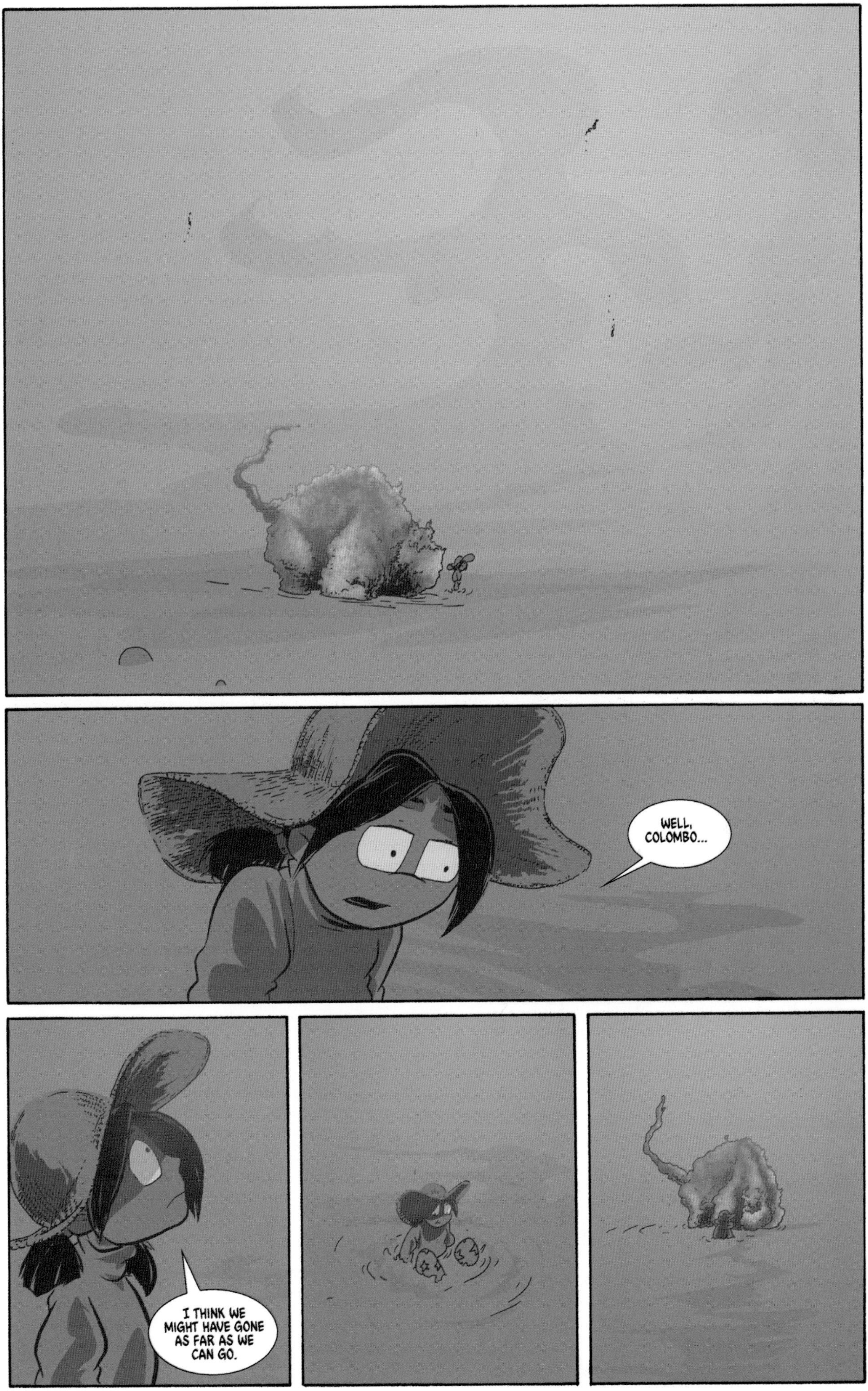
WELL, COLOMBO...
I THINK WE MIGHT HAVE GONE AS FAR AS WE CAN GO.

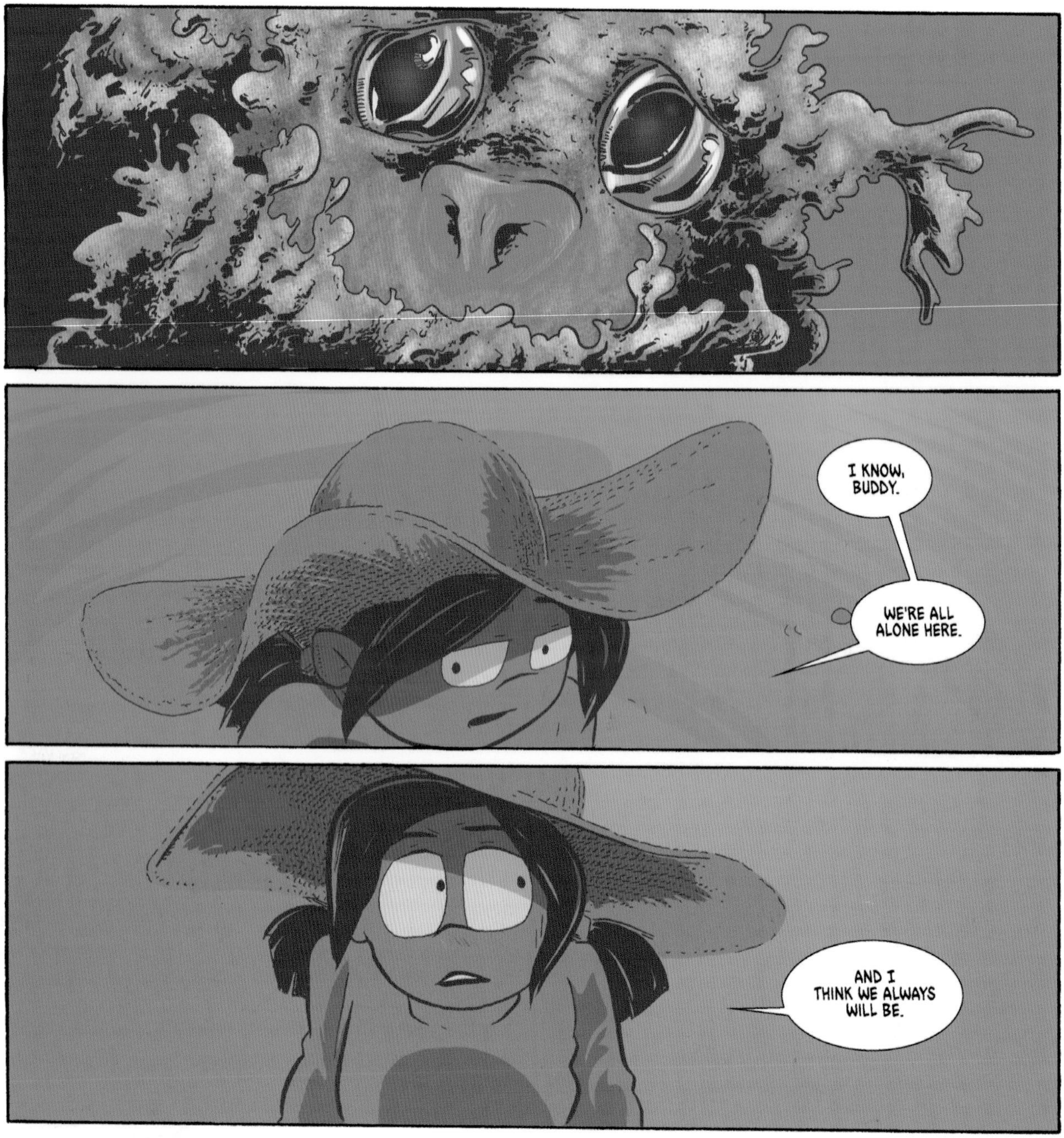
I KNOW, BUDDY.
WE'RE ALL ALONE HERE.
AND I THINK WE ALWAYS WILL BE.

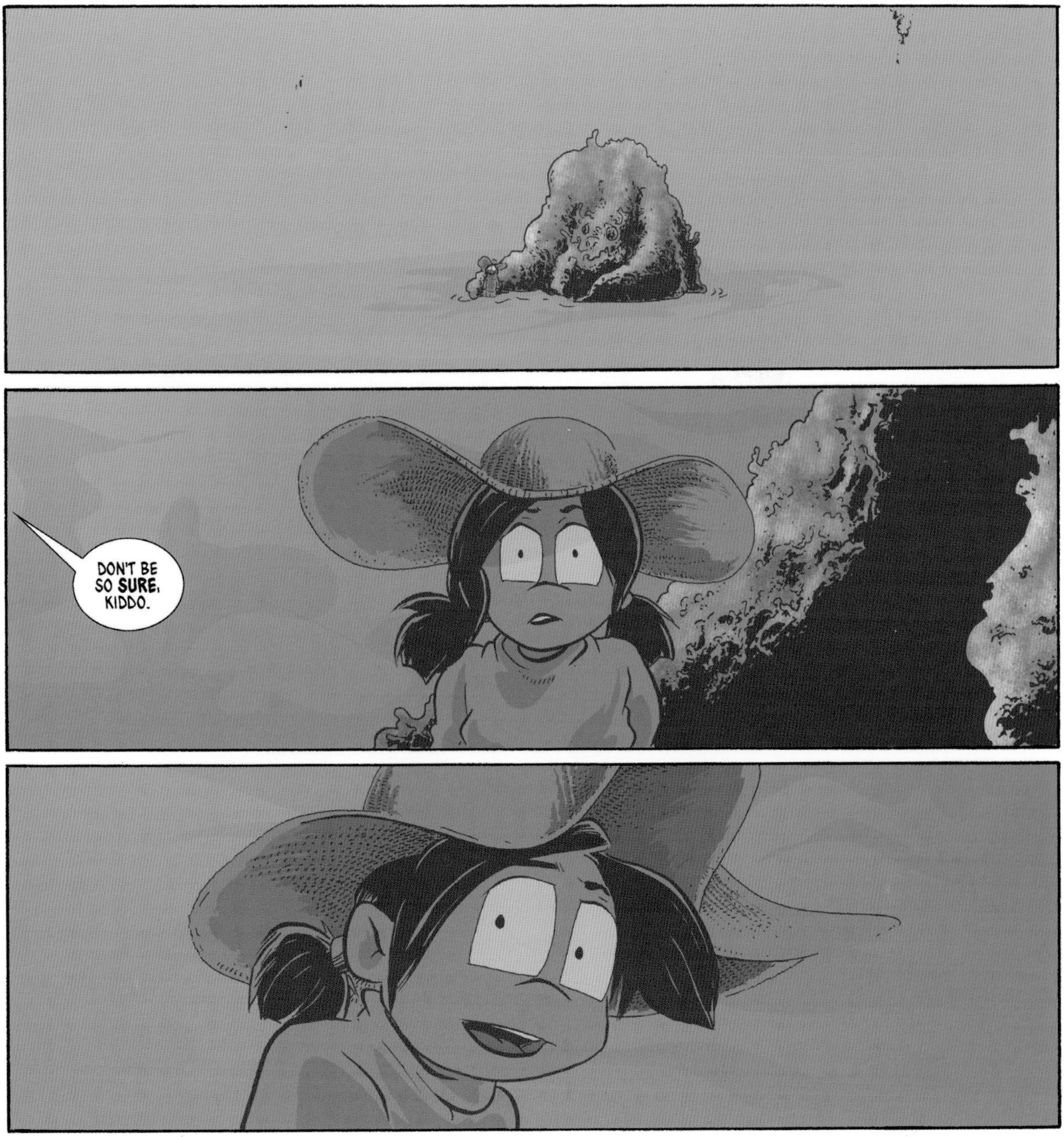
DON'T BE SO SURE, KIDDO.

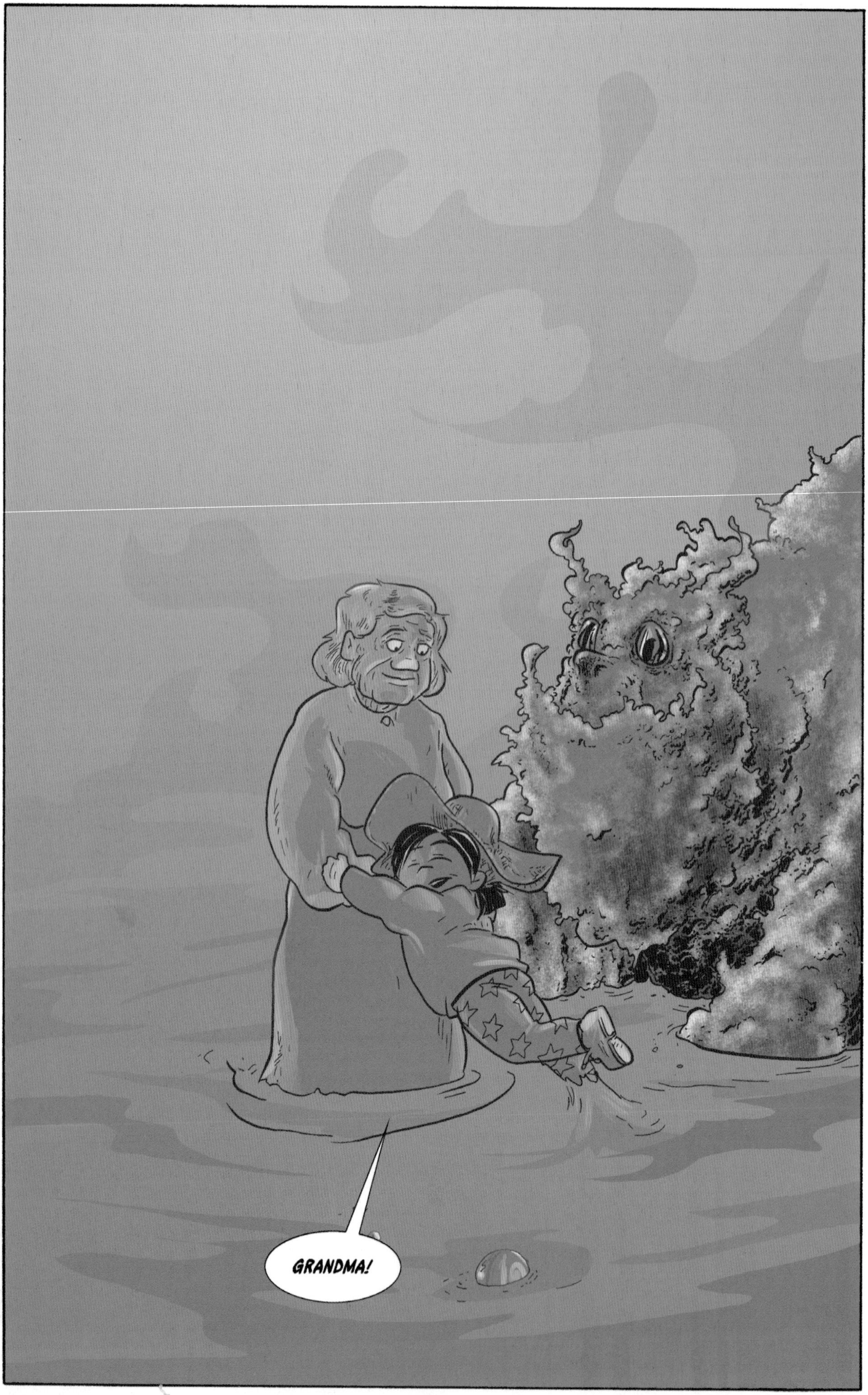
GRANDMA!

TO BE CONTINUED.